MW01686322

Andrea B. Lamoureux

Zephyra

Book One of The Elemental Diaries

Zephyra
Copyright © 2017 Andrea B Lamoureux
All rights reserved

ISBN-13: 978-1-7751006-1-4

Without limiting the rights under copyright reserved above, no part of this publication may be reproduced, stored in or introduced into a retrieval system, or transmitted, in any form, or by any means (electronic, mechanical, photocopying, recording, or otherwise) without the prior written permission of the above author of this book.

This is a work of fiction. Names, characters, places, brands, media, and incidents are either the product of the author's imagination or are used fictitiously. The author acknowledges the trademarked status and trademark owners of various products referenced in this work of fiction, which have been used without permission. The publication/use of these trademarks is not authorized, associated with, or sponsored by the trademark owners.

Cover Art @ Fotolia
Cover Design: Art4Artists www.art4artists.com.au
Map: John Renehan
Formatting: Integrity Formatting

For my mom, who has always believed in me; and my dad, whom I dearly miss.

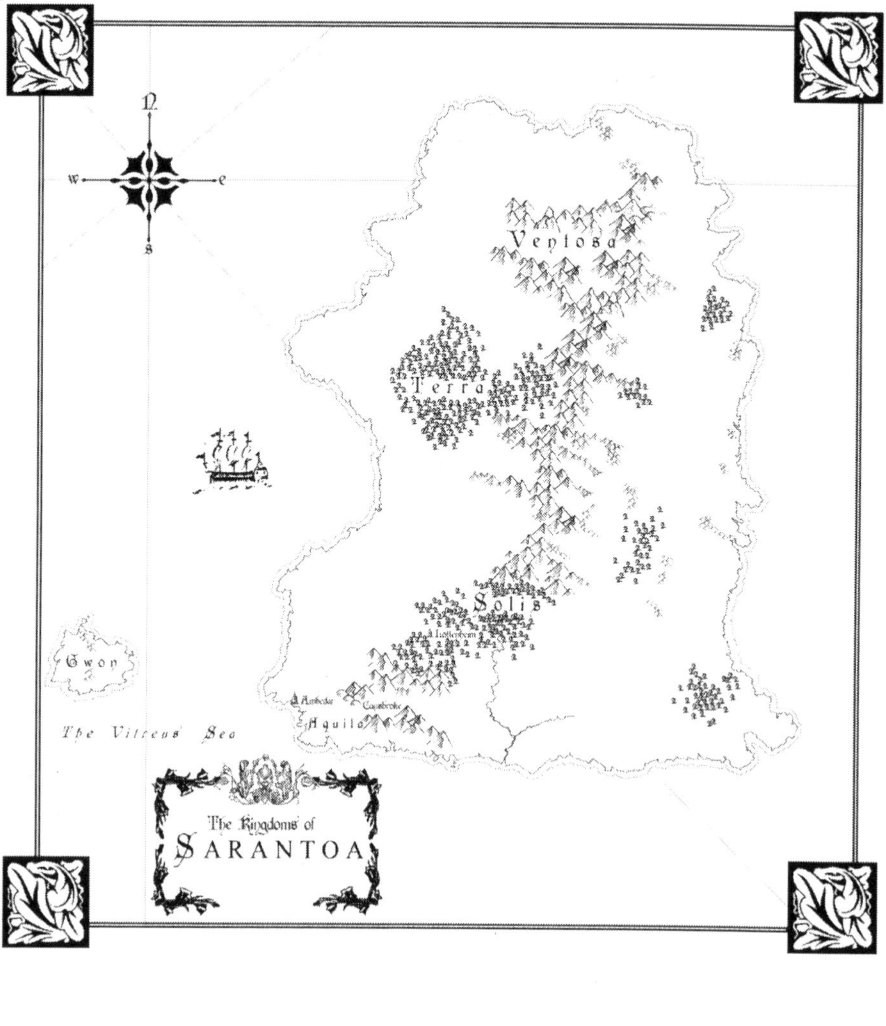
N
w
e
s
Ventosa
Terra
Solis
Gwon
Aquila
The Vitreus Sea
The Kingdoms of
SARANTOA

Some say our destinies are written in the stars, others believe we're in control of our own fates. I believe both to be true. While my own choices led me down the path I took, certain people and situations were put in my way to lead me there. To help you understand how I discovered my own destiny and the great importance of it, I will start from the beginning. I am Zephyra Caldura, and this is my tale.

** ***Warning*** **

This book contains sensitive scenes that may be troubling to some readers

CHAPTER 1

I ONCE THOUGHT living at court was tough. Little did I know, what Celestia had in store for me would be even more trying.Born with royal blood in my veins I was, of course, brought up with the proper etiquette for a lady of the court. At Solis, the kingdom I am from, the females of royal blood always take the throne. When I was a child my grandmother, Jelena Caldura, was the reigning queen of Solis. Because she only had two sons and no daughters, the next in line was my cousin Adelaide, who was a year older than I. After her, it was I who was in line to take the throne.

Though that throne and crown weren't too far from my reach, I never had any desire to be queen. I loved and looked up to Adelaide, so I hoped she would live a long and healthy life. Besides, I believed she was going to make a great queen due to her kind heart and strong spirit.

Myself on the other hand…well I just couldn't fathom the thought of all the responsibility and stress that comes along with being a queen.

Each of the four kingdoms in the land of Sarantoa were named after one of our goddess Celestia's four elements. Solis was named after the sun because it represented the element of fire.

The people of Solis were known for their golden or red hair and pale, sometimes freckled, skin. While Adelaide was blessed with beautiful golden blonde curls and not a freckle in sight, I was the complete opposite. I was cursed with my father's bright red hair and a dusting of freckles upon my nose and shoulders. I went through an awkward phase as a child where I was teased for my looks. "Zephyra, how are *you* from the same blood as Princess Adelaide when you have that ugly red hair and dirty-looking skin?" the other children would ask me with disgust upon their faces. Children are cruel; sometimes on purpose and sometimes unknowingly. This I now know… back then I did not. So I would go running to my sweet cousin and cry to her, "Why can I not be more like you? Everyone loves you. Everyone hates me and I didn't even ask to be royalty!"

"Dear Zephyra, they're just jealous because you get special attention while they only lead common, boring lives. Don't let them make you cry. They are beneath us. Besides, you will always have me and I love you, sweet cousin." She would comfort me and give me a peck on the forehead.

Though she was only a year older than I, because of her role as princess, she was forced to be more mature and wiser.

Her words of comfort and special attention would always make me feel better…until the next time.

There is one day I can clearly recall…I usually can remember the times when I was most embarrassed. Though they are memories I wish I could forget.

My handmaiden, who was a young woman from a small village outside of Solis with plain brown hair and olive skin, had just dressed me in a poofy, pale yellow gown and braided my long red hair in the Solis fashion. This was one big, loose braid that ran down ones back.

Being that it was the beginning of spring, Queen Jelena was throwing a feast at midday to celebrate the blooming of the flowers, as she did each spring. All of those at court were, of course, invited.

The feast was held in the palace gardens, which were in full bloom with an array of colourful flowers. There were lilies, irises, snowbells, moss campion, rusty alpenrose and many different types of orchids. Aside from the flowers in the garden, the apple and cherry trees were also blooming and gave off a sweet scent when the breeze blew the right way.

The gardens were one of my favourite places at Solis. During part of the spring and summer they were breathtaking with the splash of colours and cobblestone pathways. I would come here alone sometimes and just listen to the serene, trickling sound of the stone water fountain and stream that ran through the gardens. I would breathe in the aroma of all of those beautiful flowers and forget all of my troubles, if only just for a moment.

Today, though, I wasn't alone and today I would not forget all of my troubles.

The feast itself was delightful. We sat in amongst the flowers at a long table covered with white linens. The food was delicious. There was an abundance of breads, nuts and cheeses. For sweets we had tarts and fruit with sweet juice from oranges to sip on. All of this food was placed on shiny, golden platters and we used small, white linens as plates to place our food on. During this feast, a beautiful harpist played a bell-like tune in the background. If my grandmother knew how to do one thing well, it was how to put on an amazing feast.

I was seated between my mother and father, Mirrabel and Lucian Caldura. Across from us sat Adelaide and her parents, Faya with her petite build and copper hair; and Bardin with his pale skin and blond curls. Both of her parents were stiff and proper, but both had a kindness to their hearts which shone in their eyes. Mine on the other hand…well my mother, at least, had a tongue like a whip; and my father didn't have much time for the rest of us as he was grandmaster of the royal army. Though we hadn't been at war since before my birth, he was still always busy training new soldiers and making sure the old ones stayed in shape. Just in case.

At the head of the table sat my magnificent grandmother, the queen. Her hair, once copper-red, was now a shade of pearlescent white. Today she wore it up in elaborate braids with sparkling gems entwined throughout it. Her dress was a pale peach to keep with the theme of spring, and it was made of the most exquisite silk and lace. Even though she was aging, now in the beginning of her sixth decade, she still looked majestic with her head always held high and a twinkle in her eyes. If I looked up to anyone in this kingdom, other than Adelaide, it was Queen Jelena. She ruled with a just heart and a fairness that was respectable. Her smile alone could brighten one's day.

After we had eaten our fill and the adults were talking of matters that bored me at the age of nine, we children had decided to play a game of tag. It seemed that during this game it was everyone against me as the other children were always tagging me and never each other. So as I was tagged, I was running along to catch one of the boys who'd taunted me when all of a sudden I slipped on something slimy. Fish guts from the kitchen's trash. My yellow gown was now covered in disgusting, smelly fish guts. I peered up with tears of hatred burning my eyes and saw all of the other children laughing at me.

"The princess isn't here to save you this time!" one of them roared.

Adelaide wasn't playing tag with us because, as princess, she had a duty to not take part in such childish play.

"I hate you all!" I cried.

"*Zephyra!* You are a royal, and this is no way for you to behave!" My mother scolded me as she walked up to me and dragged me out of the stinking fish guts.

"But Mother, they set me up." I argued.

"I don't want to hear it. You should know better than to take part in such childish behavior. I do not care what they did to you. That is no way to speak to your peers."

"Yes, Mother." I sighed and walked with her back to the palace in silence feeling anger and hurt well up inside my chest, but I didn't dare let it out. I was a royal, and that was no way for a royal to act…according to my mother.

My mother was a woman with aspirations. She'd married my father because of his royal blood, and knowing that she could never be queen herself, she hoped to one day become queen mother. I didn't feel like this was likely because of Adelaide being the next in line, but I humoured her by letting her bring me up as her princess.

Though sometimes hard and cold, my mother was a beautiful woman with long golden locks and fair skin. Adelaide shared more of her features than I, even though they weren't blood related. The only part of me that I'd inherited from her was my burning, bright, green eyes that looked like high quality emeralds.

"You will apologize and thank the queen for the wonderful feast, of course. Once you have bathed and changed, that is." She grimaced, "That dress is ruined. I will have Gisela get rid of it."

I pouted silently. I had liked the pale yellow colour of the dress, but I understood that the stain and smell of fish guts would never come out.

"They planned for me to slip in the fish guts," I claimed, now knowing that was the reason I kept being targeted.

"I don't care what they planned. It would not have happened if you had stayed at the table instead of playing foolish games. Besides, I'm sure their parents will punish them as they deem necessary."

I really hoped so.

CHAPTER 2

I SAT IN the palace's royal bathing room in warm, lavender-fragranced water while my handmaid, Gisela, scrubbed my wet skin with a sea sponge. She was a kind and gentle lady, who had reached her second decade a couple springs ago.

The royal bathing room was a grand spectacle with its floors and walls that were made of marble swirled with shades of cream, pink and gold. There were dozens of candles placed along the walls which made the whole room glow with a soft, flickering light. The bath itself took up half the room. Just to get into the water one had to descend its stairs. It was deep enough to stand in with the water reaching the tops of most people's shoulders. I, not yet being full grown, sat upon one of the steps.

"I don't understand why my mother must be so harsh with me when I'm the one who is suffering. All I wanted was to have a little fun and to be included."

Gisela smiled as she poured water over my hair, covering my eyes with her delicate hand. "Lady Mirrabel just has high expectations for you, my lady. She only wishes the best for you. You are her pride, you know." It wasn't a question but a statement.

"If I were her pride she would treat me kinder. No, she is not proud of me. I believe if she could she would trade me for Adelaide. She believes my cousin is perfect. 'You should try to be more like Adelaide,' she's always telling me. Do you know how much it hurts to have your own mother want you to be more like someone else?" I looked at her, my lower lip quivering.

"You are royalty. She has high expectations for you. Try not to take it so hard. She means well."

"I wish I could believe that." I sank lower into the water.

"One day I hope you will, my lady. Now let's get you to your room so I can comb your hair and dress you for your meeting with Queen Jelena."

As I stepped up and out of the bath, she wrapped me in a pale pink cotton robe and led me to my chambers to prepare me for my audience with the queen.

With a fresh, clean dress on and my hair combed and re-braided, I made my way to the throne room. This dress was a simple lilac one made from linen. With its straight, long sleeves, a skirt that came to my ankles and neckline that rested on my collar bones, this dress was simple and suitable for ordinary wear. It wasn't one of the many extravagant dresses that I owned for special functions, but nonetheless, I thought the colour was pretty. Plus it was light and unconstricting.

As I approached the throne room, in the hall that was lit by the glowing lanterns, one of the royal guards nodded to me. "Lady Zephyra."

The royal guards at Solis wore chainmail under a tunic featuring the royal colours of Solis; red with the symbol of a yellow sun on the chest.

"Good day, sir. I'm here to see Queen Jelena. Please admit me."

"Of course, my lady." With that, he swung open the large, wooden door to the throne room and led me inside.

The throne room contained shelves full of leather-bound books, stone tables with scrolls scattered on their surfaces, long diamond-shaped windows and a magnificent stone throne. The throne had a long back with wide arms. The seat and back were covered in vibrant, crimson velvet. Celestial suns were carved into the stone, and upon its arms were two statues of golden dragons, one on each side.

The queen looked regal as always, still in the peach silk dress from the feast. It had full skirts and long sleeves that came to a point at her middle fingers. The high neckline came to her jaw, and the bodice featured an intricate pattern of lace. From her ears dangled pearl teardrops with diamonds looped around them. A matching necklace of diamonds with a pearl teardrop at its center rested between her collarbones.

"Your Majesty." I picked up my skirts and curtsied with my head bowed.

"My dear Zephyra, must you always be so formal? We are blood. You know you may call me Grandmother."

"Mother says we must always be formal, no matter to whom we are speaking. I'm of royal blood and my manners are of utmost importance," I replied with more conviction than I felt, my head held high.

"Bah! No matter," she waved a slender hand. "Your mother is not here right now, and I would prefer if you dropped the formalities. I am, after all, the queen, and so you must listen to me." She gave me a wink.

I did the only thing I could think to do at that moment and smiled back at her. "As you wish, Grandmother."

"Good. Fergus, you may leave us." She waved a hand at the guard who had led me in. He bowed deeply with his hands behind his back and walked back to his post outside of the door.

She turned back to me, her hazel eyes glittering, "Now dear, to what do we owe the pleasure of this visit?"

"I wanted to tell you that I enjoyed your feast and give my apologies for my misbehavior, and for not saying thank you."

"Ah, no bother. It was my pleasure. I'm glad you enjoyed yourself. I don't believe you misbehaved, though. Tell me, what happened to make you believe it so?"

I swallowed and looked down at my feet, feeling a bit ashamed. "I just thought it would be fun to play tag with the other children. There were some fish guts from the kitchen spilled where I was running, and I slipped and fell in them." My cheeks grew hot. "It was foolish. I should have been watching where I was going." I looked up at my grandmother through my lashes, feeling tears welling up in my eyes.

Queen Jelena stared at me with tight lips for a moment. Then, with a sigh, she closed her eyes and said, "And how do you think those fish guts got there, Zephyra?"

"I don't wish to accuse—"

"Forget accusing!" She interrupted me. "Those brats planted them there for you to fall in! You shouldn't be sorry for trying to get along with those of your own age. I will be speaking with their mothers and fathers. I don't understand the other children's need to torment you."

I was shaking a little, for though my grandmother was on my side, her iron voice and stern expression were still intimidating. "I—I believe it is because I look nothing like the princess. They say that I have gross, bright, red hair and that my freckles look like dirt."

The queen sat back with a pleased smile and folded her hands. "If only they knew that you got your bright red hair from me—and those freckles. Sure, my hair has whitened with age, but once it was the colour of crushed garnets. The princess takes after her mother, who is not even of royal blood. No matter. I will see to it that those children never hurt you again. You are correct about one thing. You are of royal blood and you will not be treated in such a manner."

I bowed my head. "Thank you, Grandmother."

"No bother. Perhaps you should stay away from those cruel children anyways. Those outside of our bloodline tend to be jealous."

"I don't wish to see them anymore, anyhow. Adelaide is my only true friend."

"You will find as you grow older that it is hard for us royals to come by true friends. There will be some who love you for you, though. Hold on to those people."

I smiled up at her as she looked down at me. "Meetings with you always make my day better, Grandmother. I will take your advice. You're the smartest person I know in this world."

That got a cheerful laugh from her and she replied, "I am glad I brighten your days child. Now, go and find Adelaide. I must finish reading through these agreements before dinner is served."

The queen stood up and smoothed her skirts before walking slowly to the table with scrolls spilled over it and began opening one of them.

This was her way of dismissing me. Normally, one would have bowed to the queen and bid her farewell, but I simply said, "Goodbye, Grandmother," as I quietly slipped out the door to let her be in peace.

I walked back down the halls to my chambers. Adelaide's were situated right beside mine. Instead of stopping at my own door, I went on to hers and knocked softly.

Adelaide opened the door to her spacious chambers, in which I spent as much time as my own. My beautiful cousin, only a year older than I, wore a delicate sunset coloured dress. It was long and wispy in the skirt, with sleeves to match. Her long, golden curls poured over her shoulders and ran down to her hips. While my hair was long, hers was even longer.

She gave me a wicked smile and opened the door wider to allow me entrance. "You disappeared after the feast. I heard you fell in fish guts," she stated, giving me a pointed look.

I let out an exasperated sigh. "You heard correctly. I was tricked into running through them. I guess I should know better than to believe the other children would actually want to play with me."

She frowned and pinched her pink lips together. "That's unfair. Though you are right, it isn't unexpected. Ah well. What happened to you afterwards? I had expected you'd be in your chambers."

"I was bathed, changed, and then went to see Grandmother. My mother told me I had to apologize."

She scoffed, "Of course she did. Your mother thinks of herself as a queen, ruling over you just because she can."

I let out a small laugh. "How right you are, but still…it hurts. She has never been on my side. I have always felt like I'm just a tool to her—which she can use to her own advantage."

"Forget her. I'm reading about the history of Solis." She changed the subject, just like that. I didn't mind though. I needed to get my mind off this afternoon's unfortunate events. "Noctis De Celestia is ten sunrises from today. I figured it would be good for me to freshen up on the past events of our kingdom."

Adelaide, having recently turned a decade this past winter, was going to attend the annual celebration of our goddess, Celestia, for the first time. I was excited for her. I had heard many stories about how wonderful the night's festivities were. The whole palace would be beaming with excitement in the days before the celebration. Terra would host this spring. Those invited from the other three kingdoms would travel there by horse and carriage.

"Ah, yes, you must be so excited. There's only four more sunrises 'til you leave. I shall miss you." I pouted.

Adelaide took my hand in hers. "I shan't be gone long. Gisela will keep you company, and you'll have your lessons each day…here, take this book. I'm mostly finished, and you can practice your reading while I'm gone. You are, after all, going to be attending next spring." She gave me a wink, the corners of her lips curling upwards towards her rosy cheeks.

I accepted the book from her and was about to thank her when the three bells' signal for the day's third meal echoed throughout the palace.

I set the book on her night stand. "I shall return for this after."

"Of course; now come, let's eat. I'm quite famished."

CHAPTER 3

FOUR SUNRISES LATER, I awoke to Gisela's voice. "Milady…Milady!"

I opened my eyelids a crack and moaned.

"The royal carriage is to leave soon. If you wish to say farewell, you must get up now!"

At those words, I sat up straight and swung the heavy blankets off of my body. Still in my white linen nightgown, my mass of red hair all tangled, I ran from my chambers and down the palace halls.

My bare feet pattered on the cool stone as I scampered down the grand staircase to the main hall. I saw them just outside of the main entrance. The whole royal family, excluding me, was about to climb into the carriage that would take them to Terra. The top was draped with rich red velvet, the symbol of the yellow sun upon each side. Pulling the large carriage were two magnificent white horses. Their coats shone brightly and their long manes flowed down their arched necks like pearlescent waterfalls. There was no doubt that these horses were built for endurance and belonged to royalty. Anyone could see that they were worth a great deal.

"Zephyra, there you are. I was beginning to think you would sleep through our departure. Goodness girl, you couldn't even make yourself presentable before being in the presence of Her Royal Majesty?" my mother scolded, looking down her nose at me sternly. She wore a bright yellow dress with blue patterns embroidered into the bodice. Her blond hair was piled elegantly on top of her head.

"It is of no matter. I am simply pleased she made it to say farewell before we had to be off," the queen stated in a matter of fact tone. Her gown was red; over it, she wore an exquisite white fur cloak to keep her warm.

I hadn't even thought of the state of my appearance until now. I gave a quick curtsy and blushed. "Apologies. I over-slept and was worried I would miss you if I did not come at once. I wish you all the best on your travels and look forward to your return."

"Zephyra! I shall miss you!" Adelaide pushed past my mother. The princess also wore a red gown, though hers was a deeper shade than the queen's bright crimson one. Her cloak was made of black wool and was pinned between her collar bones with a brooch of rubies and diamonds. The sides of her golden curls were pinned back, while the rest of her hair fell down loosely. She wrapped her arms around me and squeezed. She gave me a warm smile as she let me go.

"Listen to Gisela and your tutors while we are away. We will see you when we return," my mother said as she put her hand on my shoulder and gave it a slight squeeze, the only affection I would get from her. Mirrabel wasn't only proper; she was also a cold woman.

My father did bend down, though, giving me a quick hug and a peck on the cheek. His rusty beard tickled my soft face, and the leather he wore creaked with his movements. "Take care of yourself, my dear. And yes, your mother is correct. Gisela is here should you run into any trouble."

"Yes, Father." I bowed my head to him.

"Well, then, we must be off. We have a lot of travelling ahead of us. You will be in our thoughts, Zephyra. Next spring you will be able to take part in Noctis De Celestia, and it will be our turn to host." My grandmother looked down at me. Was that a hint of sadness I saw in her eyes? She turned and spoke to the others before I could confirm it. "Let us take our leave now." One of the royal guards took her hand and helped her up a step and into the grand carriage. Following her were Adelaide's parents, Bardin and Faya, then my parents.

Last was Adelaide, but before stepping up, she kissed me on my cheek.

"Goodbye, Addy." My lashes were wet with the tears threatening to spill out.

She entered the carriage too, and they were off, with only the driver and a royal guard sitting upon the driver's seat.

"Farewell. Safe travels." I waved. I stood there watching until I could barely see the carriage anymore.

I sighed and walked back into the palace, suddenly feeling very lonely. During the past Noctis's, I hadn't much cared about the rest of my family leaving for a while. I'd had Adelaide, and we didn't have to worry much about our royal duties with our parents being away. This time, there was a pang in my heart from her absence.

Back in my chambers, Gisela was awaiting me.

"I think I'll take a ride," I told her.

"Yes, Milady. I shall fetch your riding gown."

Once I was dressed in a brown riding gown loose enough in the skirt for me to sit with one leg on each side of the horse, Gisela braided my hair back to keep it out of my face. She then brought me my leather riding boots. "I know this is your first time without the princess for this long. Don't worry though; I will do my best to keep your mind from getting lonely." My plain but sweet handmaiden smiled at me reassuringly.

"Thank you, Gisela. Perhaps you could tell me a story later. For now, I just wish to clear my head and see my Nova."

"I will send for an escort at once, Milady." She curtsied and left me in my chambers.

Upon being escorted to the royal stables, I came upon the burly master of horses, Serell. He had shaggy brown hair and a scruffy face. He was holding my beautiful dappled grey mare, a gift from my grandmother. Her silky mane and tail were brushed smooth and neat. She was already saddled and ready to go.

"My lady," he gave me a deep bow. "Nova is ready for you."

"Much thanks, Serell."

"Do you wish to have one of my men accompany you today?"

"I don't. My family has left me alone, so I think I should be okay to ride alone as well. Besides, I wish to clear my head and be one with Nova today."

"As you wish, my lady. Please stay within the royal grounds. I don't want to have to send a search party out for you should you get lost…or worse. The queen would have my head."

"Not to worry, Serell. I shan't go far, and I shall return by midday."

He bowed once more and held Nova still for me to mount her.

It felt natural being upon Nova, like we were a single being. I touched her sides with my heels and we trotted out of the stables and into the field.

The sky was completely blue with not a cloud in sight. The sun warmed my face and the air smelled fresh and crisp. I could hear crickets and other creatures chirping away. We took off at a canter and I forgot about the rest of the world. In this moment there was only myself and my beautiful mare. I felt utter happiness spending time with her. She was a docile and well trained horse. Serell had trained her himself to ensure she was best fit for royalty and not at all dangerous, and everyone knew Serell was the best horse trainer in all of Solis.

As we cantered through the field outside of the stables, I thought myself lucky that I wasn't the princess. Adelaide wouldn't have been allowed to take a ride unescorted. Sure, I wasn't allowed to veer too far away from the stables, but at least I was allowed to be alone if I wished. There were so many responsibilities for those who wore the crown, and no freedom at all. I never wanted that.

As I came to a clearing of trees on the edge of the field, I spotted a couple of farmers working. I decided to ride up closer to them to get a look. I had never seen anyone farming before.

"Aye missy! Get off my field! Your horse's feet are trampling my seedlings!" a gruff looking farmer hollered as he made a shooing motion towards Nova and me.

"Girls don't know these things, Father; perhaps she is lost." The son was a smaller version of his father. I would have guessed him to be around fourteen.

These men obviously didn't know I was royalty. I thought to take advantage of that fact. How fun it would be to see how it felt to be treated like a commoner!

"Forgive me, lads. I'm not lost. I simply don't know anything about farming. I'm sorry for trampling your seedlings. I was only interested."

"Farming is of no business to little girls. Besides that, she looks too young to be out and about on her own," the father said to his son as if I weren't even there.

"I have permission to ride alone. Again, please forgive me and I shall go."

The boy smiled at me, "You're forgiven, Miss. Now please go before my father gets any angrier. He has a bit of a temper sometimes."

"Ah!" the father scoffed, his freckled face growing redder than it already was.

I laughed and touched Nova's sides, and we were off at a gallop back towards the palace. Perhaps they would see the direction I went in and the father would feel shame for the way he treated me. I did not know. Nor did I care. It felt different to be treated as a regular little girl, regardless of the scolding. I didn't feel any jealous resentment from them. Suddenly, I felt regret. People would always dislike me for my royal blood. I could never truly trust anyone…except for those who shared my bloodline.

Serell escorted me back to the palace himself. He wasn't happy that I had veered away from the palace grounds.

"Keep an eye on her. She likes to disobey," he spat at Gisela when we reached my chambers.

"Sir, may I ask what she did?" My sweet handmaiden looked up at the master of horses who towered over her.

"She left the palace grounds! If something had gone wrong Her Majesty, Queen Jelena, would have had my head!"

"Sir," she gave him a curtsy, "I will be sure to watch her."

"Humph!" He spun on his heel and stormed off without another word.

"I'm sorry! I saw farmers and I was interested. I've never seen farming before. It wasn't *that* far from palace grounds," I argued, giving Gisela an innocent look.

"Hush. No excuses. What's done is done. You'll not go anywhere outside of the palace walls unescorted until Lady Mirrabel and Lord Lucian are back. Now come. Let's get you into something suitable for the second meal. The duo bells are to chime any moment now."

I sighed, seeing no point in arguing any further. "Alright, but you're to eat all of my meals with me, Gisela," I ordered her. "I shall not eat alone."

"As you wish, Milady."

Was that mockery I heard in her voice? I decided I didn't care. I rarely ordered her to do anything. It was usually the other way around, being that I was still a child, and it was her duty to take care of me. I was still royalty though.

Once we had food in our bellies and time to cool off, we were both happier.

"I shall teach you to play chess. It'll help pass time while my family is away. Adelaide and I often play. It is a thinking game, and the only one we're allowed to play. Mother says dice and cards are for men."

"That would be lovely, Milady. Perhaps after the third meal? You are to have your harp lesson soon."

"Ah, yes, of course." I smiled at her, looking forward to teaching her something.

The days passed and I did as I said I would and taught Gisela to play chess with me. She caught on quickly and even beat me once, which was quite an accomplishment, considering I'd been playing the game since I was six and she had only just learned it. She also told me stories of her own childhood and of her home village.

Between times spent with my handmaiden, I had my lessons. I was learning to play harp, and to read and write. Luckily, I wasn't learning royal etiquette anymore. I had taken those lessons from the age of five until only one spring ago and now possessed all the etiquette skills that there were to learn. It was the dullest of all of the lessons I'd taken.

I still spent some time with Nova, though Serell had one of his men ride with me each time I had taken her out.

I thought about the farmer and his boy and how simple their lives probably were. I wondered what it would be like to be a common child and not have all these lessons and rules. I tried to stop thinking on it, as I would never know.

Chapter 4

FINALLY, THE EVE of Noctis De Celestia came. Noctis De Celestia always fell on the first full moon of spring. Tonight the palace would be quiet, as Solis wasn't hosting the celebration, and those who remained at home would be celebrating in their own ways. Peers of the realm who resided at court would be with their families, as would a lot of the palace staff, save for a few guards who'd be at their posts.

I awoke in the late morning, the sun shining through my small diamond-shaped window and spilling light into my bedchamber. With the rest of the royal family gone, Gisela had seen no need to wake me early.

I stretched, peeled the covers off my body, and went in search of Gisela so she could ready me for the day.

I found her in the servant's quarters with the other handmaidens. They all chatted and giggled amongst themselves. Gisela and another handmaiden, whose straight hair was almost as red as mine, looked up as I entered.

"Good morning, Milady," Gisela greeted me, curtsying. The other ladies followed suit.

"Good morning, ladies. Gisela, would you prepare me for the day now?"

"Of course, Milady," she answered before turning to the others. "Ladies, happy Noctis to you all."

"Happy Noctis," came their unified reply as she took my hand and led me back to my chambers.

"Today we wear white," my handmaiden told me as we entered my chambers. She grabbed a decorative comb and beckoned for me to sit.

Sitting on my wooden chair in front of my golden framed mirror, I declared with surprise, "I have never been told what colour to wear before."

"Ah yes," she paused, "but that's because I have a special surprise for you. Being that this is the last Noctis De Celestia before you are old enough to attend the celebration, I thought I would take you to Celestia's temple so you can see how us who aren't of royal blood celebrate this night."

"You would celebrate this night with me?"

"Of course. I would be honoured to share this night with you—if it would please you, that is."

I thought for a moment, and then smiled at her in the mirror's reflection. "I would very much like that."

I remember how humble I felt in that moment when my sweet handmaiden had decided to celebrate the night with me. Being that it was a special night she was free to do as she pleased, she had still chosen to spend it with her mistress. It made me feel as though we were truly more than just mistress and handmaiden, regardless of our age difference; we had become friends.

That night, once the sun had set, my handmaiden and I made our way to the Temple of Celestia. The night was fairly warm; a cool, calm breeze sometimes blew my hair causing it to tickle my cheek. We walked down the dirt path leading from the palace courtyard to the large stone temple. The simple white gown that Gisela had picked out for me earlier felt light compared to the others I had usually worn, and my unrestrained hair made me feel free. It made me want to skip with laughter like the little girl I was, but I knew better...

"We are to stand before Celestia in our most simple form," Gisela informed me. "She does not care for fashion and glamour. She loves us just as we are."

I thought about that fact and felt myself loving my goddess for it.

As we neared the temple, I saw its stone archways come into view. It was an elegant building with three spires that reached up to the stars.

I saw a line of people outside of its tall entrance door, all waiting to give thanks to our maker, our goddess.

"Good people of Solis, Lady Zephyra, daughter of Lucian and Mirrabel, cousin of Princess Adelaide and granddaughter of Queen Jelena is here to give thanks to our goddess," Gisela announced.

I felt my cheeks grow warm at her words. I suddenly felt like I was on display.

They all bowed or curtsied and moved aside to let us pass. Surely this would make them resent me even more. Who was I to be able to pass the line? Sure, I was of royal blood, but I was no queen or princess. Besides that, I had never celebrated at the temple during previous years. It only seemed fair that I should wait in line too. I bit my lip and decided to keep my silence as Gisela led us through the entrance. I would discuss this matter with her later. I knew the temple was no place for quarreling.

Once inside, a priestess with long flaxen hair greeted us with a deep, straight bow. "Greetings, children of Celestia. Welcome, and happy Noctis De Celestia to you both." She pressed her lips to each of our foreheads gracefully, her long white robes swirling around her like mist.

"Greetings, Priestess Saturnine, and happy Noctis De Celestia." Gisela bowed her head to the beautiful priestess, who looked to be in her third decade.

I followed suit and bowed my own head. "Happy Noctis De Celestia."

"Please remove the leather from your feet and don these robes," she replied as she handed us two white robes which were long like hers but of a simpler fashion.

As I looked around I saw symbols etched upon the stone walls. I knew these to be the symbols of each of Celestia's elements. I had begun learning them shortly after I had begun to speak.

Now in our robes and with bare feet, Priestess Saturnine handed us each a candle, incense, a small bag of sand and a pitcher of water, a peaceful expression etched on her face. My handmaiden and I made our way to the white marble statue of our beautiful goddess.

The packed dirt floor felt cool on my bare feet as I approached the statue. Above her, I saw a large stained glass window in red, blue, green and purple. It depicted Celestia in all her glory, with one element in each of the four corners. Fire was red, water was blue, earth was green and air was purple. The moonlight from the sky above made the window cast a sparkle down on us.

The sight took my breath away. This was my first time inside the Temple of Celestia. Children were not allowed inside unless an adult had invited them, and no one had invited me with them until now. My own mother didn't believe I understood the temple's significance when I had asked to go with her to pray a few summers ago. This was the gift Gisela had given me; she believed that I was mature enough to understand now.

Standing before the statue, Gisela whispered to me, "Do as I do."

"On this night of our goddess, our mother, our maker, we give thanks to the earth that keeps us." She poured the sand at the statue's feet, so I did as she asked and followed suit.

"To the water that quenches our thirst." We poured the water from our pitchers at her feet.

"To the air that gives us breath." She then bent and used a lit candle already beside the statue to light her incense and placed it at the feet. I did the same, the sandalwood scent filling my lungs and making me feel even more at peace.

"And to the fire that keeps us warm." We then did the same with our candles and laid them in the empty candle holders already placed at her feet as well.

"We give thanks to Celestia on this night for the elements she has created to bring us life." She bent and kissed the hand of the statue, which was held out with its palm facing upwards. As she rose, I noticed tears of love glistening in her eyes. I now repeated the last line and kissed the hand too.

Our own hands now empty, the two of us walked back to the entrance. We thanked the priestess and returned our robes. She accepted them back with grace.

Back at the palace, we sat together in one of the private dining halls. It was small, but cozy. Its large windows were covered by long red velvet curtains. The square table in the center was made from a dark wood. There were silver dishes on the table holding miniature lavender cheesecakes, prepared as a special treat only served on Noctis De Celestia.

I took one and bit into it. I closed my eyes, salivating at its rich flavour. I had never tasted anything quite like it...so creamy and sweet.

"I see you are enjoying the lavender cheesecakes. Now, are you ready for a taste of the official drink of Noctis De Celestia?" my handmaiden asked as she went to a small cart that was sitting in the corner. She grabbed two crystal goblets and poured a deep, sparkling, red liquid from a silver pitcher into each.

"Oh, yes!" I exclaimed with excitement.

She smiled as she passed me the goblet. "This is a drink we call Celestia Sanguis—which means Celestia's blood."

"We're going to drink blood?" I asked incredulously.

"No, no. It's not really blood, Milady, 'tis only a name. It's just a special type of wine made from purple grapes during the coldest of seasons. This makes this wine sweeter than other wines. It also sparkles, whereas most wines don't."

"I have never tasted wine. My mother said I'm not yet old enough. Are you sure this is allowed?"

"Ah, this is a special occasion though. It may be our last Noctis De Celestia together. Besides, you will be allowed next year once you are a decade old anyways." She paused, a pensive look on her face. "But it will be our little secret." She gave me a big grin, her golden brown eyes lighting up.

I smiled back at her. "You are so good to me. I don't know what I would do without you and Adelaide. I'm good with secrets. I shall keep ours." With that, I held the goblet to my lips. The crystal felt cool against them, but as the wine entered my mouth, it felt warm and bubbly. And the taste! Oh, the taste was miraculous! Just the right amount of sweetness, it was. I could taste the hint of grapes, and it felt as if the very essence of life poured down my throat with that taste. An instant after, I felt my cheeks grow warm, and everything truly seemed perfect for the first time I could remember. I would never forget my first taste of Celestia Sanguis.

"That's wonderful!"

Gisela closed her eyes and breathed in with delight. "I know. There is nothing like it. You must understand though," she grew solemn, "we only drink this once a year. It is a sacred drink. And so we also give thanks to Celestia for this...our food and drink...our health." She closed her eyes once more, so I did too.

"Thank you, Celestia, for this—for everything." I opened my eyes. "Will you tell me the story of Celestia and how we came to be of this earth? I have not heard it for many seasons." It was true; Gisela had told me the story as a younger child quite often before bed, but that was at least two springs ago.

"It would be my pleasure; 'tis a perfect way to end this night." She sat back and started, "Before this earth existed, there was only the universe. In the universe, a beautiful goddess lived with her brother, who was her polar opposite. We call him—" she leaned in and whispered the next word, as if she was afraid to speak it out loud, "Vesirus. Being opposites, it is no surprise that Celestia and her brother never got along. She was the light and he was the dark. So they each decided they would not speak to one another. In fact, *he* wanted to be as far away from his sister as he could because he could not stand the light that eternally emanated from her. Celestia grew lonely nonetheless, so she decided she would use her power to create the elements; and so then the birth of Fire, Water, Earth and Air came.

"They were her first children, and they had a purpose. She first asked Earth to create a place where life could grow. Earth created a planet, and Celestia was so proud she named the planet after that child. Now that earth had been created, Fire decided the planet would need warmth, and so it created the sun. It was a great accomplishment, and Celestia was amazed with her child, Fire. Now that there was a planet that was warmed by the sun, Air said that it could use its power to allow for breath on earth. And so it did; and just like the other times, Celestia was proud.

"Finally, there was just one more element left that needed to give its power to the planet. That element was Water. Water decided to recreate itself on earth so that life could grow and be sustained.

"With all of the elements' powers now in place upon the planet, Celestia was able to create her second children—us. She told her first children, the elements, that they could stay and live beyond the planet earth with her as they enabled her to create us.

"At the beginning, the elements were happy to stay with Celestia and grant their powers to vessels on this earth who were worthy protectors of the human race.

"It was then that Celestia's brother came back to her. He saw what she had done and he was furious, jealous that she had created something to take care of and keep her busy while he was left on his own. He told her she would pay for what she had done. He told her that it was only ever supposed to be the two of them in the universe.

"So he put a curse on Celestia's second children. It was a curse of dark temptation. He stated that anyone who gave in to their dark temptations would be taken to the dark world once their life was over, the place in which he now resided. Some were not able to resist these dark temptations and succumbed to evil, killing their brothers and sisters.

"Celestia was devastated. She sadly asked her first children to revoke their gifts to the humans so that their powers could never be used for evil again. While she wasn't able to break the curse, she found one way to battle it. She created a spell that made it so after a century in the dark world; a human soul would be reborn, allowing it to redeem itself and one day return to her in death. This is the way it has been since this earth was created and the dark lord cast his curse on us."

I was silent for a few moments after Gisela had finished. She took her last sip of wine and leaned forward, touching my hand. "Such a sad story…our goddess only wanted to love us and for us to love each other, and her brother took that away. So that is why we give thanks to her every spring…for all she has done for us."

"It is sad indeed. I do love Celestia. I hope she knows that," I replied with sincerity.

"She does."

"I grow weary. I think it is time I retire to my bedchamber. This has been a most wonderful night. I thank you for it. I shall never forget it and what you have done for me."

"Milady, I'm glad you enjoyed it. It humbles me to be your servant—and your friend," she added.

I nodded, and with that we rose and went to ready me for slumber.

Chapter 5

THE FINAL DAYS before my family returned crawled by. I still had my lessons and spent much of my time with Gisela and Nova, but alas, I still missed Adelaide dearly.

Gisela tried to keep my mind occupied. "Do you wish to play chess, Milady?"

"Not today, Gisela. I don't feel like playing."

She looked at me with sympathy. "Come with me."

I didn't ask why, and I didn't care. I simply followed her silently. We wound through the dimly lit halls of the palace, going up stairs and around corners; finally, we reached a closed door.

Gisela grabbed a torch off the wall and pushed against the heavy door. It was unlocked and creaked open against her weight with a whining sound, as if it had been asleep and didn't want to move.

As we stepped inside, the smell of dust met my nose. I noticed that the room had no windows. "Where have you brought me?" I asked her.

"Look around and you will see." She held up the torch to illuminate the room.

Once my eyes adjusted to the dim light, I noticed that the walls were all covered in beautiful paintings. The paintings looked to be portraits of very important people.

"There's so many of them!" I exclaimed in wonder. "They're gorgeous! Why are they hidden up here in this dark room?"

"They are kept here because they mustn't be near sunlight. If the sun's rays were to touch them day after day, they would eventually fade. Do you know what they are?"

"Why of course. They are paintings."

"Indeed they are, but do you know who they are paintings of?"

"…Royals?" I guessed.

"You are correct. This is Solis's collection of royal portraits. Every queen has her portrait painted at some point during her reign. Those portraits are kept here."

"They're beautiful."

"I think so too. This is one of my favourite places in the palace—do you see this painting here?" She went to the largest portrait hanging on the center of the back wall.

"Who is she?"

"That, Milady, is Queen Caldura. It is she whom the royal family is named after. She was the first queen of Solis. When her father learned she had the power of fire, before Celestia had her elements revoke their powers from us humans, he decided he would build her a kingdom of her very own. He threatened anyone who tried to stop him by saying his daughter would use her powers to burn them. He purchased slaves and had them build this palace. He kept these dark secrets from his daughter. When Caldura grew older and learned of how the kingdom was built, she burnt her own father out of rage." Gisela shuddered.

She continued on, "Once she came out of her rage she locked herself inside of this palace for many seasons. It was this abuse of power amongst many other evils that made Celestia realize that she couldn't let her second children carry such great power. Not with the evil temptations that her brother had created for us humans."

"…Another terribly sad story. How do you know so much of our history?" I looked up at her questioningly.

"I've had much time to study it since your mother hired me, Milady. Besides, when I found out I would be coming here to be a royal handmaiden, I thought it would be best for me to learn as much about Solis as I could."

"And now you are teaching me."

"'Tis one of my duties to teach you."

"What happened after?"

"After what, Milady?"

"Well, I know that only females can rule Solis. So who became queen after Queen Caldura?"

"Oh," She turned away from the painting and smiled down at me. "She eventually forgave herself. She made peace with Celestia once she realized her powers were gone. She fell in love and had three daughters. Thus, the royal family was born."

"That's good. I'm glad she had a happy ending."

"And so too shall you. This room is a good place to come if you ever want to be alone. A lot who live at the palace don't even know about it, and those who do rarely come here."

"I'm grateful you've showed it to me."

"'Tis my pleasure, Milady." She rubbed my back in a friendly manner. "You have been a good mistress, not some little brat that always needs reprimanding."

"I have been raised to be a proper royal. Mother would have not stood for having a brat as her daughter," I said in a matter of fact tone.

"You are quite right about that. Your mother, on the other hand, has not always been the most pleasant employer."

I snickered. "No, I would assume not."

At last, the day came when my family returned. I was asleep when they arrived, for it was late at night. Even though I was trying to stay awake until their arrival, my eyes had failed me, and I had drifted off into slumber. I didn't even hear the bell that rung to announce them.

"Psst! Zephy…Zephyyy." I woke suddenly to my cousin's whisper as her hair tickled my cheek.

"Addy!" I squealed with glee.

"Shh. You're going to wake the whole palace."

"Oh." I lowered my voice to just above a whisper. "I've missed you so much."

"And I've missed you." She was kneeling beside my bed and now decided to climb in beside me. She must have been back for a while, because she was already dressed in a lavender night-gown.

"How was the celebration? Tell me everything."

"It was most wonderful! The trip there was uneventful, except for when your mother stepped in a puddle and got all wet and dirty." At that, we both giggled. "But it was good. We had a large tent, so sleeping was fairly comfortable. I wanted to sleep under the stars, but my mother wouldn't let me. She said it was too dangerous and I'd get bitten by bugs. So I slept inside of the tent with everyone else. The guard stayed outside to keep watch. He slept inside the carriage during the day. When we arrived there was a welcoming party to greet all the visitors—"

"What was Terra like?" I interrupted.

"It was nice. It was in the forest, and there were tons of big trees and colourful flowers and singing birds there. The palace itself was made of a grey coloured stone. It wasn't as hot there as it is here. The trees blocked out some of the sun…anyways, the party was fun, and everyone was most kind."

"Tell me about the celebration of Noctis De Celestia."

"Of course. I was getting there." She narrowed her olive-green eyes at me.

"Sorry, I'm just excited to hear everything."

"Yes well, the celebration was wonderful. It was in a grand hall. There were statues that represented each of the elements. Hundreds of candles lit the room, and there were so many different colours of linens on the tables. There was music, and bards who told stories, and a singer with a beautiful voice. There was dancing, and by Celestia, there was amazing food! There was this drink…Celestia Sanguis, it was like drinking the heavens themselves!" She threw back her head onto the pillow and sighed dramatically with a smile upon her pink lips.

I so badly wanted to tell her that I'd tried the sacred drink too, but I did not wish to give my handmaiden's secret away for fear of getting her in trouble and thus breaking her trust.

I smiled. "It sounds wonderful indeed."

"Oh Zephy, I'm so excited for you to be able to attend next year! We're going to have so much fun together!" She rolled over and propped her chin up on her palm, beaming at me.

"Me too, Addy. Me too."

"Now tell me, what did you get up to whilst I was away?"

"Nothing as amazing as yourself, but I did enjoy my Noctis De Celestia here too."

"That gladdens me. Did you spend it with Gisela?"

"I did," I replied, growing solemn. "She took me to the Temple of

Celestia and showed me how to give thanks…she also told me the story of Celestia."

"'Tis a sad one."

"Indeed."

"Well, I'm glad you experienced it in your own way. It is an important night for everyone…no matter how we celebrate it."

"The most important," I agreed.

With all of the details of our time away from each other now shared, we took to talking of the usual wishes and dreams we had for our own lives and eventually fell to slumber.

My princess fell asleep beside me that night. It had been a long time since we had fallen asleep together. We'd always been able to sneak into each other's chambers without the guard posted at Adelaide's door noticing, thanks to the secret passage that lay between them. But, alas, our handmaidens did not like it. Coming in to one of our rooms to find it empty had always been quite a scare. They had always feared one of us had been kidnapped, or something of the sort, so we were told we must sleep in our own chambers. On this night, though, we'd missed each other dearly and simply did not care. If we were to be reprimanded, we would deal with it on the morrow.

CHAPTER 6

SUMMER CAME AND went without much ado. I kept to myself when around the other children to avoid being teased. I spent most of the season riding with Adelaide and always with an escort, of course. I had lessons in reading, writing and harp.

As summer faded and turned into autumn and then autumn into winter, the snow began to fall. The snow always fell early at Solis due to the high altitude. The gardens, though not as beautiful as in summer, were a sight to be seen during winter. No flowers bloomed, but all of the trees and plants shimmered with iridescent ice crystals. It was a peaceful place, and I still spent much time there, even in the winter.

I would wear the white fur cloak my father had gifted me and sit upon the bench to practice my reading. Ever since Gisela had told me about the history of Solis I became interested in the other stories history had to tell.

I learned that the four kingdoms had once been at war with each other. The rulers were fighting for power, trying to conquer one another. It wasn't until King Chauser of Terra had died over three decades ago, making his son Tynin the new king, that it came to an end. He saw the damage war was causing all of the kingdoms, and so he negotiated with the other rulers and came up with a treaty of peace for all of Sarantoa. Each of the four kingdoms agreed to the treaty as they were tired of the death and despair the war had brought to their people. Many of the people were beginning to feel Celestia's absence as they gave into their dark temptations of greed already. King Tynin had seen this and was the only one with the power to convince the others in power to sign the treaty. Each kingdom would rule itself, bringing peace to Sarantoa.

That winter I also began my dance lessons. "You shall need to know how to dance for your decade day as well as Noctis De Celestia," my mother had informed me.

I found it quite difficult at first, for I was lanky, with long legs that made me clumsy. I often left my lessons frustrated. Eventually I got it though. I still didn't feel as graceful as I out to be, but at least I could perform the steps without tripping over my own feet.

At last, the day of my decade came. My father came to me that afternoon as I was chatting with Adelaide and our handmaidens, who were readying us for the night's festivities.

"Zephyra?" He opened the door.

"Father! How good to see you." I went to him, and he wrapped me in a warm embrace.

"Happy birthday, my dear—uh…would you give us a moment, ladies?"

"It's okay, Father. Let's go into the hall."

"Of course; I can see you ladies are getting yourselves ready. Excuse my rudeness."

The two handmaidens giggled, not sure what to say.

Adelaide announced in a formal tone, "You are excused."

That had them giggling even more, and with that, we left the room.

My father shook his head with a smile.

Outside of the room, my father got on his knee so that he was closer to my level and said, "My dear daughter, I regret to inform you that I won't be able to attend your celebration tonight." He looked disappointed, the corners of his mouth drawing downward.

"I'm not surprised, Father. You have missed the last three of my birth celebrations, though it makes me sad you'll not be at my decade day," I told him truthfully, trying not to be a pouty child. I knew that wasn't proper behavior for a royal.

"I know, my sweetness. It saddens me as well. But, alas, I must travel to an outside village to commission new men for the royal army."

"But there's been peace ever since the treaty was signed," I argued, using my new knowledge of history.

"Yes, my dear, but just because there is peace within Sarantoa doesn't mean that we won't be attacked from those outside of our four kingdoms. If one of the other three kingdoms were to be attacked, we might have to give aid. A royal army is always one of the most important elements of a kingdom."

I sighed and looked away, not wanting to meet his eyes. I didn't want him to see the hurt they held, nor did I want him to ruin my day.

"I wished to see you before I left and I wanted to give you these." He pulled a shiny pair of new leather riding boots out of the satchel that he had placed on the floor.

"Oh, Father, they're beautiful." I couldn't help but give him a small smile. My father, at least, knew how much I loved riding.

"I saw your old ones were looking worn and figured you could use these."

"They're perfect." I kissed his cheek. "Thank you, Father."

"You are welcome. Now, have fun tonight and don't let your mother get to you for once. She means the best and she loves you…even if she is hard on you."

"I shall try," was all I could say. With that, he gave me a peck on my forehead and left me alone in the hall. Still feeling disappointed, I reentered the room to finish getting ready.

"My father has gifted me with new riding boots," I said to the others.

"Oh! Those are lovely, Milady," Gisela said with excitement. "Just what you need."

"Yes, they are great boots, but I rather wish he would attend the celebration…" I pouted now, not caring what those in my dressing chamber thought.

"He isn't coming?" Gisela asked with shock.

"No, he has men to commission he says."

"No mind, my dear. We'll be having so much fun you'll barely have time to think on it." She winked at me.

"What do you think of my hair, Zephy?" Adelaide piped up in the background, changing the subject. My Addy was good at that. Anytime the air got tense, she seemed to lighten the mood.

"It looks perfect."

"Come and sit. Gisela will do yours. We haven't much time to waste." She patted the chair beside her and continued to check her hair out in the mirror.

I did as she bade and decided to forget about my father for the night. Anyways, what more could I do?

Once we were all ready, Adelaide in her silk lavender gown and I in my pale blue one, we went down to one of the many halls the palace held. Though this wasn't our grand hall, it was still spacious. We held a lot of celebrations here as the grand hall was reserved for events such as Noctis De Celestia and royal weddings.

As we entered the hall I saw its large windows were draped with sheer purple curtains. Our parents and their peers were already there, talking amongst themselves, their children looking at me with as much hate in their eyes as I'd expected. I had no doubt they were only there because their parents had forced them to attend…I wished they hadn't. I knew this celebration of my decade day would only continue to make them more jealous of me.

My mother looked stiff and proper as usual in her high-collared, bright orange and gold gown. Her blonde locks were pinned up in curls while Adelaide and I both wore half our hair cascading down our backs. She turned her head as I entered. I swore I heard her neck creak as she did so. "Zephyra…Princess Adelaide," My mother curtsied to Adelaide as she greeted us. "We are awaiting the queen and then we shall feast. Please have a seat."

"Thank you, Mother," I replied as Adelaide led me to the large rectangular table, draped in crisp white linen.

It wasn't long after we sat that the Herald announced Queen Jelena's arrival. As she entered, we all stood and curtsied or bowed.

"Ah, I thank you all for coming to my wonderful granddaughter's decade celebration." She clasped her hands together and smiled at the room before laying her eyes on me. "Happy decade day, my dear, sweet Zephyra. Now, please be seated, everyone." She gestured with her palms up and arms out and sat down at the head of the table.

"Thank you, Your Majesty," I said.

"You are most welcome, my dear. Now, shall we eat?"

I grinned ear to ear and nodded.

What a glorious feast it was! There were all kinds of fresh vegetables, succulent grouse, warm bread and many kinds of flavourful cheese. A servant came around and poured each of us a goblet of white wine as we ate.

"Zephyra, this is to be your first taste of wine. You are now a decade;

thus, you are old enough to enjoy delicious drink. You must heed my words though; too much of this and you will be feeling ill later on. It is only to be drunk a little at a time and mostly only on special occasions," my mother warned me gravely.

Little did she know I'd already had my first taste of wine, but I had no intention of ever telling her that.

"Yes, mother. I hear your words, and shall drink with care."

With that the queen lifted her own goblet. "A toast, then. To Zephyra! On this day of her decade!"

"To Zephyra!" Everyone else cheered, even the other children, who were at least a decade themselves. I'm sure they did so only because of the queen's presence. They weren't fooling me.

As I drank my wine, I noticed it tasted notably different than the red Sanguis Celestia. It had a stronger flavour that made me wrinkle my nose after swallowing. After a few sips, I got used to the boldness and realized I could actually enjoy its citrusy aroma.

Once we were finished feasting, I was presented with many gifts. My grandmother had given me a set of pens with ink that I could use for writing, now that I was getting quite good at it. And my mother…my mother had a sly smile on her face as she presented me with her gift.

"Oh…It's a dress!" I said as she held it up before me.

"It is. Well go on. Have a look at it."

I took it from her to get a better look. It was an exquisite red dress made from soft velvet with a bodice that had suns, stars and moons etched in gold thread upon it. It was really very pretty. Too bad I looked terrible in red…

"I had it made for you…for Noctis De Celestia. It is our kingdom's colour and more suitable than all of your current childish gowns."

I knew not to complain of the colour. I was to be grateful for this gift from my mother or else I would be scolded later for it. "It is lovely. Thank you, Mother. I'm excited to wear it for the celebration of our Goddess."

"Wonderful." She clasped her hands together and smiled at me, though it was more of a forced than genuine smile.

I had many other gifts from the peers; most of them baubles and books and the like. Not long after the last gift was presented, some of the servants brought out a large cake with pink and white icing on it. As we ate the sweet, moist cake, we talked of peaceful subjects such as the weather and marriages that were to happen in the coming season.

All seemed innocent, and I'd finally begun to relax when one of the boys across from me sneered, "How is it fair that *she* gets to have this big of a celebration when my mother is a cousin of the queen, and my coming of a decade was only a small dinner with my parents and a few friends? It's not like *she's* the princess or anything…just another relative like me!"

The other children glared at me in agreement. His own mother gasped in astonishment at her son's outburst—right as my Addy chucked a piece of her cake at him and laughed it off with one of her light, airy giggles.

There was a moment of silence and then Adelaide's mother, Faya, spoke up with wide eyes, "Adelaide!"

"What is wrong with a little fun now and then? After all, this is a celebration, is it not?" My grandmother questioned the room. Then, to my dismay, she picked up her piece of cake and tossed it at Faya, hitting her right in the side of the face with a *smuck* sound. And then, all hell broke loose. The next thing we knew, there was cake flying through the air in every direction, and everyone was laughing—even the other children. My princess had saved the day. What a risk she had taken though! Who knew it would turn out well and not backfire in her face? Then again, it was Adelaide, and everyone did love her. I would not forget the risk she took to save me from humiliation.

Once we wiped our faces clean of cake, it was time for song and dance. I was about to go off with Adelaide, when my mother grabbed my hand and pulled me aside. "That was quite a mess you caused."

"I know I may have been the cause, Mother, but you cannot blame me for it. I said and did nothing to provoke Adelaide to throw her cake."

"Either way; just know I only allowed it to pass tonight because it is a special occasion. From now on, though, you will be seen as not only as a royal…but as a royal adult."

"Yes, Mother." I looked down at the floor.

"So I expect you to act as a royal adult. I will not have you embarrassing this family."

"Don't worry, Mother. I hear you and will do as you say." I knew if I wanted to enjoy the rest of my night, I must not argue with her, even though she was being unfair.

"Good." She patted my back. "Now, go dance the night away."

As I went to find Adelaide, a fast-paced song with fiddles, a pipe, tambourines and drums started up. I spotted her talking and laughing with another girl, so I grabbed her arm and we all began dancing to the catchy rhythm. By the end of the song, we were breathless and laughing with glee.

The next song was slower; played with a harp, flutes and a triangle. Just as the song started a boy with copper-coloured hair approached us. “Good evening, Princess.” He bowed to Adelaide. “May I have the pleasure of having this dance with you?”

“You may.” She looked back at me and winked as they strode deeper into the crowd.

I was left standing alone.

As I was about to leave the dance floor, Gisela caught my arm; she had been invited to the dance at my mother’s request. Probably to make sure I behaved well. “May I have this dance, my lady?”

I pressed my lips together and looked up at her with regret.

“Oh, come on,” she insisted. “There’s no sense moping about.”

“’Tis a slow song though,” I argued.

“Bah! No matter,” She waved her hand, “I’ll lead.”

I spotted my mother watching us. Perhaps she wanted me to show off my dancing skills. I didn’t wish to displease her, so I gave in. “Alright…”

I was thoughtful as she led us through the steps. “Why must Adelaide dance with that boy? We were having fun. It was rude of him to interrupt.” I stumbled a bit not paying attention to my feet. Gisela caught me and we continued.

“Ah, my dear lady, you must understand—it wasn’t meant to be rude. Adelaide is of that age now where boys will begin to court her.”

“But why does she have to agree to it?”

“It is in her best interest, my lady. She is the princess and expected to marry one day.”

“I don’t see why she must marry, just because she’s the princess.” I rolled my eyes. I knew I was being unreasonable, but it wasn’t fair that I had to share my Addy with a boy.

“Because she will be queen one day, and queens are expected to have children to take the throne when they leave this earth for Celestia…otherwise you would continue to be next in line for the throne, and then if you don’t have any children—”

"Okay, I get it," I interrupted and broke our dance. "No, I don't wish to be queen…ever. It just makes me sad that she left me for a *boy*. All of the boys in this kingdom have been cruel to me. I thought she knew that."

"She is only doing her duty. Try not to take it to heart."

"I will do my best." As the song ended, I walked away. Gisela stood there looking sympathetic. I did not want her pity, so I went to the place where I knew I could be at peace; I went to the gardens.

I sat on the bench for a while, the moon and the stars my only light. I contemplated what my life was going to be like once Adelaide had a true consort and eventually a husband. I felt it would be very lonely.

I was so deep in thought, I almost didn't hear the footsteps coming up behind me. "There you are. I knew I would find you here." My Addy had come to look for me after all. This made me feel slightly better.

"I didn't think you would notice I had left," I said, feeling sorry for myself.

"Well, of course I noticed. Don't be silly."

"What happened to that boy you were dancing with?"

"I told him I needed to find you, because this is your night and I needed to be with you." She looked down at me with big doe eyes.

I sighed. "I'm not angry with you. I understand it is your duty to find a consort."

She wrinkled her nose at me and burst out laughing. "A consort? By heavens, Zephy! No, not yet. I'm still too young for that. I was simply being kind. It would have been rude to refuse." She stopped and sat down beside me. "Even when I do begin the act of courtship, I'll never forget about you. You, my dear Zephy, are my best friend and my family."

My eyes welled up with tears. "Oh, Addy! I know!" I hugged her and buried my face in her golden hair, which smelled of roses. "I just feel so lonely sometimes. Like no one else will ever accept me because of my royal blood and because I'm still not important enough to matter."

"One day they will all see how wonderful you are, like I do. Until then, don't worry. I'm here."

I nodded, sucking in a deep breath.

"Now come. Let us go get ready for sleep. Our handmaidens went to bed already. I told them we could take care of ourselves tonight."

"And they let you?"

"They have no choice. I am the princess, after all." She smirked.

I laughed, feeling lighter, as we walked out of the gardens and back into the palace.

CHAPTER 7

ADDY AND I tried to stay out of the way as much as possible the week before Noctis De Celestia. The whole palace was abuzz with preparations for the celebration.

Servants were busy with cleaning and polishing the entire grand hall and everything that we were to use that night, cooks were busy picking fresh vegetables from the garden, men were hunting for dinner and the royal family was busy deciding what to wear for the celebration.

I didn't need to worry about having a new dress thanks to my mother's gift. Though I didn't think the colour suited me, nor was my body fully grown for the style of it, I would wear it to avoid my mother's wrath.

"What are you wearing to Noctis De Celestia?" I questioned Adelaide one afternoon.

"You will have to wait and see," she answered, peering down at her tea with a distant expression.

"You seem distracted lately."

She looked up then "Oh! No…just thinking."

"About what?"

"Hmm?"

"Addy!"

"Oh, nothing—just about Noctis." She waved her hand in dismissal.

"Well, *I'm* kind of excited for it to be over. I'm tired of feeling like I have to hide in order to be out of the way of everyone; they're so busy with preparations. Maybe it would have been more fun to travel somewhere else for the celebration like you did last Noctis."

"No it wouldn't. I mean it was fun to see a new place, but the travelling itself felt long and boring."

"Kind of like how it feels here right now." I raised an eyebrow at her.

She set her tea down then, her long single braid swinging to one side. "Come with me. Let's go exploring. No one will even notice, seeing as how they are all so busy."

My face lit up and I jumped up off of my seat. Finally, I had gotten her attention.

As it turned out, we didn't find much excitement exploring either. I asked her if she knew about the palace art collection and she already did. In the end, I decided we should go outside for a walk. We came across my father, who was training new men in archery.

He noticed us right away. "Girls! ...Uh, g'day Princess," he bowed quickly, catching himself. "You shouldn't be out here. Tis dangerous. You could be hit with an arrow, and then we'd all be done for."

"But it's so boring everywhere else right now," I complained childishly. Good thing my mother wasn't there to scold me.

"Can't we learn to shoot an arrow? It would be good if we could protect ourselves, would it not?" Adelaide backed me up.

"No, don't be silly. You have guards for that. You shouldn't even be in the training grounds. Go to the stables or something. I must get back to training." He made a shooing motion at us.

"Can we at least watch from a distance?" He paused, so I added, "Please, Father," giving him the saddest expression I could muster.

"Oh alright. But from a good distance. Go over there by those trees and watch if you must, but not for too long. If your mother finds out you're here, she'll have both of our hides."

"Yes, Father."

Addy snickered as we made our way to the trees, which were beginning to bud with green leaves. "Even your father is scared of your mother."

"Wouldn't you be?"

"Yes, I suppose I would," she answered.

"Look at those men. So intent on doing well for your father," Addy exclaimed, changing the subject, as we found a patch of grass that was soaked in sunlight to sit on.

"It looks more fun than what we get to do on an average day. What I wouldn't give to be someone without royal blood."

"You say that now, but I doubt you'd last a week as a commoner." She looked at me pointedly, as if daring me to try it.

"You may be right but, alas, we shall never know."

Adelaide was quiet for a moment, a thoughtful expression again taking over her face. "Some of those *men* aren't much older than us. Perhaps one of them would be our protector." Her eyes seemed to light up at that notion.

"Oh, by Celestia, is *that* what you've been thinking about all day? *Boys?*"

"Some of them are nice," she cooed, fiddling with her skirt.

"Gross! And not true. I've never met a boy who has been nice to me. Not one. They're all rude and hateful. No one would ever want me anyways; I'm just the princess's ugly cousin."

She grabbed my arm, hard, and looked me straight in the eye at that, her pretty face contorting so much that it took me aback. "Don't say that! You are *not* ugly. Besides, we're still young. Mother says we will still grow into our bodies and become even more beautiful."

"I'm sure *you* will."

"Don't argue with me. I command it, as your princess."

At that I rolled my eyes and threw some grass at her, which led to me getting up and running away and her trying to catch me. Boys were a forgotten subject.

At last, the day of Noctis De Celestia came. I was woken that morning by Gisela's gentle shakes. "Milady, 'tis time to get up. We must begin preparations for the night's celebrations."

I yawned and stretched as she threw open my heavy burgundy curtains and let the sunlight in.

"Okay, then. May I at least break my fast first?" I grumbled

"You've missed first meal. I've brought you some biscuits and tea, but you must make haste."

I sat up and rubbed my eyes, my hair a tangled mess. "I missed first meal? Why did you let me sleep so long?"

"You needed your beauty rest for tonight. No matter. Here, eat." She handed me a golden biscuit that was no longer warm, but still felt soft and fresh.

After I ate my biscuits and drank my tea, Gisela took me to the bathing room where she scrubbed me and combed out my fiery locks. Afterwards, she rubbed scented oils that smelled of fennel and violets on my skin. She then brought me to my dressing room and helped dress me in the red velvet dress my mother had given me. It was very pretty, though it would have looked better on a full grown woman; my chest was still too flat and my hips too narrow. To myself I looked like a boy in a red dress. I wrinkled my nose at my reflection in displeasure.

There were no sleeves to the dress, so I wore a sheer white sash over my shoulders. Now clothed, it was time to do my hair. Gisela was very good at doing hair. As she twisted and pinned pieces of it up, I asked her, "Where did you learn how to do hair so beautifully?"

She took a pin out of her mouth to answer me. "My mother. She was a handmaiden for one of the duchesses in my village. She knew all the tricks and secrets of beauty."

Just then, she put the last pin and handed me my silver-backed mirror so I could see her work.

In my reflection, I saw a girl with bright red hair all done up in twists with curly pieces framing her face. Some longer pieces fell down her neck. I almost didn't recognize myself. If only my dress looked as good as my hair did.

"It's wonderful. I love it!" I smiled up at her. "I only wish I fit my dress properly and that it were a different colour. Red clashes with my hair."

"I would have chosen blue for you, but, alas, it's not one of Solis' colours. You must wear a colour of fire…your hair makes up for it though." She winked at me.

"Yellow or gold would have been better."

"Mayhap next year. Now, off with you." She patted my back. "Go find your parents. It will be time to go to the grand hall soon and begin the celebrations. I hear people from other kingdoms have already begun to arrive."

"Will you be there tonight?"

"As much as I wish to be there with you, I must attend the Temple of Celestia tonight to give my thanks. It is my tradition."

"I understand. Would you say thanks to our goddess for me, seeing as how I can't join you this time?"

"Yes, my lady, of course. You may also say thanks at the end of your night. You don't need to be in the temple to say a prayer to our goddess."

"I will, then. Thank you, Gisela."

I rose and left slowly, trying not to step on my dress, as I made my way to my parent's chambers to meet them.

As we waited outside the grand hall for the herald to announce us, I studied my parents and their glamorous attire. My mother wore a red gown like mine, though hers was darker—like garnets, while mine was more the colour of rubies. Hers accentuated her body with its silky material and v-shaped neck line that showed off her pushed up bosom, unlike mine, which lay square across my flat chest. She wore matching garnets in her hair, which was all braided and pinned up in a fancy style. She looked stunning. I wondered if mayhap I wasn't her child at all and she had actually stolen me from my real mother.

My father looked like a proper royal tonight as well. I was used to seeing him in the leather he wore every day for training. Tonight, though, he wore a white tunic under a dark red doublet that matched my mother's dress. On his legs, he wore brown trousers with shiny black leather boots. His rusty beard was even trimmed neatly. I couldn't recall a time where my father had looked so cleaned up. Then again, this was my first Noctis De Celestia celebration.

"I'm glad you wore the dress I gave you. It is a touch too big, I see, but it will do." My mother looked down her nose at me. She was always so proper…even when we were alone. I despised that fact.

"Yes, Mother, it is a lovely dress. Thank you." *…And I hate it,* I thought silently to myself.

"Come, then," she dismissed me, "The herald is about to announce our names. Let us enter."

With that, two guards opened the high golden double doors and we stepped into the grand hall.

I had never set foot inside this room before, and as I did now, it took my breath away. The floor was made of black marble, with shimmering, golden veins running throughout its surface. On the far wall, opposite the entrance, was a large sun-shaped window framed with gold. From the ceiling hung matching golden chandeliers, the candles within them causing them to glow with warmth. There were square tables around the edge of the room with an open dance floor in the center. The tables were draped with black linens, golden dishes scattered upon them. The whole room was an array of black and sparkling gold. I gasped in delight and felt my mother place her hand on my back.

"Lucien Caldura, son of Queen Jelena. Mirrabel Caldura, wife of Lucien Caldura and Zephyra Caldura, daughter of Lucien and Mirrabel Caldura and granddaughter of Queen Jelena." The herald's voice boomed throughout the hall.

Now announced, my parents and I made our way towards one of the tables.

"You will sit here, Zephyra, with those of your own age from the other kingdoms of Sarantoa. Tonight is for socializing and making new friends." My mother pushed me towards a table with two girls and a boy, who did indeed all look close to my own age.

I didn't want to sit with these strangers. I wanted to sit with Adelaide—or even my own parents would have been better. I didn't like meeting new people, especially those of my own age, who were sure to tease me.

I went anyway. I knew better than to defy my mother. She would make me pay later if I argued with her—especially here in front of all these people.

Now that I was taken care of, my parents went and took their seats with another important-looking couple, with pale blonde hair and skin even fairer than ours, probably from Ventosa.

The two girls at my own table, I guessed to be from Terra. Their brown hair, brown eyes and darker skin gave them the earthy look of their kingdom.

The boy who was seated beside me had hair as black as ebony…I hadn't seen his eyes because he was seated beside me and I wasn't comfortable making eye contact with complete strangers. Almost everyone with hair that dark came from the kingdom of water though, so he must have come from Aquila. I couldn't be sure, simply because none of them bothered to introduce themselves to me.

Shortly after I was seated, the herald announced Faya and Bardin, followed by Adelaide. I felt my lips part in awe as I took in Adelaide's appearance. She was more beautiful than ever in a shimmering coral gown that caught light from the flickering candles as she descended the great staircase down into the hall. Her golden curls were an array of loops and braids, and upon her head rested a golden tiara that made her truly look like the princess she was. I noticed the other guests all had their attention focused on her as well. I smiled inwardly, for I saw only adoration in their faces. She was going to make the loveliest queen one day and I felt pride at that.

As she made her way to the head table, where the rest of the monarchs from the other kingdoms were sitting, she caught my eye and gave me a quick, reassuring smile. I felt the corners of my own mouth turn up in response, but then I looked down at my silverware and pretended to study it. I didn't wish her to see any sadness at the pang of regret I felt from not being able to truly share this great night together.

My mind still on my cousin, I almost didn't notice when one of the servants walked by our table with a tray full of little crystal goblets. Each held a deep red liquid that sparkled like the blood of the divine; Celestia Sanguis. I quickly picked one off the tray and downed the red liquid with one swallow. I felt it instantly calm my nerves and warm my heart. I closed my eyes and sighed with pleasure.

"Aye! Do you even know what that is, girly?" one of the girls from Terra shot at me. She had straight sable coloured hair and fierce eyes.

"It sure looks like she does," said the other girl, who looked almost identical, except her hair was wavy and her eyes softer.

"I wasn't talking to you, Ephera," she glared at the girl beside her before turning back to me. "Now, speak for yourself, girly. Hmm? Do you or do you not know what you have just drunk without a second thought?"

"I—Uh—Yes, I do," I stuttered, feeling my nerves return. "I have heard stories of its delicious flavour and was excited to try it. That's all."

The straight-haired girl narrowed her eyes at me, when the other girl, Ephera, laughed. "Don't be so sour, Shausana! Forgive my sister. She can be harsh sometimes. Of course you are excited—as are we!" She took a goblet for herself. "Come now, Shausana, let us try Celestia Sanguis too." She handed her sister one of the tiny goblets, then took one for herself.

The boy beside me, who still hadn't uttered one word, took one too. He looked a few years older than the rest of us girls. This was probably not his first taste of the sacred drink.

"Go on, Zephyra, have another. We shall make a toast. It won't kill you to have more than one." Ephera tilted her chin towards the tray.

"Too many, and you might get sick—or so I've heard," I said, thinking of my mother's warning.

"These goblets are tiny. Surely one more shan't cause any harm." Shausana looked me in the eyes and raised her brows, daring me to take another and join their toast.

"Alright, one more for now." I picked up another goblet, not wanting to disappoint the other girls.

"To Noctis De Celestia!" Ephera lifted her glass.

"To Noctis De Celestia!" the other three of us repeated and clanked our tiny goblets together before drinking them down.

I felt the liquid warm my heart once again and thought perhaps those of my own age from the other kingdoms were more accepting and wouldn't make fun of me.

Just then, a horn sounded and we turned to hear the herald announce, "And now, ladies and gentlemen, the queen of Solis! Queen Jelena Caldura!"

My grandmother entered through the large black and golden doors. She descended the stairs, flanked by two of her ladies-in-waiting. The sight of her brought tears of joy to my eyes. She was dressed in a magnificent gown of yellow and orange encrusted with tiny topaz jewels. Her silver hair was pinned up and upon it rested a golden crown with a sunburst at its center. She looked like a sun goddess and I was beyond proud to be able to call her both my grandmother and my queen.

Queen Jelena made her way to the center of the head table and sat with Adelaide and the other kings and queens of Sarantoa. Now seated, Queen Jelena spoke in a voice that carried throughout the grand hall. "Kingdoms of Sarantoa, on this Noctis De Celestia, we give thanks to you for coming to celebrate with us—and to our goddess, Celestia, who loves us and who we love dearly. Now, to begin the celebrations…let us eat!"

With that said, a number of servants in simple black silk brought trays filled with steaming food to each of the tables. The whole hall was abuzz with the sound of goblets clanking and people conversing. The aroma of the food made my mouth water. It wasn't long before a tray filled with fresh vegetables, bread, stew, duck and salmon sat before me. It all tasted as delicious as it smelled. Our kitchen staff had done a wonderful job in preparing the food for this night.

I sat in thoughtful silence as I ate my dinner while the other three talked of their home kingdoms.

After our dinner was finished, trays were cleared, and then the servants came back around with more goblets of Celestia Sanguis. I had one more. Then they brought out the tiny lavender cakes that were still smaller than any other cake I'd ever seen before. Seeing the cakes, I thought of Gisela and how she must be at the Temple of Celestia by now. While I was happy that I finally got to celebrate the night as an adult, a part of me wished I could be with my handmaiden. With that thought, one of the mini cakes was set in front of me on a cute little golden plate. As I picked my little cake up and went to take a bite, something caught my eye. Across its surface crawled a disgusting brown bug! I gasped in horror, dropped the cake, and let out a blood-curdling scream.

The others at my table were silent, but only for a second, before Shausana burst out laughing so hard she couldn't catch her breath.

"Shausana..." I heard Ephera trying to stop her sister as she herself was covering her mouth. The boy beside me shook his head and spoke his first words to me. "It's only a little bug. No need to be so dramatic."

I stood up and looked at them all, not even noticing that the whole hall's attention was now on me. Hot tears burned my eyes. I didn't know how that bug had gotten there, but at that moment I was sure that it had been no mistake that it had been on *my* cake, out of all of the cakes in the whole hall.

Suddenly I became aware that the whole hall was watching me, including my mother. In my disgust and embarrassment, I wailed at the three at my table, "By Celestia, you will *all* pay for this!" I heard gasps as I turned and ran out of the hall.

Perhaps I had overreacted in the moment. It probably wasn't any of my table-mates' faults. But the fact that they had laughed at me during my moment of weakness had hurt. It was a wound that had grown and festered from the many years of ridicule I had endured by the peers of my own kingdom.

This time, I'd felt something inside of me break, and as I ran up the stairs and down the halls of the palace, I felt a searing heat growing from within my body.

I thought perhaps this was an effect of all the Celestia Sanguis I had drunk. It felt as if my own skin was going to burn off my body. That heat grew from within and radiated outward. I thought for a moment mayhap I would burst into flames and join Celestia in the heavens, but then I reached the stream in the gardens and jumped into its cool waters. I felt the water steam off my skin and take the scorching feeling away with it.

So there I sat in the middle of the stream within the palace gardens, soaking wet and bawling my eyes out, when my mother found me.

"Look at you," she tutted. "You have *ruined* the dress I gave you! You have *ruined* this night for *me!* You have *ruined* everything! This is unacceptable, Zephyra. You cannot *curse* other people like that—"

"I apologize that I have ruined everything, Mother. I'm sorry that I'm such a *disappointment* to you," I interrupted, not wanting to hear anymore of her cruel and unforgiving words.

She pulled me out of the stream by my arms. My dress was indeed ruined and sticking to my body. My hair was a sopping wet mess, and had come undone.

"An apology is simply not enough this time, Zephyra. This is the last time you will ever embarrass this family. This time, I must punish you."

"Whatever you see fit to punish me with, I'll understand." I expected her to lock me in the tower for the night or take away my books. What she said next…I didn't see coming.

"Good. Then you will understand that I must send your dear Gisela back to her home land—"

"*No!* Not that, Mother, *please* not that! Anything else!" I fell to my knees and begged her, unable to believe that she would do such a thing.

She smiled in triumph at me. "I know you and she have become close like friends, and right now, you deserve to have something meaningful taken from you."

Hot tears streamed down my cheeks. "It's unfair to her! You cannot do this!"

"Well, she has you to thank for that, now, doesn't she?" She pressed her lips together tightly.

"Fine." I raised my chin defiantly to her. "I shall *never* attend another Noctis De Celestia celebration again. I'll spend each one at the Temple to honour the time Gisela took me there to give thanks to our goddess."

"As you wish. At least that way you won't be able to embarrass this family during Noctis again." That said, she spun on her heel and left me.

I sank lower to the ground, defeated. I wanted to lay there and cry forever, but I knew if I did, I would never get to say goodbye to my handmaiden. I picked up my wet skirts and I ran to the Temple of Celestia to find her.

CHAPTER 8

I APPROACHED THE temple, still soaking wet. The commoner awaiting their turn with our goddess peered at me. I ignored them and pushed straight through the wooden entrance doors.

One of the priestesses noticed me and gave a greeting. She was older than the priestess I had met the previous year, but she was just as graceful in her white robes. She took one look at me and rushed to my side with concern.

"My goodness, girl. Are you alright?"

"N—no," I sobbed, while trying to catch my breath. "I must speak with Gisela. Is she—"

Gisela appeared from around the corner with a worried look. "Zephyra! What are you doing here?" She lowered her voice, remembering where she was. "Not here. Come with me." She handed her robe to the priestess. "My thanks, Priestess. Happy Noctis to you."

The priestess bowed her head, clasping the robe in her hands. Gisela took hold of my hand and led me out of the temple and away from its surroundings so that we could speak in private. She knelt in front of me, took both of my hands in hers and looked up at me with questioning eyes.

I burst out, "Sh—sh—*she's* sending you away!" I wailed, not caring about how childish my actions were.

"Who? Sending me away where? Zephyra?" She spoke softly, but I saw a flash of panic in her eyes and felt guilty.

"My mother! It's all my fault! She's sending you home to punish *me…*"

"Oh dear." She took a deep, shaky breath to steady herself. "What in Celestia's name is she punishing you for?"

I told her about the bug and how the girls at my table had laughed at me—and how I had overreacted and cursed them before running from the hall. I decided not to tell her about the burning sensation that had taken over my body. I wasn't sure if it had been real or my imagination playing a jest on me.

"Don't blame yourself, my lady, 'tis a harsh punishment; one that you couldn't have foreseen. Alas, I'm employed by your mother; if she wishes to send me home, then home I must go."

I tried to swallow back the tears. I was sick of crying. "But you are one of my only friends, and it's not fair to you to be punished for my actions."

"Don't worry about me, my lady. I shall be fine." She smiled up at me reassuringly. "I will get to see my family again. As for friends…of course I'll miss you too, but you are going to make so many new friends as you go through life."

I didn't believe her, but at this point I didn't want new friends anyways, so I let it go.

"Look at you. You're soaking wet, my lady. Let me at least dry you and prepare you for slumber as my last task as your handmaiden."

I nodded as she stood up. "I would like that very much."

We walked back to the palace and up to my chambers, hand in hand.

Now dry, I wore a clean night dress as Gisela combed out my wet hair.

She finally thought to ask me, "So how did you end up soaking wet, if you don't mind my asking?"

"I—oh—I fell in the stream," I lied, my eyes cast downwards. "After I ran from the Grand Hall, I went to the gardens to be alone and accidently fell into the stream because I wasn't paying attention to where I was going. It was there that Mother found me," I added.

Before she could answer, a loud knock startled both of us. Gisela rose and went to answer the door to my chambers. I heard my mother's voice as soon as the door opened and knew Gisela was being told of her end at court.

Once they finished their exchange, Gisela returned to combing my hair.

Growing impatient with her silence, I asked, "What did she say? When are you to leave?"

"I told her I wanted tonight to say goodbye to you and gather my belongings, but I must leave in the morning…before you awake."

"I understand." I sighed, closing my eyes.

"Now, now; everything will be good and well. You'll see. You shall have a new handmaiden, who you can teach to play chess. And I'll get to see my mother and sister, whom I haven't seen for nearly four springs."

"Why have they not come to visit you here?" I turned to look up at her as she put my silver comb down and started braiding my hair.

"'Tis hard for them. They simply can't afford to hire transportation. Besides, long travels are tough on my mother's old body."

"Did my mother not pay you and your family well for your services?"

"She did, but most of that went to buying livestock for the farm so that they could live easier and continue to grow their own food. Besides, not having me there was one less mouth to feed."

"I see. It must be hard for commoners."

"'Tis not easy, that's for sure." She finished off my braid by tying it with a yellow ribbon and admired her work.

"Still, I would rather that than having to deal with royal formalities and jealous peers." I rolled my eyes as I spoke the last word.

"Ah, but my lady, you mustn't think that way. Many would trade you places in a heartbeat. We all must be thankful for the destiny Celestia has given us."

"I suppose so." I furrowed my brow and considered her advice.

"Now, my lady, you're ready for slumber and 'tis late. I need to prepare my things and get some rest before my travels home on the morrow."

"I understand," I felt tears threatening to well up in my eyes again as I hugged my handmaiden… my dear handmaiden who had taken care of me since I was just a babe. "I shall miss you, Gisela. One day mayhap I shall come find you. One day when I'm old enough to make my own choices."

"Ah, my lady, though I wish I could see you again, I doubt that could be true. You need to stay here were you are safe. Please promise me you'll take care of yourself."

"I promise. Tell your family I'm sorry you got sent back."

"'Tis not your fault." She gave me a glum look.

"Tell them anyways." I looked away, blinking back tears.

With nothing left to say, she kissed the top of my head and left me alone.

Feeling miserable and defeated, I collapsed onto my bed and cried myself to sleep.

That night, I dreamt my own spirit rose to the heavens above. There, I met the divine Celestia. She was pale and bright like the moon, with silk-like hair the colour of stars. Her eyes, an endless ocean of indigo, seemed to hold all the secrets of life. She held me in the palm of her hand and I was speechless; my breath taken away by the very presence of her.

"You are a special girl, Zephyra." I heard her voice in my head. It sounded light and pretty, like bells singing in the wind.

Confused by her words, I asked, *"Special? How could I be special?"*

But she did not answer my question. She only smiled and said, *"Control your emotions, my child. You must not let your anger burn too bright, Zephyra…"*

"Zephyra…Zephyra!"

I awoke to Adelaide shaking my shoulders and calling my name. It must have been the wee hours of the morning. The sun had still not begun its rise, and Adelaide wore her night dress.

"Adelaide…what do you want?" I asked, still half-asleep and annoyed by the interruption to the most vivid and amazing dream I'd ever experienced.

She backed up. My words seemed to lash her like a whip across the face. "I wanted to make sure you were okay, is all. What happened? I heard you scream and saw you run, but no one would tell me what actually happened."

"I overreacted. There was a bug on my cake and the others at my table laughed at me, so I left. And, no, I'm not okay. My mother has sent Gisela away." I felt anger pushing up inside of myself, threatening to burst, and remembered my dream. I took a deep breath and closed my eyes, willing it to dissipate.

Adelaide's big olive eyes widened at that. "Oh—my…Zephy, I'm so sorry."

She truly looked sympathetic. I didn't want her pity. "Never mind,

I'm tired of thinking on it. It's been a long night, and you've awaken me." I rolled over, wishing she would leave. I knew it was cold of me to do so. She was only concerned for me, but I knew if I thought about it any longer, that red hot anger within me would return.

Adelaide noticed my dismissal and left me to myself. It didn't take long before I fell into slumber once again. This time I did not dream though, and when I awoke the next day, Gisela was long gone.

Chapter 9

As time went on, I drew even further into myself. I didn't even seek Adelaide's company out, and when she called on me, I often made up an excuse so I didn't have to spend time with her. I was simply feeling sorry for myself and wished to be alone.

I suppose I couldn't blame her when she eventually quit coming to me and started spending time with the boy who had asked her for a dance on my decade day; Wrenth was his name. Still, it hurt that she chose to replace me with a *boy*. I grew even colder towards her, and tried to avoid her at all costs.

I spent a lot of time reading books on history and fairytales. My mother had hired me a new handmaiden. She was an older, serious woman named Awyn. Her copper hair was mostly silver with age, and her sense of humour was almost nonexistent. We got along well enough, but I wouldn't call her a friend, not like Gisela had been. I knew if I made another friend, it would've just been another thing my cruel mother could've taken from me.

My mother seemed happy as ever now that I was acting a proper royal, even if it meant I was melancholic. In her eyes, I had matured into someone she could control and someone who wouldn't be an embarrassment to her.

My father and mother began to fight a lot after she had sent Gisela away. It led me to believe that my father didn't agree with her decision, but there was nothing he could do about it now. Eventually, he spent even more time with his men than ever before, and took any excuse he could to leave the kingdom. This, regretfully, resulted in me hardly ever seeing him. The seasons seemed to come and go with a blur...until one summer day when I was fifteen.

I'd just come back from a lone ride with Nova. I was now old enough to be allowed to take rides unaccompanied—that, and now I knew better than to leave the palace grounds alone. Leading Nova into the stables, one of Serell's grooms, who was only a young boy, approached me. "I can take her from here, Milady."

"If you don't mind, I would like to unsaddle and rub her down myself. It would be most kind of you to bring me a wet cloth, if you please." I gave him a wink while I rubbed Nova's long, velvety face with my palm. She closed her eyes, telling me that she enjoyed my attention.

"As you wish, Milady." He left to fetch a wet cloth for me.

I took the leather bridal off Nova and tied her to a post. Just as I had finished unsaddling her, the groom returned with the wet cloth in hand.

"My thanks, good lad."

"'Tis my pleasure, Milday. Should you need anything else, I will be close by." He rubbed his nose, leaving behind a small mark of dirt.

I smiled at him and turned back to Nova.

Just as I was finishing with Nova, I heard voices echoing from somewhere close by. I thought this strange because no one, besides me, had been out riding today. I usually never ran into anyone at the stables unless there was a hunt going on, which today there wasn't.

My interest was piqued, so I decided to follow the voices. On my way out of the stables, I called to the young groom, "Sir? I'm finished with Nova now. You may take her back to the pasture."

I didn't wait for an answer. I walked out of the stables and around the corner to where the sound of voices had been coming from.

I stopped cold in my tracks. There by the willow tree I saw Wrenth kissing a red haired girl who was not my Addy. I cupped my hands over my mouth and ran back to the palace. I was sure they hadn't seen me; they were too busy with each other to have noticed anyone else.

Though Adelaide and I had grown apart, she was still my cousin and I loved her. I didn't wish her to be betrayed and so I knew I must tell her of her lover's unfaithfulness.

The first person I saw was a guard, of course. "Where is the princess? Have you seen Adelaide?" I asked impatiently.

"No, Milady, not since this morn. Perhaps her mother could tell you though. She's in her chambers."

"Thank you, sir."

"Milady." He bowed his head in reply as I turned and ran up the stone steps to find my Aunt Faya. Her guard let me pass. I didn't bother to stop for formalities in my haste.

Bursting through the door, I found my Aunt Faya sitting upon a velvet draped chair. She was sipping tea from a gold rimmed porcelain cup. The cozy room smelled of burning incense. She set her tea down, noticing me at once. "Goodness, child, you startled me coming in unannounced like that. What reason is there for this rudeness?"

"I must find Adelaide. Where is she, Aunt Faya?" I stopped and gave her a quick curtsy. "Forgive my rudeness. I have news for her and must find her at once."

Faya set her tea cup down and smoothed her skirts with an exasperated sigh, her copper brows furrowed. "She is in the mezzanine with her ladies."

"My thanks, Aunt Faya."

I felt adrenaline coursing through my veins as I ran down the hall and headed for the mezzanine. I had to find her before Wrenth came back from his dally with that wench.

Faya had told the truth. I found Adelaide painting with a couple of her ladies. They were joking and laughing and looked to be having the most joyous of times. I had no time to envy them, though I may have had the circumstances been different.

"Addy, I must speak with you privately." I said sternly, standing behind her.

She turned around and wrinkled her petite nose at me. "Zephyra…can't you see I'm busy?" Her ladies giggled behind their hands while Adelaide turned her back to me once again and faced her canvas of bright colours.

"'Tis important! Addy, *please!*"

"Oh, well, alright. If you say it is important," she replied with an annoyed tone, then added to her ladies, "I shall be right back. Wait for me here." She tossed her hair over her shoulder as we turned and headed away from them, just out of hearing distance.

"Now, what is *so* important that you would come seek me out after avoiding me for so many seasons? Hmm?" She leaned in towards me and held my eyes accusingly.

"Yes, I know I've been rude." I looked away, feeling guilty. "I'm sorry, but there's something I must tell you—only because you are my cousin and I love you."

"You *love* me?" She scoffed. "You could've fooled me. I barely feel like you even *like* me anymore." She raised her brows, daring me to deny it.

Ignoring her, I grabbed her shoulders so she had to look at me, "Listen! I saw Wrenth kissing another girl, and I'm sorry, but I thought you should know." I pressed my lips together and stepped back, letting my words sink in.

She stopped and stared at me for a moment. When she spoke again, it wasn't the words I'd expected to hear. "You saw nothing."

"But Addy—"

"Don't!" She put up her hand. "It would only be an embarrassment for me to admit that he is being unfaithful. I will have to pretend I have heard nothing. He is a man, after all, and men are weak when it comes to temptation. We must forgive them. As your princess, I command you to keep your mouth shut about this."

I couldn't believe my ears, but what more could I do? I had told her the truth, and she decided to ignore it.

So I gave her my best fake smile and curtsied. "As you wish—Princess."

I saw her jaw drop at my formal mockery, and then I spun on my heel and left her standing alone. Fine; if she wanted to act like a spoiled princess, I would treat her as one. I felt hot anger growing inside of me and decided I needed to stop caring about her happiness if I wanted to remain in control of my emotions.

I didn't hear anything from Adelaide for the next few days. One night, while I was in my chambers reading, I heard the faint sounds of sobbing. I knew it was Adelaide; hers was the only chamber next to mine. I decided to sneak through the secret passage between our rooms, which I barely fit through anymore, and see why she was crying. Even though I had tried to stop caring for Adelaide, I knew deep down that I never could—not truly.

I found her on her bed, blankets all tangled around her, bawling her eyes out into her pillow.

"Addy?" I asked gently.

"Go away," she sobbed into her pillow.

"Not until you tell me what's wrong."

She lifted her head from the pillow and looked at me, her eyes red and swollen. "I ended it with Wrenth. I told him it was because I was bored of him. I couldn't allow him to know it was because he was with another girl. No one must know that he chose to be with someone else when he was with the *princess*."

"Oh, Addy, I'm so sorry." I went to her and rubbed her back as she put her head back down. "He's not worthy of you."

She sat up and hugged me. "Thank you, Zephy. I know I was cruel yesterday, but I mustn't show weakness in front of anyone else."

"I understand. It's not like I've been sunshine and rainbows lately either. I had a hard time coping when Gisela was sent away. I didn't want to feel happiness, lest it be taken from me yet again."

"No, you haven't." She looked at me with a tear-streaked face. "I understand it was hard for you to lose Gisela, but that was ages ago now. I hope we can be friendly with one another again." She paused before adding, "Just know that outside of this room, I must act strong in the eyes of the public."

"Yes, of course."

"Good." She kissed my cheek. "I think I shall try to sleep now. You have lightened my heart. Thank you for caring when I needed you the most."

"Always and forever, my dear Addy. And don't worry, you will meet a man who's worthy of you soon. I'm sure of it. Sweet dreams, Princess."

"Perhaps. Goodnight, Zephy."

With that, I left her to herself. In my own chambers, I didn't sleep easily. I tossed and turned for hours before sleep finally took me. I couldn't shake the feeling of guilt at the distance I had let grow between myself and Adelaide. If only I had stayed by her side, perhaps she would not have fallen for Wrenth and had her heart broken. I was no oracle though, so who knew if that was really true.

As it turned out, Adelaide was kinder to me after my visit to her chambers, but she was still always surrounded by her handmaidens and other ladies of the court. It didn't take long before word caught on that she was now without a suitor and other men started courting her. She was the princess, after all, and they all wished to be hers—whether for power or for her beauty.

Wrenth ended up with the girl I saw him kissing by the stables. Adelaide simply ignored them, and they eventually left court for his family's estate.

It took Adelaide until the next spring before she settled on one man. Peyton Ventaspeer was his name, and he was kindhearted. It turned out he was only three springs older than her, and had just recently reached his second decade.

Now that I was sixteen, my body had begun to fully develop into that of a woman's. I was no longer the lanky, clumsy girl I had once been. Though still tall and slender, my hips and bosom were now filled out. Though I still had freckles and flaming red hair, Awyn often told me I had a pretty face. Still, I didn't feel pretty in comparison to Adelaide. I thought myself to be plain and boring.

One sunny afternoon, I was strolling through the courtyard with Awyn. The sky was blue, the grass was green and the trees were in full bloom. I could hear the birds singing as we wandered the stone pathways and passed by the arches that surrounded the courtyard. Walking onward, we came by a group of three men sitting under one of the archways. They were playing dice and barely noticed us when we neared them.

Not until Awyn said, "Good day, gentlemen," did they look up. I saw one of them was Peyton. He looked me straight in the eyes, and I had to look away. I was still uncomfortable making eye contact with those who I didn't know well.

"Zephyra, right?" He got up and came towards me. He was quite the opposite of ugly, with cropped flaxen-coloured hair, a lean figure and strong facial features.

"Yes—that is correct. And you are Peyton, the princess's new lover." It wasn't a question. I'd seen him with her a lot lately, so I knew who he was.

"That I am, though I hope to be more than that someday." He put his hand on my forearm and smiled at me…*charming*, I thought. "I know how important you are to Princess Adelaide, and I hope we can be friends."

I looked into his sharp hazel eyes then. It turned out he had a strangely comforting effect on me. With a smile of my own, I replied, "I would like that very much."

"Wonderful! If there should ever be anything I can do for you, please let me know. Now, please excuse me, Lady Zephyra—"

"Please, just call me Zephyra," I interrupted.

"Alright then—Zephyra. Apologies, but I should get back to my game. I will see you around soon, I'm sure."

"That you will." I nodded, and Awyn and I left them to continue our walk.

As we walked on, I felt Awyn's eyes on me. "What is it, Awyn?"

"It is just that I've never seen you speak so kindly to a man who wasn't your father or your uncle, especially one who you have just met. I'm simply pleased, is all."

I shrugged and smoothed my skirts with my hands, "I have a good feeling about him. He is the first *man* who has gone out of his way to be kind to me. Besides, he makes Addy happy."

"He does seem quite the gentlemen. I heard he has come to court because his father was friends with King Furraro…"

"Ah. Well, no matter his reason for being here, I'm sure Addy will be glad to learn that I finally have accepted one of her—" I paused, trying to find the right word. "Suitors."

"That she will, my dear. That she will."

Chapter 10

Entering the main dining hall later that evening, Adelaide came running up to me and attacked me with a tight embrace, almost knocking me over. "Oh, Zephy, I'm so happy!"

I laughed and saw she was beaming with a smile that went from cheek to cheek. "I'm most glad."

"Peyton has told me you've met, and that he thinks you're most delightful! You must have made a very good first impression. Do you like him? Oh, please tell me you do!" she pleaded with me impatiently, a yearning look in her eyes.

"Yes, of course. He is kind and charming and—I'm happy for you," I reassured her.

She took my hand then, still beaming and tugged me. "Come, you must sit by us tonight."

I looked toward the dining table and saw my mother watching me through narrowed eyes. I looked away from her and back at my cousin. "Yes, Addy, I would love nothing more than to sit and dine with you and Peyton."

"Marvelous." She clapped her hands together and with that we went to the dining table, draped with bright red linens, and took a seat. My mother sat on the same side as us, but a few people sat between us so she was blocked from my view. I was happy for it. My mother and I had never really mended our relationship, if you could even call it that, since she had sent Gisela away. We simply tolerated each other. It was the *proper* thing to do.

Taking my seat, Peyton greeted me warmly. "Ah, Zephyra, we are so glad you have decided to sit with us."

"No, thank *you.*" I lowered my voice too just above a whisper. "You've saved me from having to sit by my mother."

"Not getting along well with her these days?"

"She is a wretched woman," Adelaide piped in. "She sent Zephy's handmaiden from her when she was only a decade…during her first Noctis De Celestia, at that."

I thought my mother must have overheard what Adelaide had just said, she kept quiet nonetheless. I wished I could have seen her face then, how distressed she must have been to find that the princess still held that against her.

"Oh my." Peyton raised his brows and took a sip of ale.

Aunt Faya, who sat beside me, ended her conversation with one of her ladies and elbowed Adelaide. "Hush. You don't want to cause a scene at dinner now, do you?"

"I suppose not," she pouted, then decided to change the subject, picking up a bread roll. "Where is Queen Jelena, by the way?"

"She's not feeling well today…had one of her ladies bring her dinner to her chambers," Aunt Faya answered.

"Perhaps I should visit her."

"Not tonight. Let her rest."

Peyton and I enjoyed our meal in silence as Adelaide and her mother argued over whether or not the queen needed a visitor or not while she was unwell.

After dinner, I had just thanked Adelaide and Peyton for inviting me to dine with them, and was about to retire to my chambers when Peyton touched my arm. "You should come to Noctis De Celestia with us next year. It's in Terra, so it won't be too far of a journey."

"What a wonderful idea, my love," Adelaide answered him. "Zephy, you *must* come! It will have been seven springs since the one you attended here. Surely things are different now. Besides, you will have us to keep you company." Adelaide batted her long, dark lashes at me. I almost gave in to her charm.

I considered it for a moment, but then I reminded myself of my dear Gisela and my promise to my mother, that I would never attend another Noctis De Celestia celebration again. "I thank you for your invitation, but no… I simply cannot."

"But Zephy!" Adelaide complained, used to getting everything she wanted.

"No! I'm truly sorry. It's just that it hurts too much still. That night is my night for remembering Gisela and our time together."

"Oh Zephy, it's not like she's dead."

Her words stung and I had to take a deep breath to avoid lashing out at her for her careless attitude. It wasn't her fault she was used to getting everything she wanted. "To me, it feels that she is, for I'll likely never see her again."

"Come now, my love, it's not as if there won't be other joyous celebrations we can attend with your lovely cousin," Peyton pleaded with Adelaide.

She sighed and gave in. "You're right, Peyton dear, of course. Zephy, forgive me. I understand that night is hard for you. I only want you to be with us for all joyous occasions. Perhaps Grandmother's birthday. 'Tis only a few weeks away. I hope she's feeling better by then."

"Yes, of course I'll be there and I would love to spend time with you two on that night—as well as many others to come," I assured her. "Now, if you'll excuse me, I would like to retire to my chambers. It has been a good day, but I would like to read some before sleep takes me."

"Always reading. Alright then, have a good night. I'll see you on the morrow."

"Goodnight to both of you," I replied.

"Goodnight, Zephyra." Peyton bowed his head at me, and then I left them.

I thought about what a good influence Peyton was on Adelaide on the way back to my chambers. He had, after all, stopped me and Addy from a possible argument. Was he too good to be true? I didn't know, but I was glad for my princess. If I couldn't find happiness, at least I could find peace in hers.

As was I about to push open the door to my chambers, I heard a woman from behind call my name in a desperate tone, just before I felt a hand grab my wrist. I spun around and came face-to-face with my mother. I hadn't allowed myself to be alone with her for a long time. I hated her, and I didn't want to speak to her. I wondered what nerve she had, seeking me out now as I was about to retire for the night. What could she possibly want from me?

There we stood, staring at each other in silence outside of my chambers in the stone hallway. No one else was in sight. There was no escape from her here, so instead, I stared coldly at her in silence for a moment. Finally, my lips found the ability to move, though the words came out strangled. "What do you want from me?" I pulled my wrist from her grasp, realizing she still held onto me.

She let go and looked down, fidgeting with her velvety orange skirts.

"Zephyra—I know I haven't been the kindest mother—"

"No, you haven't. So leave me be." I didn't want any kind of apology from her, especially after it had been so long. Why was she coming to me now?

"Please, daughter—" she begged.

"Do *not* call me *daughter*. You lost that right when you sent away my *only* friend!" I was losing my patience, and I didn't care if I was being cruel. I couldn't control my rage with her and I didn't want it burning me up inside.

I saw her green eyes go bright with tears at my words. She put her palms over her face, her slender shoulders shaking. It was the first time in my life I saw my mother cry, or show any kind of weakness, for that matter. It made me feel awkward and I didn't really know what to do, so I rolled my eyes and said, "What do you want?"

She sniffed, pulling her hands from her face and looked at me with red rimmed eyes. "The princess hates me for what I did to you. I can't stand to have lost her favour. It has been six springs, and you still hold it against me. As long as you do, I believe the princess will too. So I'm begging you to please *forgive* me. You don't have to forget, but *please* forgive." She looked at the floor, unable to meet my eyes any longer.

It must have taken great strength for her to beg for my forgiveness. Even so, it hurt that she only wanted my forgiveness just so Adelaide would also forgive her.

I felt hot anger growing and failed to push it down. "You selfish woman," I started quietly, but was unable to control the volume of my voice as I continued. "I'll *never* forgive you! And neither will Adelaide! Now get out of my sight." I pushed her back with my arm and heard her gasp as I turned and slammed my door behind me.

Hearing her footsteps running away from my chambers, I plopped down on my bed and cried. I hated that she could still make me cry, but at least I had waited until I was out of sight before I let my tears fall. I didn't want her to see that she could still affect me in such a way.

Still feeling hot from my anger, I opened the shutters to my window and screamed.

It wasn't long before I heard a guard pounding on my door. "Lady Zephyra? Are you alright?"

I cracked the door open a little. I didn't wish him to see my tear streaked face, "Yes, sir. I just had an argument and was frustrated is all…nothing to worry about."

"Would you like me to fetch Awyn for you, Lady?"

"No, no, that's alright. I wish to be alone right now. I can ready myself for slumber tonight. My thanks, sir"

"Goodnight, Lady. Take care."

"Goodnight, sir." I closed my door, undid the stays from my corset and unpinned my hair. Once in my undergarments, I fell onto my bed and fell fast asleep.

I woke to the smell of cooked ham and eggs. I cracked open my eyes and saw Awyn setting down a tray on the wooden stand beside my bed.

Noticing that I was now awake, she placed her hands on her hips and reprimanded me, "Goodness, girl, you slept in your undergarments? And look, you left your nice dress all crumpled on the floor. Next time, you must let me attend you so I can ensure you are in your night dress and things are put away properly."

"Oh, Awyn, I had a rough night. Please let it go."

"I'm sorry to hear that, my lady. Would you like to talk about it?"

"It's nothing, really." I sighed and sat up, taking the tray from the stand. "It's just my mother. She expects me to forgive her, but not because she cares what I think. She wants me to forgive her so that she can be in Adelaide's good graces."

"Oh my, after all these seasons…" She inclined her head.

"Well—she probably heard Adelaide talking to Peyton about her at dinner. I think that's what set her off," I explained.

Awyn sat on the bed beside me with a distant look in her eyes, the silver in her hair catching in the sun's rays beaming in through my window. "I'm going to tell you a story about your mother—a story she would be too embarrassed to have you know," she said, looking pointedly at me.

"Okay. It has been a while since I've heard a good story. Do tell," I urged her as I picked at my food.

"You must understand, my lady," she went on, "Your mother grew up learning only to please. Her own mother died giving birth to her, so she was raised by her father, who I worked for at the time. They were one of the wealthiest families around, you see, but her father was friends with King Furraro. When he agreed to fight alongside him in the Great War he only asked one favour…that his daughter be taken care of. That is how your mother and your father became betrothed. And it's a good thing they were, for her father, along with the king, died during that war.

"Your mother was still too young to hold a land title, so her father's land went to his sister, who didn't care much for your mother. It was likely that once her aunt took over the titles, your mother would have been tossed out on the streets and would have become a vagrant with no home—or worse, she would have ended up dead. Celestia only knows she probably wouldn't have made it very far on her own." She turned to me and put a reassuring hand on my knee.

"I'm not asking you to forgive her. All I'm saying is, maybe don't be so hard on her. She never learned how a mother should behave. I believe she feels power is the most important thing in the world, so she tries hard to make sure herself and her family is always in favour of those who hold it."

I shook my head to clear it of what Awyn had just told me. "That's no excuse! She could have acted cold and proper without sending my friend away. Even now, she only cares about herself. She cares nothing for *me;* her *family.*"

"Perhaps she thinks she is—"

"Stop defending her!" I put down the piece of ham. "Anyways, I'm finished talking about this. You will ready me for the day now. I wish to go for a walk, and when I'm gone you will clean and hang my dress from last night." I knew I was being as cold as my mother at that moment, but I didn't agree with Awyn's sympathy for her and I let my emotions get the best of me.

"Yes, my lady." Her formal response came from tight lips. I knew that I'd hurt her, but I didn't care, as long as it made her shut up about my mother. All I wanted was to forget about her and think of something else.

Now in my cream-coloured day dress, I walked around the palace gardens, taking in the sight of the pretty leaves. They were turning shades of amber and crimson. A sign summer was coming to its end. I breathed in the crisp air and tried to clear my head of this morning's discussion with Awyn.

Deep in thought, I barely noticed Adelaide and two of her ladies having a picnic underneath two large oak trees. They seemed to be enjoying a cheerful conversation and were laughing amongst themselves. As I grew near, Adelaide noticed me. She stood up and said something to her ladies before approaching me.

She gave me one of her sweet smiles and linked her arm with mine. She looked as beautiful as always in her simple, pale rose-coloured dress. "May I walk with you, dear cousin?" she asked politely, even though I knew she would no matter what my answer was.

"As you wish; what about your ladies though? Aren't you supposed to be entertaining them?"

She waved her hand and brushed off my answer. "They'll be fine without me. I can spend some time with you if I like."

"Alright."

"I'm so glad you and Peyton are getting along," she continued, not noticing my dark mood.

"He is quite lovely. I'm glad you're happy, Addy. You should wed him," I said, forgetting my own troubles for the time being.

She sighed as we came to a clearing that opened up to one of the meadows I sometimes rode Nova through. "One day, I hope to. It's complicated for me, being the princess. I can't be married before I am queen. 'Tis one of our laws. 'The regent of Solis must be independent when she is crowned, lest she look weak,'" she quoted.

"Oh…I suppose I should know that." I thought I probably had been told duriung lessons when I was younger, but a lot of the time, I wasn't paying attention. I remembered finding the lessons on rules and laws quite drab.

"Oh well," her tone lightened. "Peyton is a patient man. He knows I'm the princess and that our relationship must be different because of that."

"Good. I suppose as long as you get to be together, marriage doesn't matter much."

"Exactly! Mayhap my positive thinking has finally begun to influence you." She sounded delighted by the notion.

I smiled and tightened my arm on hers. I was glad we were on friendly terms once again; she made life seem brighter.

CHAPTER 11

SUMMER TURNED INTO autumn, and autumn into winter, before the spring sun finally started to pry away winter's icy grip.

I grew closer to Peyton. He became somewhat of a brother to me. I spent much time with him and Adelaide. My mother left me alone, which I was grateful for. In fact, I believe she was trying to forget my existence all together. I was perfectly fine with that.

One brisk spring day, as I was having biscuits and stew for midday meal with Peyton and Adelaide in her chambers, Peyton brought up the subject of finding me a suitor.

"So, Zephyra, don't you grow lonely on these chilly spring nights? Perhaps you would like a man to keep you—" he paused, searching for the proper word, "Company?"

I felt my cheeks grow hot and looked away. We had never breached the subject before and I was happy to have avoided it. "I don't want a suitor…or even a lover, for that matter. Besides, no one wants a plain-looking, socially awkward girl like me."

Peyton looked like he was about to choke and swallowed hard before saying, "Do you jest? You should look in the mirror; you're a truly pretty girl. Any man would be lucky to have you. And no one cares if you're socially awkward."

"He's right you know, Zephy," Adelaide chimed in, supporting her partner.

"No, I don't need to be with anyone. I'm fine; now, can we please talk about something else? You are making me quite uncomfortable," I stated firmly, not believing that he was actually bringing up my love life—or lack of it.

"I'm sorry I brought it up. I only want you to be as happy as me and Adelaide," he mumbled.

"What are you wearing to the spring feast?" Adelaide changed the subject, sensing the tension. That was my Addy, always trying to keep the mood light. She was a sweet girl, and I loved her for it then more than ever before.

I told her of the green dress being made for me and that I'd chosen that colour to represent life. We talked of whom we thought might be attending the festivities and of other pointless gossip that was going around the palace. Peyton didn't put much into the conversation. He seemed content nonetheless, or at least, he pretended to be. I knew he probably thought I'd been rude. The thought did make me feel uncomfortable, but I let it be.

The next day, I was informed that Queen Jelena required an audience with me.

She was in deep conversation with her treasurer when the guard let me into her throne room. She looked up from the scrolls that they had been contemplating.

"Oh...apologies, I didn't mean to interrupt. I was told you wish to speak with me." I bowed my head.

"No, no, my dear, do not worry. You are not interrupting, these other matters can wait," she waved a hand at the scrolls scattered about the wooden table. "Please give us a moment," she said to her treasurer. "We can finish this discussion later."

"Of course, your Majesty," the tall man with a curly mop of ginger hair bowed deeply as he backed into his office.

My grandmother made her way to a sofa covered in red velvet, which was placed under the kingdom's official coat of arms; a red shield with a yellow sun. She patted the space beside her. "Come, sit with me."

I obeyed, folding my hands in my lap and awaited her next words.

"How are you, my dear granddaughter?" Her green eyes searched my own, an expression of concern etched on her features.

"I'm well enough, my thanks for asking. How are you, Grandmother?"

“I am fine.” She sat back and decided to get right to the point, “The reason I have asked to see you is because Adelaide has told me you do not wish to obtain a suitor for yourself—ever. Is this true, Zephyra?” Concern drew the corners of her mouth down and crinkled her fair, aged skin.

I looked down at my hands as I fiddled mindlessly with the folds of my silky maroon dress. “Is that a problem? I’m happy enough on my own, and I figured it would not matter, being that I’m not next in line for the throne.”

“While it pleases me to hear that you are happy, I regret to inform you that it does indeed matter. You see, if Adelaide were to fail to have a daughter, the responsibility would fall on you to continue the Caldura bloodline. If you recall your Solis history, you must know that my own parents were not the queen and king. It was my aunt who held the crown, but she was unable to have any children.” She held my eyes with a look that told me she was serious and waited for my reply.

“So it was your mother’s responsibility to produce a daughter for the crown. I understand.” I sighed, feeling the weight of the world suddenly rest upon my shoulders.

“Good. You do understand. Now,” she clasped her hands together and continued, “You may choose who you wish, as we do not believe in arranged marriages here. We wish our family to find love and happiness, not to be forced into something because of duty. It is still your duty to at least *try* to produce a daughter to ensure the kingdom’s stability. We would hate to have Solis fall into the wrong hands because there is no woman heir to succeed the throne from our bloodline.”

I gave her the most reassuring smile I could manage. “I will try to find someone who I like to help me continue our bloodline. Thank you, Grandmother, for your explanation—and your patience with me.” I hoped the dread I felt didn’t show through my voice.

“Ah, my dear, of course. I do not wish to hasten you. I only worry now because I did not know you wished to remain without a suitor for your entire life.” She stood, her red and purple skirts rustling around her. “You are dismissed. I should get back to my treasurer; he is not as patient as you and I,” she winked.

I giggled as we kissed each other’s cheeks, a gesture only royals gave to one another.

Once I was out of the throne room, I paused to lean against a wall and take in what I had just been told. Feeling the cold stone against my back, I squeezed my eyes shut. *How could Adelaide have told our grandmother on me?* It seemed I had no choice now but to accept Peyton's counsel about finding a suitor. I only hoped that he might be able to help me find one because, Celestia knew, I certainly couldn't find one on my own.

Of course when I told Adelaide and Peyton I had changed my mind about finding a suitor and decided to let them help, they were overjoyed.

"I know of someone who I believe will be perfect for you," Peyton exclaimed with pride. "His name is Saffiero, and he is the son of Lord Trumont of Affendale. Lord Trumont is a friend of my parents; we spent much time at their manor when I was a child. Saffiero has recently come to court."

I could tell that Peyton was excited about the whole idea of setting me up with his childhood friend, but I myself couldn't even pretend to be. I was already dreading the introduction. I was so far away from comfort I may as well have been in another kingdom.

I took a few deep breaths, trying to slow my quickened heartbeat. "Tell him to meet me in the courtyard tomorrow, when the sun is at its most western point." I didn't wish for this to happen when the courtyard was abuzz with the peers and their gossip. If we met shortly before the third meal of the day, most others would be inside preparing themselves for eating.

"As you wish. Please be there," he added, eyeing me with suspicion. "I would hate to look a fool if you didn't show up."

He must have been able to see the look on my face, so I quickly tried to mask my panic and gave him a smile. "Don't worry; I shan't make you look a fool."

Now that the meeting was set in motion, I took my leave. I wished to be alone for the rest of the day. My nerves were upsetting my stomach just thinking about the whole ordeal.

As promised, I stood in the courtyard wearing a white gown with red lace on the bodice the next evening. Faint gold flowers were etched into the white fabric. I loved the material. Awyn had done a wonderful job preparing me, mooning over me the whole time. I just wanted to get this over with. *Why did I have to be born a Caldura?* I groaned as I paced. Life would have been so much simpler if only I could have come from a less important bloodline.

As I watched the sun begin to descend behind the mountains, turning the clouds different shades of pink and orange, I began to hope he wouldn't show.

My hopes were soon crushed.

"Lady Zephyra?"

I almost jumped out of my own skin when I heard my name. A ruddy man with wavy strawberry blonde hair approached me.

I assessed him as he came closer. His hair was cropped fairly short, coming only just below his ear lobes. He looked to be only a few years older than myself…probably Peytons's age. He wasn't unattractive—but he also wasn't my type. I didn't even know what my type was, but he wasn't it. His face was scruffy, with a beard that matched his hair, and his overly large muscles made him look too gruff.

"I am she." I didn't know what else to say except, "You must be Saffiero…Peyton has told me you are childhood friends."

"Ah, yes, that we are, though I have not seen him for many years until recently. It's a pleasure to meet you, Lady Zephyra." He took my hand and kissed it, which I found it to be a bit trite—but again, what did I know?

Feeling awkward and not really knowing what to do with myself I suggested, "Shall we walk?"

"A fine idea, my lady." He put his arm through mine as we started. I thought it was a little forward for having just met, but then reprimanded myself for being so judgmental.

"So why have you come to court, Saffiero?" I asked in a stiff voice. My nerves were rung tighter than ever with the closeness of his body.

"My father thought it would do me good to learn about the ways of the kingdom; how to be a true gentleman and possibly find a mate," he winked at me. "I think he will be proud to find out I have met the princess's very own cousin," he said proudly, as if I were some prize.

"Ah…" I stared straight forward, keeping my eyes on the path in front of us. So he wished to woo me because of my status. Perhaps that was all I would ever be to anyone, save my family; 'the princess's cousin.'

"Perhaps I can convince him to attend Noctis De Celestia this year in Terra! It isn't too far from here and then he could meet you." He squeezed my arm closer to his body in what I imagined was a possessive manner.

I was beginning to feel like a piece of property and we had only just met. "I don't attend Noctis De Celestia anymore," I informed him in a matter of fact tone.

"What? That is blasphemy!" He stopped and turned to look at me. "If you are to be my suitor, you must attend. You're royalty and must take part in such celebrations."

"I do take part—in my own way. I visit the Temple of Celestia each year to give my thanks. I feel that is more important than getting all dolled up and attending a *ball.*" I didn't wish to tell him the truth of why I didn't want to attend the celebration. It was none of his concern, and as matters stood now, I wasn't comfortable telling him about my past.

"I'm feeling quite weary," I made up an excuse, putting my hand to my face. "I wish to retire to my chambers."

"But we've only just met. I had hoped to spend more time together," he pleaded, disappointment drawing his features down.

"My apologies. Perhaps another time." I didn't wish to see him again, but at the time, I would have said anything to be away from him. I'd seen enough to know he wasn't the right suitor for me. Mayhap no one was.

"As you wish, Lady Zephyra. I'll walk you back to the palace," he offered, but I could hear the regret in his voice.

"I'm fine, thank you," I said, turning and pulling my arm from his.

I walked back to the palace at a steady pace, not turning back even once. If he followed me, he did not say a word.

CHAPTER 12

I SAT PLAYING the beautiful golden harp my grandmother had given me for my sixteenth birthday, when I heard a knock on my door.

I paused, my fingers stopping on the pearlescent strings, "Who is it?"

"It's me—Addy."

"Come in," I said, closing my eyes. I had purposely missed breakfast, wanting to avoid any discussion about the previous night. It seemed my attempt had failed.

Adelaide entered and sat on my bed with a bounce, her golden curls bouncing with her. "Why did you miss breakfast? Peyton and I wanted to hear all the details about your meeting with Saffiero."

"I wasn't hungry," I lied, stepping away from the harp. I began brushing out my hair with my silver jewel encrusted comb.

"Okay then…so how did it go last night?"

"I'd rather not talk about it."

"Oh, come on! It can't be that bad," she looked up at me, waiting for my reply.

"Fine, it went okay. We just walked and then I left," I shrugged.

"That's it? Well, what did you think of him? Stop brushing your own hair. That's Awyn's job."

"I can brush my own hair if I want." I sighed and stopped to look at her. "He was pushy. I didn't like it. I feel that he only wants to court me for my status…as if I'm some prize." I rolled my eyes and turned back to my large oval mirror.

"Oh dear." I saw her eyes widen behind me in the mirror's reflection before she sat back with a pensive expression. "I should tell Peyton. They were childhood friends, but perhaps he doesn't know Saffiero as well as he thought—"

"No!" I cut her off and went to her, putting my hands on her slender shoulders so she had to look at my face. "Please promise me you won't breathe a word of this to anyone. Perhaps I'm overreacting. I have never been courted before. I'll give him another chance and try to be less judgmental."

The last thing I wanted was for Peyton to find out what I thought of his childhood friend. I loved Peyton for how well he treated Addy, but I couldn't trust him not to tell Saffiero how I felt. I didn't want this kind of gossip going around the palace—nor did I wish pity from anyone.

"Alright, if you are sure…"

"Yes! All is well. No sense worrying Peyton over my silliness. Now, off with you. I'm going to get ready to take Nova for a ride." I shooed her out of my chamber.

"A ride, you say? Would you mind if I joined you? It has been quite a while since I myself have taken a ride," she asked with excitement, already forgetting our conversation.

"Sure, meet me at the stables when you are ready."

"See you there. Ta-ta," she called as I closed the door behind her.

It wasn't long before my second chance came. While I was reading in the courtyard, I noticed a person's shadow appear over me. I peered up from my book, my white hat shading my face from the sun, and saw Saffiero standing before me. His strawberry-blond hair was messed up from the wind, but he was dressed well in a red and gold doublet and brown breeches.

"Lady Zephyra, how wonderful to see you," he bowed as I stood up.

"Good day, my lord," I replied politely.

"Please, call me Saffiero."

"As you wish. Are you enjoying life at court so far?" I decided to pretend like our last visit hadn't ended awkwardly.

"Aye, I am. I would enjoy it more so if you would agree to attend the jousting tournament that is to happen five sunrises from today."

"If that would make your life here more enjoyable, how could I refuse?" I didn't bother telling him I was already going to watch my father jousting against my Uncle Bardin—and that Adelaide had already asked me to attend the tournament with them.

"Perfect. I will be taking part in the tournament. Your presence wll be good luck," he said, giving me a wink.

Flattery didn't work on me, but I let him think it did for the moment and gave him my sweetest smile. "You are too kind." I was beginning to make myself feel sick with my pretend flirting.

He took my hand and kissed it. I resisted the urge to pull it away. His demeanor seemed somewhat insincere to me…mayhap, just as false as I was being towards him.

"Five sunrises then, Lady Zephyra," he bowed again, backing away.

He turned his back and left me alone with my book once again. I let out a sigh and tilted my face toward the sky. "Celestia, give me strength," I whispered under my breath.

Time seemed to drag on until the day of the tournament came. I was anxious to get the whole event over with so I could quit dreading it. What had I gotten myself into, letting Peyton set me up with a potential suitor? At least if I had tried to find one on my own, I may have been able to stand his presence—if nothing else.

I checked my reflection as Awyn left my chambers, her task of readying me for the tournament now complete. I was all gussied up in a frilly bright orange and yellow dress. My hair was twisted up and pinned on top of my head, showing off the amber jeweled earrings that dangled from my earlobes.

I made my way downstairs, where Adelaide and Peyton awaited me at the palace's golden framed entrance doors. Adelaide looked like a true princess in a lacy peach and pink dress, a golden tiara resting on her head. Peyton looked elegant in a beige and gold colored doublet with white breeches. His teal eyes held a look of awe as he watched our princess. I smiled at the happy sight.

"I bet you one gold piece my father beats yours today," said Adelaide, linking one arm with mine and one with Peyton's as we stepped outside the doors and made our way to the arena where tournaments were held.

"Alright, bet's on," I agreed, feeling confident in my own father.

At the arena, I saw my mother and Aunt Faya seated with our grandmother. "Let's sit over here," I beckoned towards the other direction, wanting to sit as far away from my mother as possible.

Everyone in attendance was dressed up in bright, beautiful colours that made one think of a garden of flowers. I looked down as we took our seats on the benches and saw my father talking candidly with a pretty lady in purple near the front.

"That's Lady Brice," Adelaide whispered in my ear, covering her mouth with her hand. "They say your father has taken her as his mistress. I guess he doesn't have much interest in your mother these days."

"Who can blame him?" I raised my brows, though as I looked at my mother, pretending not to see my father, I felt a pang of sympathy for the both of them. "Perhaps that's because they were betrothed and my father never really loved her. Queen Jelena told me we're allowed to choose our own suitor so that we may find love and happiness, but that wasn't the case for my father."

"He looks happy now," she commented.

"If he wishes to take a mistress, that is his business," I defended him—though I did feel disappointment that he was turning his attentions to another woman while I myself hardly ever saw him.

Just as my mind began to wander, Adelaide jabbed me with her elbow. "Look, Zephy, there's Saffiero." I followed her pointed finger and saw he was indeed there on a bay horse, helmet up and smiling up at me. I waved, knowing I had to put on a show so that Adelaide and Peyton would think everything was well between us.

"If I win this tournament, shall I receive a kiss from the gentle Lady Zephyra?" he called up to me. I heard a note of hope in his voice.

I felt my cheeks grow hot. How could he embarrass me like this? I certainly didn't want my first kiss to be in front of the eyes of the whole kingdom and I most definitely didn't want my first kiss to be with *him*. It seemed I didn't have a choice now that everyone seemed to be awaiting my answer.

I squeezed my eyes shut and gathered all the courage I could muster before answering, "You shall, good sir."

Satisfied with my answer, he bowed his head and steered his horse to the large tent to await his turn.

"Oh, Zephy, how exciting for you!" Adelaide grinned beside me.

"Yes…exciting." I tried not to sound sarcastic.

I thought mayhap she would question my tone, but then the horn sounded and it was time for the tournament to begin.

The first couple jousters, I didn't know. Each one started on separate ends of the rectangular dirt patch that made up the jousting arena. The point of the game was to knock your opponent backward. He who wasn't sitting upright was deemed the loser. Each winner would go on to compete in the next round, until there were only two jousters left. The winner of those two would be the champion of the tournament and would receive twenty gold pieces, which was enough to buy oneself a fine horse.

We watched with anticipation as each couple faced one another. Finally, it came time for mine and Adelaide's fathers to face off. They paused at each end until the announcer yelled out in a booming voice, "And go!"

They rode towards each other with great speed, and I held my breath as their lances crashed into one another. My uncle's lance slipped off my father as my father's splintered and my uncle was forced backward, though he still stayed upon his horses back.

I rose off my seat and cheered and clapped with everyone around me.

"So your father bested mine. Perhaps you get your riding skills from him." Adelaide winked and tossed a gold piece at me while Peyton chuckled beside her.

"Indeed…" Whatever else I was going to say was forgotten as the next jousters got into position.

At one end was a man I recognized as one of our soldiers, riding a white horse. At the other end was Saffiero on his bay.

"Oh, it's Saffiero!" Adelaide clapped her hands together. "Do you think he'll win, Peyton?"

"I know not, my love. I've never seen him joust before."

"Oh, well, I hope he does." She nudged me and I rolled my eyes.

"Annnnd GO!" The announcer yelled and I secretly prayed to Celestia that Saffiero would lose.

The pounding of the horses' hooves on the earth was the only sound I heard as each jouster aimed their lances at each other. A few breaths later, the cracking sound of lances breaking echoed throughout the crowd.

For a moment, it looked like Saffiero would fall backward, but he held on and pushed through. Alas, his opponent wasn't able to hold his upright position any longer and fell backwards.

It took all my strength to fake a smile, knowing he would move onto the next round.

Don't worry, there are still three more rounds, I reminded myself, but with each round, Saffiero advanced—and my heart sank deeper. Not only did Saffiero advance, my father also remained undefeated, until only the two of them were left.

"Your suitor and your father! How exciting!" Adelaide beamed, grinning ear-to-ear. Peyton watched intently beside her.

"He's not really my suitor…" I began to argue, but then the announcement for them to begin was given and they were off.

I held my breath yet again as they raced towards each other, my father and my unwanted suitor. I didn't want to watch, but I couldn't peel my eyes from the scene.

After what felt like a lifetime, they crashed into each other with such force that my father came right off his chestnut stallion and fell to the ground with a sickening *THUD.*

My eyes widened with horror and I jumped off my seat.

"Zephy!" I heard Adelaide call, but I ignored her.

I ran from the stands where we were seated and across the arena, not paying any attention to all of the dust and dirt as I made my way.

Saffiero was already dismounted and had his helmet pushed up. He gave me a stupid, lopsided grin when I neared them. He obviously thought I was running to give him his kiss. I was about to run straight past him and towards my father, when he scooped me up in his arms and pressed his warm, dry lips to mine.

I wrenched my face away from him, causing him to frown at me. "I'm only claiming my prize, which you agreed to. What's the matter with you?"

"Let. Me. *Go!*" I shouted, pushing him away. "You've hurt my father. I must see that he is alright. And I am *not* some *prize* to be won!"

Surprised by my anger, he released me, holding his hands up in surrender.

I scrambled over to my father, who wasn't far from us. There were already a couple of men with him, checking to make sure he was okay.

"Father? …*Father!*" I called on my knees beside him, shaking his shoulders.

His eyes were closed, but he moaned in reply.

"He's alive! Thank Celestia! He needs help," I ordered one of the other men at his side.

"Kennard went to fetch the healer. He will be able to tell us what's wrong," the man informed me.

Moments later, the palace's healer in his robes was at my father's side, checking him over for injuries. "He will be okay, my lady…just a few broken ribs," he said to me in a soothingly. "We must put him on a cart and take him back to the palace for healing."

"My thanks, Sylack," I nodded, still feeling glum.

"He's a lucky man to have no ribs puncture his innards. Now off with you, dear lady; you may visit him in his chambers on the morrow once he has rested. He should be alert by then. I will give him a tonic to ease his pain."

With my father now in good hands, I headed back to the palace, wishing to be left alone. What anyone else thought of the scene I had made with Saffiero—I did not care. He'd shown his true personality to me when he thought to claim me as if I were a prize to be won. Even worse, he showed no sympathy for having injured my father. How selfish he was! I would not see him again. This time, I didn't care what Adelaide or Peyton thought of that fact.

CHAPTER 13

As IT TURNED out, Adelaide and Peyton were more understanding than I had expected.

"I'm sorry he was so forceful towards you, Zephyra. I truly thought he was a gentleman. I guess he has changed much since I last saw him," Peyton explained, his brows furrowed and his mouth drawn in a grim line.

"I don't blame you, Peyton. People change. Perhaps he is only like that with women."

"Whatever the matter, I'm sorry he hurt your father to try to win a kiss from you; whether it was an accident or not, it was unacceptable."

"I appreciate that. Thank you." I gave him a quick smile to help ease his guilt.

"How is your father, doing by the way?" Adelaide piped up, now that Peyton had given his apology.

It had only been a week, but thank Celestia, he had been showing signs of improvement already. "He's fine…he won't make it to Noctis De Celestia though. Sylack says travelling would be too hard on his healing body."

"That's unfortunate." Her olive eyes grew distant as she spoke her next words. "At least he'll have you here to keep him company."

"He shall, though I do wish it were under different circumstances. It's not often I get to spend time with my father. He always seems to have an excuse to be away from the palace. I know it is only to keep his distance from mother, but 'tis still hard for me."

"Well lucky us, now we get to travel with her to Terra without your father there to keep her preoccupied," Adelaide said with sarcasm as she looked to Peyton.

He rubbed her back and laughed, "No matter, my love, you have *me* to keep you preoccupied. It'll be your mother and father who have to deal with her mostly."

"And how joyous I am to have you," she said, leaning over to give him a peck on the lips.

I rolled my eyes and groaned, getting up to leave to mezzanine we'd been lounging in.

"Where are you going?" Adelaide called after me.

"To visit my father," I called back to her. Truth be told, I would rather have been anywhere than watching them two love birds get all sappy with each other.

On the way to my father's chambers, I thought about how grateful I was that Peyton had told Saffiero to leave me alone and find another girl to court. He really didn't have to do that for me. I could take care of myself, but alas, I was still grateful. I'd heard Saffiero had tried to argue his innocence, but gave in when Adelaide had told him she would have the queen throw him out of court if he didn't do as Peyton demanded and leave me alone.

The next day, I'd seen him flirting with a dainty young lady. I was delighted to see his attentions turned to another.

While the rest of thc royal family was away for Noctis De Celestia, I spent much time with my father. Though he was no longer bed-ridden, he was still unable to perform much in the way of physical activity.

One day, when I brought tea to his chambers, I found him pacing about.

"Father?" I asked, poking my head through the door.

"Yes, dear, come in." He stopped pacing and beckoned me inside.

"I'm sorry that you are unable to attend the celebrations—or do much of anything for that matter, but look, I have brought you tea and company to lift your spirits." I gestured toward the tea cart I had brought with me.

"It's not your fault, my dear, I'm just restless," he reassured me as I handed him the porcelain gold-rimmed tea cup filled with the warm liquid.

"Thank you." He accepted the tea.

"But Father, I can't help but feel responsible for your condition. If I had but followed my own instincts and not let that horrible man try to court me, you wouldn't have gotten hurt."

He waved a hand in dismissal. "You are no sorceress that can see into the future. How were you to know that was going to happen? Please promise me you will stop blaming yourself."

"Alright…if it'll make you feel better." I decided to change the subject. I eyed his white shirt. It was strange seeing him in such plain clothes. "Has Lady Brice been to see you? I saw her taking fancy to you at the tournament."

He winced. "I'm sorry you had to see that. No, she has not. She and I simply use each other for…" he paused to search for an appropriate word, "Certain pleasures. I'm of no use to her in this condition."

"Oh." I looked away, feeling my check grow warm. This was an uncomfortable subject for me, but I felt the need to tell him my thoughts. "You don't have to apologize. I don't blame you for your interest in other women. I know you had to marry Mother out of duty, not love."

He chuckled, smoothing his coppery locks back. "And where did you hear that, my dear daughter?"

I looked down at my hands, "Awyn told me. She worked for Mother's father."

"Right, I forgot she hired someone from her past to take care of you. No matter. I figured you would find out one day. Yes, I married your mother out of duty, unlike most from our kingdom. Don't think I regret it for one moment though. I have you because of that arrangement, and I have more love for you than any other being in this world," he said as he tilted my chin towards him.

Seeing tears shining in his eyes, I embraced him. He smelled of sweet musk. "Oh, Father, I love you too."

"I'm sorry for always being absent from your life. I didn't agree with the way your mother treated you, but I didn't know what to do, so I turned the other way. I just want you to know I tried to reason with her, she just would not listen to me. I'm not an aggressive man when it comes to women. Perhaps I should have had her sent away, but I thought children needed their mothers…especially ones with fathers who are always so busy."

"I forgive you." I held his shoulders and smiled at him, peering into his warm olive eyes that reminded me so much of Adelaide's. "You did what you thought was best for me. You are here now. That's what matters."

He smiled back at me. "Would you like to take a walk with me? I'm awfully bored cooped up in here."

"I would love nothing more," I told him genuinely.

So we did just that; we walked around the breathtakingly beautiful palace gardens and breathed in the fresh, clean air.

I visited him each day, and it cheered us both up. We took walks, played chess, and I even played my harp for him. As sad as I was that he had been hurt, it was also a blessing in disguise, because it gave us time to bond.

When the royal carriage returned, my father's strength was back, and he disappeared back into his work. I didn't blame him. If I could have disappeared, I would have too.

I didn't attempt to find another suitor. Nor did any man try to court me. I had kept my eyes open, but I didn't cross paths with anyone who interested me enough to pursue. Every man I had met was boring, disgusting, or seemed to have ulterior motives.

No one pushed me to find a new suitor either—well not until my eighteenth birthday, at least.

On the night of my eighteenth birthday, I sat in the main dining hall with the rest of the royal family and some of our closest peers. The conversation was light and we had just been served our dinner, for which some of my favourite foods were prepared. There was roasted pig, different types of cheeses, warm bread, and sweet potatoes, with a crisp white wine to drink.

We were just waiting for Queen Jelena to arrive so we could start our meal when her head handmaiden entered the hall alone.

Everyone went silent; turning to stare at her as she entered with haste, her brow furrowed with worry.

"Queen Jelena sends her deepest regret that she won't be able to attend your birthday dinner tonight, Lady Zephyra. She is not feeling well, but wishes you a happy night," she said to me, and then curtsied, casting her eyes toward the floor.

I saw Adelaide pale at my side, and was that a quick smile I saw on my mother's lips across the table?

"Oh no!" I replied with concern. "May I visit her after we dine? Since it is my birthday, 'tis my wish to see her."

"Of course your wish will be granted, my lady. Come as soon as you are finished here. She rests in her chambers."

"Thank you, Vienna." I gave her a curt nod as she curtsied again and was off to attend to the queen.

"I hope she'll be okay." I didn't know what else to say. My grandmother wouldn't miss my birthday unless her health was dire. The whole scenario had given me quite a shock.

"She is obviously *not* okay. She would never miss your birthday if she was okay. The queen adores you, Zephy," Adelaide said with a shaky voice, putting my own thoughts into words.

A moment later, she shook herself, realizing that it was now her place to announce dinner so that the rest of us could eat. "We wish Lady Zephyra a happy eighteenth birthday on this night. Now, please eat...before this food gets cold."

We all picked up our forks and began our meal with awkward conversation, the queen's state never leaving any of our minds through the meal. To be honest, I'd lost my appetite, but made myself eat nonetheless. It would've been rude not to after the kitchen staff had prepared this meal especially for me.

Once we were done our meal, it was time for cake. A servant carted out a grand white cake with a yellow sun painted with icing in its center. I accepted a small piece and shoved it into my mouth as fast as I could while still looking like a lady of the court and not a starving vagrant.

Once I was finished, I set down my silver fork and rose from my seat, the folds of my bronze coloured skirts falling to the floor like rippling water. "Thank you all for joining me for this most delicious meal on my birthday. Please stay seated as long as it pleases you. I'd like to visit the queen now."

As I turned and walked away, I heard a few wishes for a good night and a few to give the queen their love. I kept my head high and walked on through the doors of the dining hall.

I made my way up the winding stairs and through the dim halls to the queen's chambers; flames from the lanterns that were posted along the stone walls flickered like dancing fireflies. The air inside the palace was cool, and I shivered as I came upon the door to my grandmother's chambers.

A guard who was posted outside of her door noticed me and stepped aside for me to enter. "Queen Jelena is expecting you, Milady." He bowed his head as I walked passed him without a word and pushed the door open.

Inside the first chamber, Vienna was sitting by the hearth that heated the elegant space, holding her stitching in her lap. Hearing my presence, she looked up and said, "Oh good, you're here. Please go on in to her sleeping chamber. She is resting in there. I've told her you were coming."

"Thank you, Vienna." As I entered the queen's sleeping chamber, I saw her in her bed, which was covered with an open canopy of red velvet. Her eyes were closed, but fluttered when I neared her.

"Grandmother, did I wake you? Apologies; I only wished to see you on my birthday. I'm sorry you weren't well enough to attend the dinner." I tried to hide my worry as I saw her state. Even though she had lived many seasons, she'd always seemed strong and graceful. Now, she looked as if she had aged a decade since I last saw her only days ago. Her body looked frail, as though it might break at the lightest touch. Her skin, which sagged from her bones, was as pale as parchment. The very sight of her made me sick to my stomach.

"No, dear, I was just resting my eyes." She gave me a weak smile with thin lips. "Don't look so worried. It isn't becoming of you."

"Apologies, Grandmother." I sat on a stool that was placed next to her bed. "I only wish you were in better health."

"No matter, my love, it is a sickness of the heart. I can feel it in my chest. It grows weaker with each beat."

I put my hand to my mouth and squeezed my eyes shut to stop the tears from spilling out at her words. This wasn't just some sickness from which she would quickly recover. If it was indeed a sickness of the heart as she said, there was a high chance she would soon die.

I felt her place her bony hand on my arm. "It is alright, dear Zephyra, we all must return to Celestia eventually. I feel my time is near, and I am quite looking forward to being reunited with King Furraro."

I looked at her then, my eyes burning bright with tears. "Oh, Grandmother, of course you must be. 'Tis only hard for those of us who are left behind. Adelaide…I don't know if she is ready for this—"

She stopped me there, "Adelaide is as ready as she will ever be. She has found a wonderful suitor and she has you by her side. You are her rock, and I am glad for it."

"I don't even have my own suitor to ensure I have a daughter to back her up!" I sighed and lowered my voice, not wanting to upset my grandmother. "I promise I'll try harder to find someone to have a daughter with…even if it is someone I don't particularly like."

Now she took both my hands in hers and looked me straight in the eyes. "My dear, you must promise me you will never be with someone whom you do not love. I do not worry for the future of this kingdom anymore. I *know* everything is going to turn out alright. I only want my family to be happy. I regret every day that my husband promised your father to your mother as his friend's dying wish. I know he did not have much choice, but I see how it has ruined my son's life. You are his only happiness, and it would be a shame if you were to lead the same fate. It would crush him. So *please* promise me you will not be with someone simply out of duty."

I nodded and pressed my lips together, coming to a conclusion. "I don't know if I shall ever find anyone who will love plain little me, but I promise you, I shall not accept someone I don't love."

She smiled, letting out a deep breath and released my hands. "You will, trust me. Celestia assures me there is someone for you out there."

"Okay, Grandmother." I thought perhaps she was losing her mind, but I decided to humour her—she was still the queen, after all.

"Now I must sleep, if you don't mind. I hope your birthday was well."

"Of course, yes—well, except for the sad news of your condition."

"Do not be sad for me. I am well enough. I have made peace with my death. I only wish my family to be happy. Can you do that for me?"

"Yes, Grandmother, and I'll come back to see you soon. I bid you goodnight for now."

I left her chambers for my own. As soon as I reached my bed, I plopped down, buried my face in my feather pillows and sobbed myself to sleep.

The next day, as I sat in my chambers, Adelaide came to visit me. I had never seen her look as serious as she did when she entered through my doorway. Her eyes were red and puffy from crying, and her skirts were a rumpled mess. I took this as a sign, and stated, "So you've seen Grandmother."

"Yes, I have, and I am scared to death! I'm not ready for this." She buried her face in her hands.

I went to her and held her in my arms, hoping to give her some sort of comfort.

"Oh, Addy, but you *are* ready…as ready as you shall ever be. I know it shan't be easy. Just know I'm here for you. Anything you need, all you have to do is say so."

"Of course, thank you. It's just so hard. I don't want to lose her," she blubbered into my shoulder.

"I know. Me neither." Though I felt sad about our grandmother, I was glad that I didn't carry the burden she did. As hard as it was for the rest of us, this would be even harder on Adelaide, who it seemed would become our queen sooner than later. "You have been raised well. And you're a smart, beautiful woman. All of Solis adores you. Besides, you will have advisors when it comes to the political stuff."

"You are right. Thank you again, Zephy. What ever would I do without you?" She held both of my arms and gave me a gentle shake.

"Ah, no matter," I waved her off. "Now go clean yourself up. You mustn't be seen showing such signs of weakness."

She nodded, gathering her wits, and then she left, the sound of her skirts rustling as she made her way from my chambers.

Once she was gone, I sighed, tilting my head back to stare at the ceiling as I sat back down. I was so glad that I wasn't the princess right now. The weight of an entire kingdom would soon be resting on my dear Addy's shoulders. I felt I myself would have collapsed under that weight. Addy was strong, and everyone loved her. She would be alright—in time.

I was painting in the gardens when I heard the sound of the bell that brought doom to our whole kingdom. The long, drawn-out sound of the loud iron bell could only mean one thing…

After about three chimes of the bell, I dropped my paint brush. Leaving my incomplete painting of roses in front of the bench, I ran into the palace. I ran as fast as my feet would carry me, up the winding staircase to my grandmother's chambers. As I ran down the hall, I heard others footsteps echoing off the walls.

When I neared the door to her chambers, I found Adelaide already there with her mother and father. Adelaide stood as still as a statue, an unreadable look on her face. Noticing my arrival, she set her olive-green eyes on me. The next words she spoke sounded as though they came from someone else, some stranger I'd never met. "The healer has just informed us—" she paused, taking in a deep breath. "Queen Jelena is dead."

Chapter 14

THE NEXT FEW days were a blur. The atmosphere at the palace felt somber. I didn't see Adelaide much; she was busy with her new advisors, making preparations for Queen Jelena's death ceremony. I did my best to keep Peyton company while Adelaide was encompassed with all of the arrangements. I doubt I was good company. I myself felt absent. All I could do was assure he would see more of her again once things had settled down.

Two sunrises after her death, we were allowed to see Queen Jelena to say our last goodbyes.

The palace's steward, a short, solemn man, came and got me when it was my turn to be taken to her body. Once inside the room with her, he left me alone.

The room was small and made completely of stone. It was well lit, with dozens of glowing white candles. An exquisite painting of Celestia hung on the wall above where my grandmother's body lay. The beautiful goddess in the painting was looking down at my grandmother with love, holding out her hands to accept the spirit back into her universe. The image gave me comfort.

I approached my grandmother's body and saw she was dressed in the finest gold trimmed red silk. Upon her neck rested a golden necklace sparkling with diamonds and rubies, and on her head was her breathtaking golden sunburst crown, encrusted with the same jewels as her necklace. The jewels, of course, were just for the viewing. Her body would be burned in the traditional Solis way, consumed by the fire from which our kingdom was born.

I looked upon her peaceful face and knew then that she had finally been reunited with her husband and our goddess. I smiled, feeling content at the thought.

"I will keep my promise to you, Grandmother," I whispered to her. "I can't promise I will find love, but I can promise you that I'll never be with anyone I do not love. May Celestia keep you for the rest of days." I kissed two of my finger-tips and pressed them softly to her forehead.

Now I had said my goodbyes and there was nothing left to do, so I took my leave, my black skirts and robe floating around me as I exited the room.

Once everyone had said their goodbyes to the former queen, it was time to send her body back to the earth.

The whole kingdom was stationed around the outer courtyard while the queen's body rested upon a wooden slab at its center. Everyone was dressed in black to show their grief for the loss of our queen, with the exception of the priestess, who stood beside my grandmother's body holding a giant torch. She was a beautiful woman with flaming red hair, much like my own. She wore a long flowing robe of white that rippled gently as the wind kissed it with its cool touch.

"On this day we thank Celestia for giving us such a kind and just queen. We thank her for the seasons with which she allowed Queen Jelena to rule this kingdom." Her voice echoed with almost an unnatural volume throughout the courtyard as she spoke. "We thank Celestia for taking back the spirit of this great queen so that she may be at peace for the rest of days. We now call upon the powers of her elements, Fire, Water, Earth and Air to take back the body for which she no longer has need. For the love of Celestia!" she shouted the last words and hoisted the torch high above her head.

"For the love of Celestia!" we all repeated in perfect unison. I held my father's hand as the priestess lowered the torch to the wooden slab.

My mother stood on the other side of my father with her head held high, her expression unreadable as the fire consumed the wooden slab and my grandmother's body within an instant. And then it was done, and we left, knowing Queen Jelena was now in our past and we had only our future ahead of us—a future with our new queen.

After the death ceremony was over, it was time to celebrate life. I sat in my dressing chamber, freshly adorned in a high-collared, pale yellow dress that I found to be most unflattering. I'd chosen it for its colour and modesty. Because we were celebrating life, only bright and happy colours were to be worn, and being that we had just burned my grandmother's body, I felt it necessary to be modest.

I adjusted the golden brooch at the center of my throat while Awyn put the last pin in my hair. A persistent tapping on the door sounded, causing us both to look at the door.

"You may enter," I shouted from my chair, which was facing my mirror.

I heard the door creak as it opened before a guard announced, "Her Royal Majesty, Queen Adelaide."

The guard bowed deeply and waved his hand at my cousin before she swept past him, rolling her eyes and sighing with exasperation, "Yes, yes, very well. We get it. Eck! Enough with all of these formalities, I wish to speak with my cousin in private. Now leave us be. Awyn, dear, if you wouldn't mind…" She clasped her hands together, beckoning with a tilted head for my handmaiden to depart my chambers.

"Yes—yes, of course!" she stumbled, not yet used to our new queen's authority. "Excuse me, Your Majesty." She curtsied and quickly swept passed Adelaide and out the door.

Adelaide sat, throwing her head back and looking to the ceiling. "Dear Celestia, will I ever get used to all of this fussing over me?"

It was more of a hypothetical question, and I was no goddess, so I ignored it and asked one of my own instead, "So, when is your coronation to be?"

"Ah…that. Not until after Noctis De Celestia. It is only thirteen sunrises away, and the palace must begin preparations on the morrow. With the death ceremony and life celebration, it's going to be hard enough to have everything ready for Noctis. No, we will wait until another ten sunrises after Noctis De Celestia before my coronation. In fact, this brings me to the very matter of my presence in your chambers." Her lips pressed into a thin line that turned her expression grim.

"Oh?" I raised a brow in question as I peered at her, still in her black dress from the death ceremony. I guessed she'd been too busy to even have her ladies prepare her for the life celebration yet.

"Yes. Well—you know how you said you would be here for me no matter what I needed?" She smiled innocently.

"Of course, what do you need of me?"

"I know you like to spend your night at the Temple, but this time would you *please* spend Noctis De Celestia with me?" She looked up at me with her big, pleading eyes and added, "Please, Zephy."

"Oh, Addy, of all the things you could ask of me, you ask me for the one thing I wish you had not." I looked down feeling shame.

She on her knees in front of me and grasped my hands."But, Zephy, I *need* you. I promise you can sit by my side this time. I swear I won't make you sit with people you don't know."

The fact that the queen was kneeling before me instead of the other way around didn't escape me.

"What about Peyton? Shan't you have him there with you?"

"He will indeed be there, but—he is not to sit at my side, as I'm not yet crowned and, alas, we are not yet married. It is not custom for me to show I have a partner at this time, while I'm still new to my sovereignty. People would question any decision I were to make and accuse me of being influenced by someone who is not royalty. No, I must appear independent until I am crowned."

"*Argh!* Alright, Addy," I surrendered in frustration, knowing she was right. "I told you I would be here for you, so okay; I shall come to Noctis De Celestia this time and sit by your side."

"Splendid!" She clapped her hands together and then held me in a crushing embrace, kissing my cheek. "You have my gratitude! You cannot know how much this means to me."

"You're welcome. You should go get ready for tonight's celebrations. You haven't much time." I shook her off, giggling.

"How right you are. Luckily, I have many ladies now to ensure I'll be prepared with haste." She paused and pulled something out of the pouch tied to her waist. "I almost forgot, I meant to give you this on your birthday. I just never got the chance because of what happened with Grandmother." From her hand dangled a shiny golden necklace with a pendant on it.

I took it from her and examined it. "Oh, Addy, 'tis most beautiful!"

The pendant was in the shape of a heart with a sun etched on it, and at its center sat a bright red ruby.

"I'm glad you like it. I think it symbolizes the love we hold for one another."

"'Tis perfect. Thank you." I squeezed her in another embrace.

"You're welcome. Now, I really must go find my ladies and get prepared for the night."

"Yes, I'll see you there."

She gave me a wink as she slipped out my door, closing it behind her.

Now alone in my room, I clasped the necklace around my neck and slipped it under my collar. It truly was a thoughtful gift. Something I knew I would cherish forever. I thought of my promise to Adelaide and closed my eyes, feeling a weight suddenly rest upon me. Of all that she could have asked of me, she'd asked the toughest thing of all.

At least this time I would be at her side and, for the most part, I would be able to ignore the peers of the realm.

I entered the dining hall and saw it had been decorated with colourful flowers that gave off the most wonderful aroma. It truly did look like we were celebrating life. Not only were the flowers colourful, but so too were the outfits donned by the people of Solis. It made for a most delightful scene. A gentle harp song played in the background and most of the attendees were in quiet conversation with one another.

I observed silently from a corner until Peyton came up beside me. "Lady Zephyra," he bowed his head.

"Good eve, Lord Peyton. How are you faring?"

"I am well, thank you, and yourself?"

"Well enough. I'm coming to Noctis, if you haven't already heard, as I'm sure Adelaide—err—the queen has already informed you." It was going to be hard for me to remember to call her by title whilst I was in in the company of others. I looked at him, ending my observation of the crowd.

His eyes widened at my words. "Truly? No, she hasn't. I've hardly seen Adelaide, the queen, since the passing of your grandmother. She's been much too busy. Tell me though, what has brought upon this decision? I know how you love to spend that night at the Temple."

"Oh…" I paused, biting my lip. "Well, I'm sure things will settle down soon and you'll see more of her. It was actually she who asked me to attend Noctis. She said she wants me by her side, and who am I to refuse the queen?"

He laughed, sensing my humour, and tossed back his flaxen hair before clearing his throat. A serious look overcame his features. "I'm glad you'll be there by her side. I fear she'll be in danger of other possible suitors trying to take her hand."

I frowned at his words. I knew he wouldn't be allowed to sit next to Adelaide, but for him to fear her choosing another suitor was just silly. "But she loves *you.* Besides, she wouldn't take someone's hand just like that—not without being courted first. You have nothing to fear."

"Be that as it may, she also loves this kingdom, and if someone were to give her an offer too great to refuse and charmed her enough to make her believe she could grow to love them…" It seemed he didn't wish to finish that thought.

"Well, you can set your mind to rest. I shall indeed be there, and no other man will be getting close to her on my account."

That earned me a grin. "You're too kind."

I was about to say something in response when my breath caught and I suddenly forgot everything. Adelaide had just entered the hall, and she was a sight that could take anyone's breath away.

Flanked by her ladies, she made her way across the room as the herald announced her. She wore an exquisite dress of emerald green. Its square neckline showed off her slender neck, and the fitted bodice with its golden beads pushed up her bosom in a way that made me wonder why I had chosen my own gown for its modesty. Her golden locks were half pinned up, while the rest was left down to tumble down her creamy shoulders and back. Upon her head rested a golden tiara inlaid with rubies and emeralds. As she hadn't yet had her coronation, she wasn't to wear the kingdom's crown; even so, she looked regal as ever. Her pink lips were set in a straight line of seriousness as she took her seat at the head of the table between her mother and father. Her chair was large and golden with a seat of red velvet; the one our grandmother used to sit in.

Now seated, she spoke was a voice that was loud enough to carry, but still as sweet as bells, "People of Solis! Welcome. Please be seated."

We followed her command and made our way to the long rectangular table, which was covered with rose coloured linens and sparkling crystal vases.

Peyton looked to be in as much awe as the rest of us. He and I took a seat beside Aunt Faya and waited quietly.

Once everyone was seated, Adelaide began her speech. "People of Solis, tonight we celebrate life, and we celebrate happiness. Though death has cast its dark shadow upon us, the light shines through once again and has consumed that shadow. I hope I will be as good a queen as my grandmother was. And if any of you would ever like a word with me, I would be happy to receive you by appointment. Now, with that said," she paused for effect before smiling so brightly it lit up her elegant features even more, "let us eat, drink and be joyous!" She raised a glass of ale and we all followed her lead.

"To the new queen!" the whole hall boomed as glasses clanked and ale was downed.

Our delicious meal was consumed thoroughly, and the ale flowed throughout the night. We all chattered with one another, having light-hearted conversations. Many told funny stories of times past, whilst others, myself included, sat and listened. After dinner, a bard told us the life tale of Queen Jelena. What a grand tale it was! It brought a smile to every face in the hall. Finally, the musicians took up a light, bouncy melody and most found a partner to dance with. I stood on the sidelines, as usual, and watched.

I had my eyes on Adelaide, watching her dance with some short fellow with curly auburn hair, when Peyton approached me. "May I have this dance, Lady Zephyra?" I saw hopefulness shining in his eyes and found I couldn't refuse him.

"Why yes, Lord Peyton, you may." I offered him my hand, and he took it with pleasure.

As we danced to a song played with fiddles and tambourines, he noted to me, "Adelaide has danced with five different gentlemen so far…"

"Yes, but none of them has been you. Why haven't you asked her for a dance yet?" I asked him in disbelief.

"She said she doesn't want it to be obvious we're still together."

"Tsk," I shook my head in disapproval. "'Tis but only a dance. If she's been dancing with other men, it is appropriate for you to dance with her too. In fact, she's probably hurt you have not yet asked her."

"Do you really believe so?"

"I do." I looked him straight in the eyes to show I meant it.

"Of course, how foolish of me," he gave a nervous laugh. "I'll ask her after this one with you."

"Good. How has your night been otherwise?"

"Ah…fairly well, but I'm distracted by thoughts of Adelaide. I'll feel easier once her coronation has taken place."

"As will I," I agreed, and we danced on, laughing here and there until the song came to its end.

"Thank you, Zephyra." He bowed his head and released me.

"Yes, yes, of course. Off with you." I gave him a wink and shooed him away.

I watch him approach Adelaide, and I saw her face light up. It made me smile to myself. I felt for him. How hard it must have been to watch his lover from a distance; pretending not to be her true suitor, even though they obviously were together before my grandmother's death. I supposed it was just as hard for Adelaide. Again, I was reminded of how thankful I was that I wasn't queen. It seemed to be queen offered no freedom at all.

Alone once again, I took the opportunity to retire to my chambers. I didn't think anyone else would ask me for a dance, and I didn't really want to dance with anyone else anyways.

Chapter 15

With Noctis almost upon us, Adelaide had convinced me to see the seamstress to create me a new gown for the night.

"And what colour were you thinking of wearing, Milady?" she asked, inclining her forehead.

"On Noctis De Celestia, we wear white," I said proudly, repeating the words Gisela had once spoken to me.

The seamstress wrinkled her nose. "*White?* That's no colour at all. Most surely, it's not a colour of the sun."

"Oh but it is. It is the lightest of all colours. Besides that, 'tis the colour of Celestia, and the colour *I* always wear on Noctis." I looked at her with defiance, daring her to deny the fact.

She sighed and dug through her fabrics. "If you truly must. Silly royals, I say. Aha! Here we go." She pulled out some white lace that shimmered as it hit the candlelight. "This will go nicely over some plain white silk, I think."

"Yes! Oh yes, 'tis perfect!" I exclaimed with glee. I was very pleased with the fabric.

"I'll add some gold and rubies to accent it. Yes, I can picture it now. At least you'll stand out." She patted my shoulder as she spoke those last words into my ear.

"Oh..." I was at a loss for words; while I wanted to wear white, I didn't wish to stand out. It seemed I had no choice. I *had* to wear white. "Perhaps you can make it quite modest then?"

"Nonsense! Leave it to me. I have your measurements. Come the day before Noctis so we can ensure no adjustments need to be made."

I sighed, resigning. I knew that arguing with her would be pointless. She was the seamstress, and she was also stubborn as a mule. "Gratitude, Madam Seamstress."

"Of course. Now, off with you. I must get to work." Her wild, silver-streaked flaxen hair bounced with her as she bobbed a quick curtsy before she turned her back on me.

I took that as my queue to leave.

As promised, I waited outside the seamstress's door the day before Noctis while she was busy with another of her customers. Moments later, Adelaide came out of the door with one of her ladies.

"Zephy! Here for your fitting too, are you?" She beamed with delight.

"Why yes, actually, I am. I trust your gown fits well?"

"It fits perfectly. I am most impressed with the dress Madam Seamstress has created for me," she exclaimed with rosy cheeks and a big smile.

"Wonderful! What does it look like, if I may ask?"

"It is a surprise, dear cousin." She fluttered her lashes at me and laughed, "What does yours look like?"

"It is a surprise," I repeated her words.

"That's what I thought." She gave me one of her winks. "Now, you better see Madam Seamstress. She is most impatient."

"Right you are. Good day, Your Majesty." I gave her a quick curtsy.

"Oh please." She rolled her eyes. "Off with you."

I chuckled and pushed the seamstress's door open.

"There you are! I have much work to do today. Come, come. Stand over here. I'll bring out the dress." The seamstress waved me over with one of her plump hands.

As short and plump as she was, she was still one of the most intimidating women I'd ever met. So I did as she bade me. I stood and waited while she went to the back of the room, staring at myself in the long mirror that stood in the middle of the room. I'd really grown into my own body, I thought to myself—finally. No longer was I the awkward, lanky girl I once was. I was still tall and slender, but now with the womanly curves that men desired instead of the sharp edges of my youth. My hair, though, was still bright as fire. I wrinkled my nose at that.

As I continued to contemplate my reflection, the seamstress came up from behind, holding my new gown in her hands. I turned around and gaped in awe as she held up the stunning dress of white silk, with gold ribbon sewn on its edges. Over the skirt was a layer of the shimmery-white lace we had chosen, and down the bodice lay a row of sparkling red rubies.

"Well don't just stand there and gawk at it. Try it on." She pushed it towards me.

I shook myself and did as she ordered, disrobing down to my undergarments before stepping into the gown. "It is most wonderful, Madam Seamstress, but—are you sure it is not more exquisite than the queen's own? It would not be acceptable for me to out-dress the queen." I bit my lip. I didn't want to offend her.

"*Psh,*" she waved a hand in dismissal, "of course not. What do you take me for? I would be blamed if you were to outshine her. The queen's dress is just as exquisite as yours—even more so." She smiled to herself, nodding, as she complimented her own work.

"Very well. Oh!" I spun around, looking at my reflection in the mirror. "It fits perfectly!"

"Here, put this on too." She handed me something else.

It was a sheer white shawl to wear around my shoulders. It complimented the gown well.

She eyed me with approval. "There, that should do. You did say you wanted to be somewhat modest, so that should do it."

"'Tis lovely," I replied. Even though the dress still accentuated my bosom more than I would have liked, what could I say? She had done a marvelous job. As modest and hidden as I liked to remain, I was still a girl, and I was pleased with my new gown.

"I'm glad you like it, Milady. Now that we know it fits, I must see to the other girls. So if you don't mind, I would ask that you take the gown off now."

"Of course, I understand," I said to her.

She assisted me with taking off the gown and re-adorning my peach day dress.

"I thank you kindly for this new gown. It is an amazing work of art." I smiled at her, touching her hand to show her my appreciation.

"The pleasure is mine, Milady. I'll have Awyn bring it to your chambers on the morrow."

I nodded and left her to her next customer. Leaving the seamstress's office, I saw two more ladies awaiting her services. I heard them giggle and whisper to each other while I walked away and felt instantly sick to my stomach. *Were they whispering about me?* I could only imagine. Having stayed away from the celebration for so many seasons, they were probably now speculating I would be attending tomorrow night's. It was obvious, being that I was here seeing the seamstress on this day. I knew gossip in the palace spread like wildfire, but I had hoped my attendance would go unnoticed until the night of. Oh how I hated being someone of status. All I wanted was a private life that no one else cared about. Perhaps I should have been careful what I wished for…

Chapter 16

By the time Noctis came, I was ready to get the night over with so I could quit dreading it.

I stood in front of my reflection. Awyn pulled tight the laces on the back of my corseted bodice until I could barely expand my lungs.

"I can't breathe," I managed to choke out.

"'Tis the price of beauty, my lady." She grinned at my reflection, tying the laces in a bow. "There. You're ready, and you look wonderful!"

Indeed, I barely recognized the reflection staring back at me. Adelaide's gift rested between my collarbones. I had paired some ruby droplet earrings with the delicate necklace—Awyn's advice. They caught the light as I moved my head, causing them to glimmer. My hair was in curls and twists and pinned up most elegantly. I used the powder that was fashionable among ladies to whiten my face, and colouring from rose petals to redden my lips. I looked, for once, the woman I had always wanted to be. Too bad I didn't feel as confident. Perhaps I could pretend to be so.

"Here. Rub this on your neck and wrists." Awyn handed me a bottle of oil that smelled of lavender.

"Thank you, Awyn. Are you sure you can't attend the celebration tonight?" I asked her with what I imagined was a pout.

"Oh no, my dear, I'm going to have a nice meal with some of the other ladies in waiting who have stayed at the palace, and then I'm going to the Temple to give my thanks."

"I envy you. Would that I could go to the Temple—"

"Hush now," she cut me off. "Tonight you may give your thanks to our goddess by celebrating in her name and by being there for our queen. Now, I shall be asleep when you return from the great hall. I will set out your night dress for you. Do you think you can manage on your own for tonight?"

"Yes. Thank you, Awyn."

"Good. You should be on your way now. You don't want to be late, lest you make a scene."

I certainly did not, so I heeded her words and headed for the great hall, my silk slippers soundless on the stone floor.

I came upon the doors to the great hall. Two guards noticed me and opened the grand doors to the hall to allow me entrance, both bowing as they each held a door.

This time I entered without my parents, and my name was announced solely.

"Lady Zephyra Caldura! Daughter of Mirrabel Caldura and Lucian Caldura, cousin of Queen Adelaide," the herald called out.

I descended the stairs into the great hall, heads turning as I came into view.

I felt my cheeks grow warm and decided to focus on the room instead of the people it contained. Outside of the sun shaped window, rays from the setting sun beamed in. It cast an ambience throughout the whole hall. This time, the linens on the tables were a deep shade of red, though the plates and candle sticks on them were still gold, like the last time I had attended Noctis. To the left side of the room sat a large dais that was decorated with intricate celestial moons, stars and suns. Upon the dais sat a throne, along with three other chairs, which sat in front of a rectangular table. I smiled inwardly, knowing one of those chairs was for me.

I turned around, and standing right in my line of vision was my mother. She stood with a couple of other ladies of the realm; her piercing green eyes were set on me. Seeing me looking back at her, she stuck her nose up and turned back to her conversation. Perhaps she was shocked I had finally decided to go back on my promise to her that I would never attend another Noctis De Celestia celebration. Or mayhap she was just jealous that the queen favoured me. I decided to think no further on the matter, but I wondered where my father was.

As if he could hear my very thoughts, he suddenly appeared at my side with his mistress. "Zephyra? I thought I'd heard you were attending the celebrations this spring. I hadn't believed it though." His mistress excused herself and left us to chat up another lady.

"The rumours were true. Here I am." I gave him my biggest smile and added, "I only came for Adelaide. She basically begged me to come after Grandmother's death."

"Ah, well I'm happy you're here. I hope it does not bother you that I've brought my mistress. She brings me joy, unlike your mother."

"I'm glad you have found happiness. Don't worry, I understand perfectly," I reassured him. "Now, you should go fetch her before she gets away. Happy Noctis De Celestia, Father." I smiled again, and he gave me a quick hug.

"Happy Noctis De Celestia, my dear daughter." With that he disappeared into the crowd of people.

A servant came by with a tray of Celestia Sanguis, I accepted one of the tiny crystal goblets. Placing it to my lips, I tilted my head back I felt its warm red contents trickle across my tongue and down my throat, warming me from within. Thankfully, it took some of my nerves away. I set the empty goblet down on a table just as the horn sounded and the doors burst open.

The whole room turned, growing silent. And then the herald's voice sounded, carrying throughout the great hall, "Ladies and gentlemen; Queen Adelaide of Solis!"

And there she was, flanked by her ladies. My, did she look stunning. She wore a most exquisite gown spun of gold fabric. Her skirts seemed to float around her as she descended the staircase. Upon her shoulders lay a cape of red silk, and from her ears dangled gold earrings with peridots embedded in them to match her eyes. A matching choker rested on her neck. She wore her shiny golden hair down, with her tiara upon on her head. I daresay she took everyone's breath away that night. I felt myself beaming with pride.

Spotting me, she came towards me and asked, "Lady Zephyra, would you please join me?"

I knew this was a formality for the public eye. It had to seem as if I was invited but our queen to sit with her only now. Otherwise, I would've had to sit with someone I didn't know, as was custom at Noctis. With the whole hall bearing witness to her invitation, there would be no question.

I curtsied while stating the obvious. "I would be honoured, Your Majesty."

She winked at me and kissed my cheek. I followed her to the dais, my Aunt Faya and Uncle Bardin following us. It seemed I had failed at not drawing attention to myself, for I was now up on a pedestal to be viewed by all. I guess that was the price of sitting with my beloved cousin. I did my best to ignore the others watching us as Adelaide downed a goblet of Sanguis.

Setting her empty goblet down, Adelaide clapped her hands together. "Greetings to all. First, I would like to thank those of you from afar for coming to our kingdom on this night of Noctis De Celestia to celebrate with us. And to my own kingdom, I thank you as well for celebrating this night with us. I wish you all a most joyful Noctis De Celestia. Now, let us feast!" She spread her arms wide before taking her seat.

Everyone cheered and rushed to their seats while the servants began to bring out our delicious meal. Golden plates were filled with small roasted hen, sweet potatoes, warm bread and fresh vegetables. More Celestia Sanguis was brought around and all was glorious. I started to feel more comfortable—or perhaps it was the Sanguis that made me feel so.

Everyone shared cheerful conversations while we dined. Musicians played a low, quiet tune in the background that added to the merry atmosphere. I could see why so many loved to celebrate on this night. It was all quite glamorous.

Once our meal was finished and the servants had cleared our plates, a bard came out to tell stories of our kingdom's past. The beautiful harpist played a tune while he spoke, her delicate fingers plucking glimmering strings as she swayed. It made me think of the gift my grandmother had given me, and I felt tears welling up. Adelaide must have noticed for she gave me a gentle smile and touched my hand. Once the bard was finished his tales, he bowed, and the musicians took up a catchy tune. It was time to dance, my least favourite part of any celebration.

I spotted Peyton and thought mayhap I would dance with him when I noticed a couple of boys around their decade age, poking at another boy and pointing at me. The boy was chubby, with a ruddy face. He looked like he wanted to disappear. I knew that feeling well and decided to approach them.

"Why, good evening, sir. May I be so honoured as to have this dance with you?" I said to the boy with a reassuring smile.

He looked up at me with a stunned expression, his friends following suit. I gave him a wink.

"Y—yes, Milady. I—It is I who would be honoured." He bowed, and I led him to the dance floor.

The other boys were left standing with dropped jaws, looking like a bunch of fish.

"Don't let others get to you. They are cruel. You shall grow older someday and they won't matter anymore."

"You truly think so?"

"I know so," I said looking down at him. He had not yet reached full height and was much shorter than I. "I was teased and tormented when I was your age too, but eventually it stopped and now here I am—dining with the queen."

I scanned the room as we danced and saw my father dancing with his mistress. Peyton was chatting up another lad, but where was my mother?

"That's good to know, Milady. Not good that you were teased, I mean," he added quickly, his eyes widening at his own words so much that I had to suppress a snicker. "Good that you are here on this night with the queen and look so beautiful. I doubt anyone would tease you now." He blushed at his own words.

"You are too kind. And I hope no one would. However, I am close with the queen. People are jealous of that."

"I see."

It seemed he didn't really know what else to say. So I laughed and danced on.

Once the song had finished, I told him to go tell the other boys that I told him he was a good dancer and kissed his cheek. I'd be damned if I'd let them little scoundrels ruin his night much like many of mine had been ruined at his age.

Letting him go, I turned to see a man who looked closer to my own age approaching me. He had a slender build and a pretty face. He reminded me of a big cat, sleek and elegant. I guessed he was from Ventosa, the kingdom of air. His hair was the palest shade of blonde and he wore a light blue tunic with a purple cloak that was clasped between his collarbones with an amethyst encrusted silver brooch.

I didn't want to dance with anyone save Peyton or my father. I felt uncomfortable with even the thought of dancing with a stranger. It was too late; I saw no escape.

I averted my eyes, pretending not to see him as he neared.

"Milady, may I have this dance with your fair self?" His voice was cool and liquid; smooth and caressing.

Celestia help me, I thought, feeling myself blush.

"Y—you may," I answered, cursing myself inside for stuttering. How unladylike was I? I wasn't used to being given any attention by strangers.

He took my hand and we danced to a slower song played with tambourines and a harp. I tried not to stumble on my own feet—or his.

"I must say, I'm a lucky man. A goddess has favoured me with a dance on this night." He peered into my eyes with his own, so crystal blue.

I felt my face growing hot again. "I'm no goddess, just a girl. To say I'm so would put me above her Royal Majesty, and that is blasphemy."

He threw his head back and laughed. "Be that as it may, you look like an image of Celestia in that white gown. I wonder. What kind of a *girl* does it take to wear white on this night, when it is not a colour of her kingdom?"

Brushing off his flattery, I felt determined to make him see reason. I squared my shoulders, forgetting the dance, and stated, "When I was a child, my handmaiden taught me that on Noctis De Celestia, we wear white."

He scoffed at that, which only made me grow angry. "Priestesses and servants might, but surely not *ladies* of the court. Why would someone of high status listen to a handmaiden, anyways?"

I suddenly felt myself burning up inside at his proclamation. *How dare he speak of Gisela that way!* I took a deep breath to calm myself before saying, "Perhaps, Milord, you shouldn't judge things you do not understand."

His eyes widened before he grinned. "Then perhaps, Milady, you should tell me of that which I do not know," he said in a condescending tone.

I'd had enough. He may have been beautiful, but that didn't give him the right to act like he was better than everyone else.

"Thank you for the dance, Milord," I said, ignoring his last comment and pulling away from his grasp.

"But wait, you didn't tell me your name," I heard him call after me.

I ignored him and rushed into the crowd so he couldn't come after me. I looked around and spotted Adelaide. There she was, in all her glory, dancing with Peyton—who looked quite majestic himself. I was happy to see them together and decided that she no longer needed me to be at the celebration, so I exited the great hall with haste.

I was through with dancing for the night and didn't want that despicable man to find and question me further. Besides, it would be the perfect time to head to the solar. There, I would give my thanks to Celestia.

Now outside of the great hall, I leaned against the stone wall to catch my breath. I closed my eyes with relief. It felt good to be away from all of the people. It was suffocating being in the company of so many.

"Are you okay, Milady?" I opened my eyes to see a guard in his red uniform looking at me with concern.

"Yes, I'm well enough. Thank you, sir. I'm just wary. I shall retire to my chambers now."

He bowed as I pushed off the wall and left him.

If I was going to give thanks to Celestia, I didn't want to go empty-handed. I knew it would be near impossible to attain water and earth without difficulty at this time of the night, so I decided it would be appropriate for me to at least offer my own kingdom's element of fire. I knew I had a few unburned candles in my chambers so I picked up my skirts and rushed up the stairs and down the hall. My silk slippers were silent on the stone floor.

Once inside my chambers, I saw that Awyn had left my night dress out for me to change into, as promised. I decided I would wait to undress until I had given my thanks. I went next to my wooden chest and opened its lid. Digging inside its contents, I came across the white candles I'd left there. I pulled one out, closed the chest and grabbed my tinderbox.

As I headed back down the hall towards the winding staircase that would take me to the solar, I passed some of the guest chambers. I knew most of them would be occupied by visitors from the celebration later, but as I walked on, the sound of voices floated at me from within one of them.

Growing nearer, I realized I recognized one of the voices. I crept closer and listened more intently. Almost upon the room's entrance now, I saw the door was open a crack, so I halted just outside. I knew the guards would think it unsafe for a lady to wander the palace unescorted with all of the visitors here, but at that moment, I didn't care.

"Can we go over it again? What is it that you're going to do? I want to be sure you don't mess it up and fail."

I gasped and quickly covered my mouth. The woman speaking was my mother.

The other voice was a man's I did not recognize. "Yes, Milady. I'm to put a drop of this poison on my arrow and hit the queen from afar on next week's hunting trip."

"Yes, but you must *not* be seen. That is very important if you want to be given a higher position. Else you will be executed. We wouldn't want that, would we?"

"No, Milady, of course not! You promise you'll be able to get me a higher position once it's done?" he replied, sounding astonished.

"With my daughter on the throne and my husband as Grand Master of the royal army, there is nothing that I shall not be able to do. Zephyra isn't fit to rule. She'll have to turn to me for advice. Solis shall be mine in all but title."

My grip on the white candle loosened, and it fell to the floor. In a panic, I bolted back to my chambers. I couldn't believe my ears! My own mother was planning to kill my beloved cousin, her own niece, to put me on the throne? And if that wasn't enough, she thought she'd be able to do whatever she pleased under my rule. Oh, I knew she could be a horrible woman, but *this*—this was pure insanity. I refused to let this happen.

Within my own chambers, I leaned against my wooden door, sank down to the floor and put my head in my hands. *Think!* I told myself. *What do I do now?* I simply couldn't allow my mother to arrange this assassination.

After what felt like eons of breathing deeply, I came up with the only plan I could think of. I knew the hunt wouldn't take place until sometime after the coronation, meaning I had time to warn Adelaide. It was also clear to me that I had to remove myself from the kingdom to ensure my mother's plans to have me become queen never came to pass. If I was gone, the next person in line for the throne would be one of our more distant female relatives who shared the Caldura bloodline. Surely that wouldn't suit my mother's wishes.

I found my feather pen and ink pot and wrote to Adelaide, scratching the words onto the piece of parchment with haste.

Dearest Addy,

I write to you to tell you that I'm sorry. I have learned of an evil plot, and I cannot stay here, because otherwise, you are not safe. I cannot explain, but please, do not trust anyone except Peyton. I also beg you to not go on the hunt next week! To do so could mean your end. Get crowned, get married and have a daughter as soon as possible. Mayhap one day, when I know you are safe, I shall return. Know that I love you and always will. And please do not worry or look for me. I shall be alright.

Your dear cousin, Zephy.

P.S Burn this once you have read it.

As much as I wanted to tell her it was my mother who plotted against her; I knew it would be a death sentence and, as much as I did hate her, she was still my mother. Besides, I didn't know who the man she spoke with was or if anyone else knew of her plans. I knew my only hope was if I simply warned her to trust no one but Peyton. Once I had removed myself from the kingdom, my mother would have no way to the throne.

Now that the letter was written, I slipped through the secret passageway between Adelaide's and my chambers. I hadn't gone through the passage since I was a child and it was a tight squeeze now that I was full grown… I made it nonetheless. Inside her bedchamber, I slipped the letter just under the covers on her bed, ensuring only she would see the letter should any of her ladies come into her chambers.

Feeling satisfied, I stole back into my own chambers and contemplated what to do next.

CHAPTER 17

I KNEW I had to get away from the palace before people began retiring to their chambers. Looking down at myself, I realized I couldn't run away in this gown. If I managed to escape in it, others would see it and come to the conclusion that I was someone of importance and possibly have me sent back here. No, that wouldn't do.

Deciding one of my older riding dresses would have to work; I went to my dressing chamber and began rummaging through my wardrobe. At last, I spotted an old brown riding gown that was a bit worn. I took it out and tore the material a little on the sleeves and at the hem of the skirt to make it look even more worn. *Perfect,* I thought as I held it up. That would do. I hurriedly undid the bow on the back of my dress and pulled the laces loose.

I shrugged out of my beautiful gown and hung it up before donning the old one, tucking Adelaide's gift under the collar. I then took off the rest of my jewelry and pulled the pins out of my hair, the twists falling out and tumbling down my back as I did. I shook it out and tied it back with a simple ribbon. I heard the midnight bell sound and felt my heart begin to race in my chest. I had to pick up my pace. I rushed to my bedchamber and found my little wooden box with hearts etched on its surface. In it were five gold pieces and eight silver. I took the pieces out and put them in the pocket of my dress. I decided to leave my slippers on. They were quieter on the stone floors than any other shoes or boots would have been.

I took a deep breath to steady myself. It was time to leave the palace.

If I had a moment to ponder, I suppose I may have lost my nerve—but I didn't.

I slowly opened the door to my chambers and peered out. I didn't see any guards—or anyone else, for that matter. I decided my best bet would be to head down to the kitchens. I knew there was a small door down there where the servants and cooks threw the daily compost. Supper was over quite a while ago, so all of the kitchen servants would either be in bed or with their families.

I grabbed a torch off the wall and descended the dark, narrow staircase down into the kitchens. There was no light, save my torch, which told me I had guessed correctly; there would be no one occupying the kitchens right now.

Once inside, I spotted a servant's black cloak hanging on the wall. I decided to take it to help disguise myself. It had a hood that would hide my face and hair, and the wool material would help keep me warm from the nights chill. I passed two empty cauldrons and a large stone sink as I searched along the wall near the back of the kitchen. Finally, I found it; a small door with an iron latch was near the corner of the back wall.

The latch creaked open, and the horrible scent of rot hit me like a wave. Almost taken aback with the stench, I pinched my nose with my fingers to block it and breathed out of my mouth. Stepping carefully over slippery, rotting vegetables and animal guts, I cringed. *At least now my new slippers wouldn't look so new,* I thought as I tried not to fall into the stinking mess. I managed to make my way through the compost and looked around at my surroundings.

I knew I couldn't take Nova. Serell would be or have his grooms stationed at the stables. Besides, I couldn't take Nova on such a long journey; she was getting old, and I didn't think she'd be able to make it too far with such haste. No, I would have to make this journey on foot.

I knew the village called Lottenheim lay just beyond Solis. I would try to find passage to Terra from there. Perhaps I could become a servant to some lord or lady in the kingdom of Earth. My identity would then be hidden from the rest of the world. I nodded in conclusion at the thought and took off towards the woods.

I knew I had reached the end of the palace grounds when I came across a line of bushes. I pushed through them, their tight branches scratching at me like an old hag's finger nails trying to hold me back. When at last I had cleared the bushes, I fell forward. My chest was burning from the exertion. Tears burned my eyes as I tilted my face up to the sky, sucking in deep breaths.

The moon was full and bright overhead, casting a silver sheen over the landscape before me. Stars sprinkled the black velvet sky with their brilliance. The scene was most breathtaking, and I found myself whispering, "Oh Celestia, I never got to give my thanks. You know I'm grateful for all you have given, don't you?" Of course I heard no answer, but I hoped next Noctis De Celestia, I would be able to give my thanks properly.

I rose and gathered myself. I took one look back the kingdom I had never left. While I wouldn't miss all of the cruel people within Solis, I would surely miss my dear Addy—and Peyton and my father too. I wiped away a tear and marched into the woods with resolve. There was no time for regrets now.

The floor of the woods caused me to stumble a few times on protruding roots and fallen branches. I prayed to Celestia I wouldn't get lost and pushed on through. I heard night animals' chirp and squawk as I made my way. I pulled my cloak tighter around myself as I hurried on, not letting myself stop to think about what was making those sounds. I slowed to a walk to conserve my energy now that I was a fair distance from the palace, but still kept a steady pace.

When I'd been walking for what seemed like forever, I began to worry that mayhap I was lost and would die out here in these woods. It was then I saw glowing light in the distance ahead. I took off towards it at a sprint, fearing that it was just my imagination and the light would disappear if I didn't catch up to it soon.

The light didn't disappear. In fact, as I grew closer to it, I saw a clearing in the trees. Coming to a quick halt, I almost laughed with glee, for before me stood the torch-light of Lottenheim.

I checked my hood to make sure it still hid my face and hair. I took a moment to ready myself and walked on, into the little village I had heard much about but had never seen with my own eyes.

The whole village seemed to be in a lull of sleep, with not a person in sight. I thought perhaps I could find a barn or something of the sort to sleep in for a bit before first light. Once people began to wake for their day's work, I would seek out a wagon to take me to Terra. Thankfully, I had thought to bring my gold and silver pieces with me for payment.

I crept down the cobblestone street and around the corner of a building and actually came across a wagon, unhitched and abandoned for the night. *Perfect,* I thought to myself. I would find somewhere nearby to rest and return here after to wait to speak with the owner of this wagon.

My eyes felt heavy, and I yawned. The very thought of sleep compelled me. I edged my way further along the building in search of a resting place, but suddenly, the scraping sound of footsteps caused me to freeze.

My heart sank, and I tried to shrink against the wall when a dark shadow came upon me. I held my breath and was about to peer behind me, but before I could, I felt a large *THUMP* on the back of my head…and then darkness enveloped me in her unrelenting embrace.

Chapter 18

I AWOKE WITH a fuzzy feeling in my head. Confused, I opened my eyes and saw sunlight peering in through the shutters of a large bedchamber I'd been placed in. I lay atop of something soft—a bed covered in white blankets. Looking around, I saw the walls were decorated with tapestries of grotesque, bloody battle scenes and others of naked women. I wondered what type of person would keep such vulgar décor in their bedchamber.

My head pounded, and as my fingers touched the spot that hurt the most, I felt a large lump and dried blood that had become matted in my hair. My cloak was still on, but the hood was now down.

Who did this to me? I quickly sat up, which I regretted immediately, because my head pounded even harder with the motion.

"I wouldn't do that, if I were you," said a deep, booming voice from across the room.

I turned my head to see a large, burly man sitting in the corner. He watched me like a hawk watched its prey. He was dressed in a red velvet coat with golden buttons down the center; something only a wealthy person could afford, I noted. He had only tufts of hair on the side of his head, while the rest seemed to reflect light with its baldness. A bushy beard matched those tufts, and his pudgy face shone with perspiration as he eyed me. Seeing me studying him, he cracked a big grin. I swore I'd seen him before, but I couldn't quite remember when. Perhaps he'd been to court.

I felt sweat upon my own neck as panic rose within me. "Where am

I? What happened to me?"

The man chuckled and stood up, he was at least a foot taller than I. "You're in my manor. I'm Lord Algor. My most favoured servant has brought you to me. Welcome to my home, Lady. And who might you be, to have been out all alone at night? A servant escaped from the kingdom of Solis perhaps? Hmm? Answer me, girl!"

I blinked fast, starting at his shout. It seemed he didn't recognize me at least. "I—I…Yes, I'm a servant. My Lady died of some sort of condition. You see, she was very old. I had nowhere to go, so I came here to look for work," I lied, not wanting him to know where I was actually headed. The story came upon my lips easily.

"Well now, how perfect is it that Winslan has brought you right into my hands? What a good servant he is, always looking to impress me."

He didn't wait for my answer. It seemed it pleased him to hear his own voice. "In the next room, you will find a wash basin and a new gown. Wash your wound and don the dress. I won't have you looking like," he gestured towards me with a disgusted look on his face, "*that* in my presence. You're *my* servant now." He let out a malicious laugh.

I looked away.

I surprised myself when I found my voice again and actually had the guts to protest. "Sir, I—ah—I thank you for the offer, but I really hoped to find a lady to care for, as that is my expertise. I've never served a lord before."

He came at me, so close to my face, I could smell his foul breath. It smelled of rot and fish. I had to hold my own breath to keep from gagging. He grabbed my shoulder hard and forced me to look into his cold eyes. "Don't test me, *girl!* You're nothing but a servant, and you'll do as I say, or Celestia help you…now go! Get washed up. I will return soon." He let me go and strode out of the room. I heard a key turn after the door shut.

I flew off the bed to the door and tried to turn the knob anyways. It wouldn't budge. He'd locked me in there. I was trapped.

I decided I would wash. The water would help to refresh me, and I couldn't go around with my hair caked in blood once I figured out a way to escape.

I dipped a linen cloth into the basin of cool water and cleaned my face and back of my head, trying to be careful with my wound, while getting as much dried blood off as I could.

A pale blue dress lay on the stone counter beside the basin. I decided I would not wear it. I wouldn't obey this monstrous man's commands. Sure, I hoped to find employment as a servant once I got to Terra, but this man wasn't treating me as a servant. He was treating me as a slave.

No, I resolved, *I must plan my escape and continue my journey to Terra.* I went to the window, where sunlight beamed through. I looked down and saw it would be too far of a jump, even if I managed to get through. I also noticed there were no other people or buildings around the manor. I was outside of the village. No one would hear my screams. I sank down against the wall and cried with defeat.

What felt like an eternity passed by. I began to think Algor wouldn't return that day, and then I heard the door click. I immediately stood and rushed to the edge of the bed and sat, holding my head high with defiance. I would not let this crude man bully me.

Algor entered, leaving the door open behind him. He looked at me with hungry eyes. I forced myself not to look away, telling myself I must remain strong.

"I see you've taken my orders to clean yourself but not to change your clothing. No matter; it will be coming off anyways." He winked at me.

I shrank back into the bed and pushed my knees up. "Don't touch me," I warned.

He laughed, a loud bellowing sound that came from his belly, and then he came at me. His hand grabbed my tangled hair, and he pulled my head back so I was staring straight into his face. His wretched breath made me want to hurl, but I kept my eyes open wide and willed myself not to cry out at the pain he was causing me.

He leaned in and smelled my neck, causing me to shiver. "You don't tell me what to do. You're mine now, *girl.*" His lips curled in a sneer as he spat out the last word.

He grabbed my ankle and started to slide his other big, rough hand up my leg, letting go of my hair.

I did the only thing I could think to do; with my free leg, I kicked him with as much force as I could, right in the jaw.

He fell back with a look of shock on his face. Wasting no time, I jumped off the iron-framed bed and bolted to the open door.

Ha! I thought. At least he wasn't bright enough to close the door behind him. Perhaps he thought I wouldn't fight back—a mistake on his part.

Just as I got through the door, I heard him call, "Winslan!"

A tall lanky man with chestnut hair, about my own age, appeared in front of me. I had no idea where he came from, but he must have been close by, guarding the bedchamber. He smiled at me before he grabbed my arm and twisted it behind my back. So this was my captor, here to take me once again.

"Oh, no you don't," he said to me before calling out, "Master Algor, what would you have me do with her?"

Algor limped out of the bedchamber, rubbing his jaw. "Take her to the dungeon! It seems she doesn't want to be my servant. So disappointing; just like all the others."

"Of course, Master, as you wish."

Winslan took me down the staircase, keeping my arm pinned behind my back the whole way. I swear to Celestia, had he not had me in such a position, I could've taken him out. I daresay he must have known it, because he never loosened his grip on my arm.

"Ow! You are hurting me!" I cried out. "Please just let. Me. Go!"

"Sorry, lassie, it's either you or I."

"Surely it would be only a mistake if I escaped from you. I can see you're not all bad," I pleaded with him, hoping he did have some goodness in him.

"Nay, you're wrong. I'm all bad. That's why Master Algor has taken me in when no one else would have such a thief in their household. I owe him everything. Besides, he would indeed punish me if you escaped. Ah! Why am I telling you anything? You're nothing but one of my master's prisoners now. Stupid girl, wandering the streets alone in the dark. What did you expect would happen to you?"

I bit my lip as I tried and failed to choke back a sob. I was so naive to think I would be okay outside of the palace.

He all but dragged me as we descended further and further down and away from the light. We reached a dark opening that was only lit by a couple of wall torches. The smell was foul, and the air was stale and cold. My eyes adjusted and I saw iron bars just as we stopped in front of a gate. Winslan pulled a key ring off of his belt and fiddled with a lock until the iron gate swung open with a whining sound, as if it hadn't been opened for many seasons. He threw me inside, and I felt the cold, slimy floor beneath my hands and knees.

I said the last thing I could think of that might make him change his mind, my head hanging down. "Please, I'm Zephyra Caldura of Solis—cousin to Queen Adelaide. She'll be looking for me, and she shall reward my return generously."

"Ha!" he spat with disbelief. "Even if that were true and not just some petty attempt to get me to let you go, it wouldn't matter. My master doesn't need any more wealth, he needs entertainment. And if I were to take you to Solis and ask for the reward for myself…well, I doubt we would even make it there before Master Algor had us hunted down and slaughtered in a most gruesome way."

He didn't give me a chance to answer. He left me, taking my last hope with him.

I laid down on the stone floor, feeling utterly defeated.

Chapter 19

When I awoke on the cold, hard floor, I had no idea as to how long I'd slept; there was no way to see the light of day in that horrid dungeon. I got up slowly, my muscles aching, and made my way to the back wall. I felt a crunch beneath my feet as I made my way. I looked down and felt instantly sick when I saw that I had stepped on the bones of some other poor soul.

"Hel—lo?" I heard a scratchy voice from somewhere in the dark and suddenly felt panic rise within me. I'd assumed I was alone in this dungeon. I had neither seen nor heard anyone else when Winslan had thrown me inside.

"Who's there?" I scanned the dark cell, holding my cloak tightly around me.

To my surprise, another woman came slowly out of the shadows, dragging her feet as though the effort of walking was too much for her. She had the appearance of a skeleton with skin draped upon its bones. Her dark eyes were sunken in, and the bones of her cheeks protruded sharply out of her face. I could tell she was weak.

"So…they've caught another." She stared at me with blank eyes, and then shook herself as if finally remembering her manners. "Forgive me. I'm Meleini, but please call me Mel."

Her ivory dress was torn, caked with dirt and hanging off her frail body. I thought perhaps she may have once been beautiful, but this place had made her look terrifying, and I felt a stab of guilt at having to avert my eyes.

"I look that bad, do I? I suppose I do, for I feel death will soon take me." She let out a sigh. "And it'll be welcomed."

I blinked at her, and at last, I remembered my tongue. "How—how long have you been down here?"

"Does snow still cover the ground?"

"No. "'Tis spring now."

"I've lost track of how long I've been here. As you see, we never see the sun. When I was taken, snow had just begun to cover the ground." She let out a nervous laugh that sounded like more like rattling bones. "So how did they catch you, sweet…sorry, what's your name?"

"Apologies, I'm Zephyra." I sat beside her and drew my knees up, hugging them tightly. "I left Solis and came here to find passage to Terra, but was knocked out and brought here."

"A shame. It isn't safe for a woman to wander around all alone, you know?"

"So I've learned."

"Too late; I suppose we shall both die here now."

I let out a sob at her words, but she kept going. "I was engaged to a wonderful man, or at least, I thought he was wonderful then. We were celebrating our engagement at his parents' house when he disappeared. When I found him, he was kissing my sister in the storeroom.

"I left without anyone noticing, paid a carriage to take me back to my own parents' house. The curtains were drawn, so I couldn't see where we were going, but I felt no need to look; I was in too much misery. Before I knew it, the carriage stopped and I was being dragged by my hair into this manor. Two men threw me in here and told me I was to be their master's new play-thing. Apparently he'd recently lost his last one."

"You mean whoever he had before you actually escaped?" I gawked at her.

"No, I mean she died—in here. That's whose bones these are—the mistresses Algor held before us. I think that perhaps no woman has ever loved him, so he locks us away when we refuse to be compliant. I talk to them sometimes. At first, it was lonely, but now they talk back to me sometimes. I suppose I'm finally losing my hold on my sanity.

"Now I have you to talk to, though; a real live person. What's a curse for you, is a blessing for me. You see, now I don't have to die alone." She gave me a weak smile and patted my arm, as if to offer comfort.

I gaped at her, speechless. This woman was barely holding on to her sanity. I wondered how long it would be before I lost my own. *No,* I scolded myself. I could not let myself lose sight of reality. *I'm going to get out of here,* I told myself.

I decided not to speak of my hopes to Mel. I didn't want to give her false hope. I wasn't sure if I would be able to escape before she passed away. Instead, I crawled to a wall and leaned against it, pulling the hood of my cloak up.

Without meaning to, I'd dozed off again. I suddenly woke to the sound of chains rattling as the gate was being unlocked.

An enormous hairy-looking man with a sword at his belt squeezed through the gate and threw down two bowls. "Here ya go, ya dogs. Dinner's served! Eat it or don't, but it's all ya get today."

He then took a water pitcher out of the crook of his arm, filled two metal cups, and set them down, too. Then he turned and went back through the gate. I heard a slam and a click as he shut and relocked the gate.

I rubbed my eyes with my fists and went to the bowls and cups he had left.

In them, I saw what looked like scraps from the last meal; there was some kind of green slimy vegetable and pieces from a chicken that looked like it had already been picked at. There was barely enough meat on the bones left to eat.

I picked up one of the bowls and took it over to Mel. She stirred as I neared, she must have been sleeping too—or perhaps she was simply too weak to move.

"No, no you take both. You should keep your strength up. I'm a lost cause—happy to be gone from this life," she pleaded with me.

"But Mel, you're weaker than I. 'Tis you who should take both."

She tossed her head back and forth uncontrollably and screeched, "No! No! You can't make me!"

I backed up, horrified by her reaction. "Okay, okay! Shh. I'll eat both."

She sunk back down and smiled, satisfied. "Thank you."

She grabbed my arm with her bony hand and pulled me closer. Her breath was foul, but I pretended not to notice. "The water, though! Bring me my water! Please."

I nodded and fetched the cups. I held one of them out to her. She took it from me without hesitation.

She held it close and sniffed it. "They put something in the water sometimes. It'll make you weak, but it'll also make you feel wondrous—for a short while. It takes you away from this place, into a dream where everything is perfect.

"You could choose not to drink it to keep your strength longer, but without water you'll die quicker anyways. Perhaps you shouldn't drink it, actually. Perhaps I shouldn't have. I would already be gone from this nightmare if I didn't. But, alas, I had no one to tell me about this magical water, and once I had gotten a taste, I couldn't stop."

I narrowed my eyes. I didn't like what she was explaining. It seemed our water was poisoned, but I didn't wish to give up and die yet. The only real choice I had was to drink it.

She drank and I saw her face go serene before she sank back down into a peaceful slumber.

I decided to eat first. I took both bowls and ate what I could from the scraps. They were cold, and the texture made me gag. I forced it down anyway. Once the bowls only held the bones from the chicken, I picked up my own cup and slowly took a sip. Nothing happened at first and I began to wonder if Mel's warning was nothing but the ravings of a girl half gone mad.

Then, I felt as if my body erupted with power, as if Celestia herself cradled me in her arms! And then reality faded away.

I found myself watching my dear Addy. She was on her throne, Peyton at her side. I was on her other side, and before us were twin girls about the age of seven. The girls were running around, giggling with glee. It seemed they were playing a game of tag. Adelaide laughed, and I knew them to be her and Peyton's children. I felt so much joy for them and knew Solis was flourishing with Queen Adelaide's reign.

Adelaide took my hand and squeezed it. "Oh, Zephy, I am so grateful you have come back to us. My world was so empty without you."

I smiled at her, feeling pure delight and heard myself say, "I'm just glad my mother's gone for good. It has given my father and me so much peace. We're as happy as could be with her gone from Solis."

"I'm delighted she is gone too. You finally seem *truly* happy, my cousin."

Peyton laughed as one of the girls jumped on his lap and squealed when he tickled her. She had long, flaxen curls; the colour obviously came from her father.

I felt as though life couldn't get any more perfect when Adelaide nudged me with her elbow. "So now, tell your queen, how excited are you to be married soon?"

Chapter 20

My eyes shot open as my breath caught in my throat. I gasped in effort to get air; it was as if I were drowning except without water. At last, air mercifully rushed into my lungs. As panic begun to subside, I felt a blanket of dread come over me with the realization that it had all been a dream. I was still locked in Algor's dungeon with Mel.

As I gathered my bearings, my hands still shaking, I caught Mel watching me with a frown. "What did you dream?" she asked.

"I—uh—I dreamt I was back at home with my cousin and her lover…except he was now her husband. Is this the future to come, or merely an illusion?"

"Your guess is as good as mine," she shrugged. "Though I have dreamt of murdering the man I was engaged to, so it's probably just an illusion. I don't expect I'll make it out of here to fulfill that destiny."

"How often do they bring the water?" I asked, not wishing to hear any more about her dark dreams.

"They always bring it with our meal—which I suppose is once a day. Without the sun, who knows how much time has passed? Oh! The water is sometimes pure, though. It doesn't always do that. I figured since it was your first meal, chances were high that it'd be poisoned this time."

"I need to get out of here."

"And just how do you plan to do that?" she whispered, leaning towards me.

"When we're fed…do they always leave the gate open whilst they give us our meal?"

"They do, but they always carry a weapon with them. Try to escape, and they'll cut you!" She made a cutting motion with her hand.

"Have you ever tried?"

At that she fell back, cackling. The sound made me cringe.

"Me? Celestia, no! I don't have the courage to try something so brave. I simply sit here in misery and rot away."

"Next time we're fed, I'm going to try. If you would be so kind as to create some sort of distraction to get attention off me, I'll send help and get you out of here, too."

"Help would be too late. I'll surely be dead soon," she said with regret.

I began to feel that she wouldn't aid me in my efforts, and I didn't think I would be able to escape all on my own.

She must have seen the disappointment in my face, because she added, "I'll help you though—so that you don't suffer the same fate as I and the other poor lasses in here." She picked up a skull and stroked its shiny cheek.

She wasn't totally insane—yet. Between her madness, sanity still lay within. I just hoped she would be able to hold onto that sanity long enough to aid me.

Now all we had to do was await our next meal, which seemed to take forever in that stale, dark dungeon. I told Mel stories, letting her rest her head in my lap. I thought mayhap I could at least make her end easier by giving her some comfort. I told her of the wonders of the palace of Solis and all about Noctis De Celestia and how I preferred to spend it at the Temple.

When I felt her body relax and heard her wheezy breath slow, I stopped talking. Soon, I myself drifted into a dreamless slumber.

A loud *BANG* awoke us both.

"Wake up, ya wenches! Dinner's here!" The same large man who had fed us last time was back.

I gently shook Mel. She sat up as the guard opened the gate and stepped inside the cell with us.

I worried for a moment that Mel would forget our plan after her slumber, but to my shock she started shrieking and throwing her head against the wall.

"Stop that! You must stay alive until Algor ends ya himself! Your life's not your own to take, wench!"

It took me a moment to remember myself because of the scene Mel was causing, but as soon as the guard headed towards her, I bolted towards the open gate.

"Hey! Halt!" I heard him yell from behind me, but I was already out of his reach.

The stone floor was sharp on my bare feet, but I didn't dare slow my pace. My heart raced, and my breath came hard. I didn't know if it was from the poisoned water I had drank or the fact that I'd barely eaten anything since I had arrived here, but I felt weak.

I rounded a corner and saw the stairs that led up and out of the dungeon; hope began to fill me.

That hope was instantly crushed when another guard came down from those stairs and wrapped his muscled arms around me, squeezing me so tightly I could barely draw breath.

"Please," I begged, hardly able to chock the word out.

"Shut up!" He grabbed me by the hair and dragged me back to the cell…back to my death.

I had never felt so defeated. I saw Mel being squished like a bug under the first guard's boot. "This one thought to hurt herself to distract me. I'll give 'er pain, if that's what she wants!"

"Enough, Gustiv; Algor will want to deal with them himself. You wouldn't accidently want to kill one of his play-things now," my captor said to the other guard.

"Fine," Gustiv spat. "No food for you this time, ya wenches! Water's all ya get! And now that Algor will be coming to see ya sooner than expected, you'll need to smell better." With that, he took the jug of water and dumped it on Mel and strode out of the cell.

My own captor shoved me to the ground and left the cell too, locking it behind him.

I heard myself scream. I screamed so hard and so loud, and I didn't even know for how long. I stopped when I felt my throat grow raw.

Turning, I saw Mel on the ground. She was sopping wet and covering her ears. I went to her and hugged her. She was shaking violently. "I'm so sorry, Mel. I didn't mean to scare you. I didn't mean for you to get hurt."

"I told you it wouldn't work!" She glared at me, and I backed off.

"Now Algor is going to come and—and—and that's the *worst!* I thought mayhap I would die before he came back down here, but now he is *coming,* and he'll have his way with us."

"He comes down here? I figured we were just his prisoners now. I didn't think masters ventured into their dungeons. Celestia knows, royals never step foot in places as awful as this."

She looked at me, dumbfounded. "Didn't you hear the guard? We are his *play-things* and now he is coming to *play.*" She let out a sob and shrank back down, burying her face in her hands.

"I'm sorry, Mel. It almost worked. I almost escaped."

"You didn't think there would be other guards close by? No, don't blame yourself. It's my fault for going along with your plan. I should've known better. I know my fate. I'm to die here—and now, you are too."

There was nothing left for me to say. I left Mel alone and crawled to a corner and curled into a ball. My stomach growled, and my throat hurt from screaming. What I wouldn't give for even a sip of water. I was exhausted from my failed escape attempt. Sleep soon overtook me once again, wrapping me in its sweet embrace.

How long I slept for, I did not know. When I woke, Mel was singing a light-hearted tune. When she caught me watching her, she stopped.

"My mother used to sing this to me when I was a child. How I miss her. Her voice always gave me comfort," she explained. It seemed she had forgiven me for my foolish plan.

"'Tis pretty. My mother never comforted me. She always thought I wasn't good enough to be her daughter, never mind a royal of Solis. My handmaiden, Gisela, raised me instead. She was kind, but then my mother sent her away. I wonder where she is now."

She looked astonished by my words. "If you're a royal as you say, shouldn't people be searching for you?"

"Indeed, but I doubt they'll find me here. I don't think anyone knows what Algor has been up to with all these girls."

She nodded in agreement, dismissing the thought at once, "You're probably right. I just want more magic water so I can dream away the rest of my days here."

Now I understood why she drank the water even though it made us weak—because this time I agreed.

Chapter 21

THE NEXT TIME we had a visitor, we were both relieved it wasn't Algor. Nor was it our old guard, Gustiv. It was the guard who had caught me trying to escape, and with him, he had our bowls and the metallic pitcher of water.

He didn't say a word as he placed our bowls in front of us and poured our water into the metal cups.

"Thank you," I called as he turned to leave in silence.

He paused for a moment, the only evidence that he'd heard me. Then he continued on, leaving us alone again.

When I turned back to Mel, I was surprised to see her stuffing her face with the day's scraps. I decided not to say anything and let her eat in peace. I gave her credit for going this long without eating. I didn't know how long it'd been since she ate, but I knew it was before I had been thrown down here with her.

I took a sip of water and felt the cool liquid fill my mouth, which now felt like sand. I swallowed and waited …nothing happened. The water was ordinary this time. Nothing had been added to allow us that temporary escape from this misery. I looked at Mel; she looked as disappointed as I felt.

What I imagined to be the next day, I heard heavy footsteps accompanied by a faint clinking sound.

"Ah, my pets. I hear you haven't been behaving yourselves."

I knew that voice to be Algor's; the sound of it would haunt me for the rest of my life.

I heard a small squeak, like a mouse, from Mel. I decided not to answer.

"So, you think you can escape from *me?* Ho, ho, you are quite amusing," he mocked, fiddling with a key in the lock on the cell door. "And my dear red-headed prize, Winslan tells me you claim to be a royal. Do you know how happy it makes me to know that I've captured myself a *royal?*"

I looked up at him, glaring through my lashes as he locked the door behind himself. I saw that the clinking I'd heard had come from the metal cane he held in his left hand. "If you've heard of my royalty, perhaps you've also thought on how much Queen Adelaide would pay for my return. She will be searching for me." Except she wouldn't, because of my note.

"Oh, my dear silly girl, she'll never find you here. Besides, I have no need for a reward. I'm already rich thanks to my inheritance. I've been left this estate and all of the gold pieces I could ever wish for, plus more! No, it's only girls like you that I *want*...toys for me to play with. Of course, I would have taken you as my mistress if you would have cooperated, but, alas, you did not." He spread out his large palms with a smug expression. "So now here we are, and I must say, it quite thrills me to know I own you."

He rubbed his hands together with anticipation as he made his way towards me. When he grew close enough, I spat on him. "You do not *own* me. You hold me against my will. I shall *never* be yours."

"Ha! How wrong you are! Shall I prove it to you?"

I didn't even have a chance to answer. He backhanded me straight across the face, throwing me to the damp floor. In the next instant, he was upon me, tearing at my gown. I realized he was going to try to push himself on me, so I squirmed and writhed and swatted at him. After much struggling, I got one arm free and dragged my nails across his face.

"Ow! Foolish girl!" he hissed, covering the place on his cheek where I'd done the damage.

Mel started shrieking and clawing at his back. He turned on her with a scowl.

"Leave her alone!" While I didn't wish to be taken by him, I also knew Mel couldn't handle our malicious captor's advances.

I scrambled to Mel, who was now nothing but a pile of rattling skin and bones, ready to defend her.

Seeing me, Algor drew a dagger from his belt.

"Don't make me use this, lassie. I will if I have to."

I swallowed hard and backed away from Mel, knowing I couldn't win a fight against him while he held such a sharp weapon. I had to think quickly.

"Why do you not use the dagger to take me, then?" I held my chin up in defiance.

He scoffed at me, "What fun would *that* be? I can take anyone with a dagger. It means more to me to use only my bare hands to take you. Now, shut up!" Finished with me, he smacked my arse with his metal cane so hard I fell to my knees. I winced, feeling the hard ground scrape my skin.

So that was it, he wanted to feel powerful. All I needed was a way to make him feel powerless, but how was I to do so when I myself was growing weaker each day? Soon, I would be a walking corpse just like Mel. Oh Mel, poor Mel.

He was upon her now, beating her with that wretched cane. She lay there, still as a rock. I could hear her breath rasping between each hit.

I felt hot tears running down my cheeks and squeezed my eyes shut, unable to watch any longer. I hated myself for being the reason that he turned on her. If only I had been strong enough to…to what? Kill him? I didn't know if I had it in me to do so. *Coward!* I scolded myself.

And then it was done. I opened my eyes to the sound of him shuffling back to the gate. "She'll be dead soon, and next time I come, it will be for you—even if I have to knock you out first, I *will* take you."

I ignored him and crawled to Mel, who was laying in the same spot with her grungy gown half off, her dark matted hair even more of a mess than it was before. Purple welts had begun to blossom on her pasty-white skin.

I heard the door clank shut and the lock click, and then the sound of his footsteps and his clinking cane faded away.

"Mel…Mel!" I cried, covering her up with her torn gown.

"I—I'm done, Zephyra." She sobbed into my shoulder, using my name for the first time.

"It'll be okay. Celestia shall take you, and you shall be free of this awful place. I only wish you wouldn't leave me. I'll truly be alone once you're gone."

"Alone, like I have been for s—so long," her voice faltered. "D—don't worry. The others'll keep you company." It seemed her sanity was once again slipping away.

I heard the click and clank of the cell door being opened again. I snapped my head around at the intruder. "She's *dying!* Can't you leave her to do so in peace?"

"My master has sent some water for the two of you." It was the guard who'd brought us our last meal.

"How *kind,*" I said with disgust.

The guard ignored me and set down our cups before leaving.

As soon as he was gone, I picked up one of the cups and brought it to Mel. "Here, drink this." I placed the metal cup to her dry lips and let it trickle down her throat.

She swallowed and closed her eyes. "It's magic water. Oh, merciful Celestia, I shan't die in this place after all. Thank you for your kindness. I hope you find peace in your death too."

"Shh, save your strength."

With that she smiled and I felt her slip away into her dream world. Her breath still came out raspy, but it seemed to grow slower…more relaxed.

I stayed with her for a long time, not drinking any of the water myself. I drifted in and out of sleep too until I felt her breathing cease. Her body went limp as her spirit returned to Celestia. I felt a single tear make a trail down my cheek, hot and wet.

I smiled down at her. "You're free now, little bird." I placed her hand, which I had been holding, on her chest before I rose and went to the cup that had been left for me.

At least she hadn't died alone. If I were to perish in this place, at least I'd been able to give comfort to Mel at her end.

Taking my own cup, I sat against a wall. Feeling the hard stone against my body, I tilted my head back and opened my throat, sucking the cool liquid back as fast as I could manage. Once I'd finished the whole cup, I let it drop to the floor.

I felt as though my whole body became filled with lightening, pure and white. The feeling quickly gave way, leaving me floating through a starry sky. It was like I'd become a spirit and the whole world fell away. My goddess, Celestia, peered down at me in all her glory. She was ethereal…larger than the moon, brighter than the shining stars. She took my breath away as she scooped me up and held me in her giant, pale white palm.

"My child, you cannot give up hope." Her voice was like the trickling of a silver stream, serene and peaceful.

"What hope do I have against these men? Can I not just stay here with you? I've never felt such peace. I never want to leave."

"No, Zephyra, you still have much to do. You will return to me one day, but now is not the time."

I felt sadness that she was denying me my wish. The way I felt right then, in her presence…I had no words to describe it.

Colours and light sparkled upon the darkness surrounding us. For the first time I could recall, I had no troubles…no worries.

"What do I have left to do on Earth anyways? I am but one small girl who's got herself caught by a horrible man."

"Zephyra." I could listen to her speak my name for the rest of eternity, the way it sounded coming from her. "You must set your emotions free. The power is within you, if you would only set yourself free."

I frowned at her words. "What do you mean? What power?"

But she was already gone, and I woke with a gasp, back in the dungeon. Reality hit me hard. I curled up on my side and cried myself into another sleep, though this time, it was a dreamless one.

Chapter 22

I CONTEMPLATED MY dream about Celestia for a long time. *What did she mean? What's this power she's trying to tell me about? Did I truly visit her, or was it just simply a dream that meant nothing?*

My guard came and went, but I didn't pay him much attention. The water he'd given me hadn't held any of the magic in it since my dream of Celestia. Each time I was disappointed. All I wished was to revisit Celestia so I could ask her more about this power.

I didn't know how much time had passed in my prison, but one day, I awoke to an awful smell. I looked over to Mel's corpse, and it dawned on me that her body had started to rot. Horror filled me as I realized that I was stuck in there with her while she decayed. I bent over and retched, spilling what was left of my previous meal out.

I stood up and wiped my mouth. Noticing my shaking hands, I felt dreadful. I could see bone clearly beneath my pale skin; I would soon be as frightening as Mel was when I'd first laid eyes upon her.

"*Set your emotions free,*" Celestia's voice echoed in my mind.

I supposed I should at least try to obey her. I strode to the gate of my cell, grabbed the iron bars and screamed at the top of my lungs, "LET ME OUT!"

Hot tears burned my cheeks, and I felt anger welling up within me, anger that I'd managed to push down for so long. To my surprise, the iron bars grew hot beneath my touch. I pulled away with a gasp.

I looked at my hands and recalled the night my mother had told me she was sending Gisela away. I remembered how hot I'd felt then—like

I was burning from the inside out, and how I'd had to jump in the palace's stream to cool myself.

Could this be the power my goddess was trying to tell me about? How could this be? Why did I seem to have this power of…heat? No one on Earth had had any of Celestia's powers for centuries.

Or perhaps I was simply going mad like Mel had.

Still studying my hands, I heard someone approaching. It was only my guard bringing my meal, if you could even call it that. Though, whoever prepared my food the last few times had been more generous. Perhaps with Mel now dead there were more scraps left for me.

When he entered my cell, I decided to see if my apparent power was real, or just in my head. I placed a hand on his arm once he was close enough and thought about how I didn't deserve to die here.

"Get your filthy hands off me!" He pulled his arm away and set my bowl down.

I looked at my hand and asked, "Why? Is my hand thot?"

"Don't be stupid. I just don't want your dirty hands on me."

"Oh," I said, feeling disappointed. If I truly did have some power, it seemed it would be of no use to me.

"Look, just eat your meal, and don't try to touch me again or I'll have to take action against you. Don't make me do that."

"Yes, sir," I looked to the floor, hearing the defeat in my voice as he turned and left me.

I picked up the tray and plopped down against the wall. Today's meal consisted of a stale bun and some cold stew that was mostly broth. I stared at the food for a moment before deciding to set my tray aside. How could I eat with the smell of decay in the air? I reached for the water instead and was surprised when I took a small sip; the effects of the mysterious potion hit me once again.

My eyelids fluttered shut, and I slumped back against the wall. This time, I did not dream of Celestia. I dreamt again of Addy.

We were in the great hall, just her and I. A beam of sunlight shone through the large window and into the hall, casting a golden shimmer over the whole room.

Her laughter rang like bells as she took my hand and spun me around in graceful dance. "How I have missed you, Zephy. Please promise to never leave me again."

"I promise," I heard myself say. "I'll stay here forever with you. There is nowhere else I'd rather be."

"That brightens my heart. This kingdom is ours, after all. We have everything we need right here, especially now that you have finally found love. I'm so happy for you."

"As am I. I never thought I'd find someone who I could trust with my heart but, alas, here he is." I felt my heart burst with so much love that it pulled me from my deep slumber. I woke with a smile on my face.

That smile faded as I opened my eyes and saw Algor staring down at me.

I quickly sat up, taking in a breath of stale air. I felt fear rising up from the pit of my stomach and swallowed it. *I must be strong,* I told myself.

"Good morning, sunshine," he said as a grin cracked his face.

I stayed silent.

"Where are your manners? I thought you were a royal, *my lady,*" he mocked, taking a few steps closer. He gripped his metal cane in his left hand; it made that awful clanking sound with each step he took.

"I have nothing to say to you. Please leave me to die in peace."

"Ah, now what fun would that be, my pet?"

Glaring at him, I noticed his eyes were brown like those from Terra, but lacked the warmth I had seen in others from the kingdom of earth.

Eyes still locked, he pounced just when I was about to kick his cane from him, in an attempt to stun him. He was surprisingly fast for his size. His hands pressed down on my shoulders. I tried to squirm free from his grasp, to wriggle away, but I couldn't gather the strength to escape his heavy body.

I'd just woken from the dream the poisoned water had induced, and I could now feel that it had indeed weakened me to the very core, as Mel had warned. I felt as though I were now an old crone, awaiting the kiss of death.

He tore at my dress; already worn, it tore easily.

What he did next brought the taste of bile come to my throat. He started fumbling with his belt, his big fingers having a bit of trouble before he got it undone successfully.

"No! Wait! I'm a virgin!" I said, thinking quickly. "You wouldn't want to soil your good clothing with my blood, would you?"

I squeezed my eyes shut, hoping he would heed my words. I didn't know what else to do. I had nowhere to run. If I could've, I would have ended my own life, but I didn't see any way of accomplishing that.

Then I heard his laughter, deep and rumbling like thunder. The sound made me shiver.

With his knees between my legs and one hand grasping both my wrists, he spat, "Well then, I'll just have to let my friend take you first."

I opened my eyes to ask what friend he spoke of, but before I even a chance to utter a word, his cold metal cane rammed right between my legs. My vision went blurry with white hot pain, and I heard a shrieking so loud it pierced my ears. As my throat began to hurt, I realized it had been from me that the awful sound was coming. Hot tears burned my eyes right before everything went black

At first, I thought I'd fainted, but then I heard him groan and felt his weight no longer on me.

"*Celestia's ass!* Damn these torches! Damn them all the way to the dark world of Mnyama!"

I was startled when the cell gate slammed shut, realizing that the torches had all gone out, leaving the dungeon in such darkness that I couldn't tell whether my eyes were even open or closed.

Had I done this? I wondered. I didn't know, but I whispered a prayer of thanks to Celestia because I felt her presence in this matter either way. Fire was one of her elements, and the fact that it had ceased to burn meant fire had saved me for the moment—though it hadn't been in time to save me from the searing pain I now felt between my legs.

I lay on the floor, shivering in the darkness, wishing for my death. Eventually, a guard came down and relit the torches.

CHAPTER 23

THE GUARD CAME and went with my scraps, which were now less than they had been. He also brought me water that, more often than not, contained the poison. Suspecting that Algor was trying to weaken me further, I tried to stop from drinking it. In the end I always failed, my thirst conquering my will.

I drifted between my lucid dreams and reality. When I was dreaming, at least I was away from that dreadful place. It was as good as it was going to get for me. So I drank and waited for the day when I wouldn't wake up.

Unfortunately, Algor came back to see me eventually. I lay there, a shriveled thing on the floor, helpless and uncaring about what he was going to do to me. It wasn't like I could do anything to stop him. I had even less strength than I'd had the last time he had visited me, and my will was now crumbling.

"Ah, my pet, you don't look so well. It'll be easy for me to have my way with you tonight. Did you enjoy my friend last time?" he asked with a malicious smile, patting that awful cane of his.

I glared at him with hate, but kept my mouth shut. Talking took too much strength. I thought perhaps this time I would meet my end, as Mel did, and then I would be free.

He shook his head at me, as if he could read my thoughts. "Don't worry, my pet, you still have awhile before you'll face death. And I will be sure you are fed well for pleasing me."

I looked away, disgusted. I did not *want* to be fed well. I did not *want* to live…for my misery to go on.

Though I wanted to argue with him, I didn't see the use.

It seemed he was satisfied with my silence, because he kept going on. He told me about how he was pleased that I'd finally come to my senses and how he was going to take pleasure from me, growing closer and closer with each word. When he was close enough, he whispered in my ear, "It's time now. The moment I've been waiting for. You are *mine*."

"Get on with it then," I uttered, breaking my silence, our gazes locked on one another.

He clapped his hands together with a gleeful expression. "Ah, she speaks." Then he tore my dress from my chest, exposing my bosom. I noticed his gaze fall there. "Oh, and look…a keepsake to remember you by."

I looked down in confusion and saw a glint of gold before he ripped my necklace off.

My necklace…*my necklace!* How could I have forgotten the one thing I still possessed that held so much meaning to me? It was the only piece of Addy I had left. I felt the loss of it fuel a fire within me that I hadn't felt since my mother had sent Gisela away. I shrieked at him, balling my hands into fists.

I awaited Algor's wrath, but instead, he released me with a yelp.

I looked up at him and saw that the hand which had grabbed my necklace was now aflame. I wrinkled my nose at the smell of burning flesh. The fire crept higher and higher up his forearm.

"Winslan! Gustev! Guards! Help me!" he bellowed, running from the dungeon in a panic while patting his arm frantically.

I sat in utter shock and felt my stomach flutter with hope. I realized he'd left the gate open and there was no one in sight.

As shock from the events that had just fallen began to wear off, I wondered, *could this be it? Did I finally use my power to free myself from this nightmare? Dare I even hope?* Oh, but hope I did as I gathered what was left of my gown around myself, covering my sacred bits by holding the material in a bunch at my midsection.

I stepped out of my cell with my breath held and noticed a figure just down the hallway, my heart sank. He was beckoning at me to come toward him. I looked the other way and saw a stone wall. It seemed towards this man was my only way out.

Drawing nearer, I noticed he didn't look like a guard. In fact, he looked to be a vagrant with his dirt-streaked, tattered clothing and long, scraggly beard. His long matted hair looked like it hadn't seen a comb in many seasons. I wondered what a vagrant would be doing here. I decided perhaps he'd also been a prisoner of Algor's.

"Make haste, my lady. The guards could come back at any moment," he said in a hushed voice. He didn't speak like a vagrant, I noted, and figured my guess had been correct.

I quickened my pace as much as I could, which wasn't much. I barely even had the strength to stand, let alone run. I suppose it was adrenaline that had given me the will to leave at all; that, or my beloved goddess.

"Here, here. There you are." He put his arm around my waist to help steady my pace. "I know a way out of here, if you'll just come with me."

I tried to shrink away from his touch, but almost fell over with the effort. He caught and steadied me before repositioning his arm around my shoulders. This time I accepted his help.

"A way out?" My voice was raspy and shook with effort.

"Shh, shh. Yes, you'll just have to trust me."

So I let this vagrant lead me down the dungeon hall. What other choice did I have? I had no idea where to go, and the other way was a dead end. In my poor state, I couldn't have fought this man off anyways.

I felt the sweat of anxiety wet my brow. I thought for sure we would be caught. That was until the vagrant stopped and bent down to push a large boulder aside, revealing a hole just large enough to fit a person through.

"Okay, I'm going to jump down first, and then when I say, you climb in the hole and I'll catch you."

I looked at him, unsure. He added, "It's not a far way down, and you're very light. I promise I'll not drop you."

Again, what choice did I have? Anything had to be better than this place, and if I did die from a fall…well, that wouldn't be so bad either.

He disappeared into the hole. A moment later, I heard his voice echo from below. "Alright, my lady, whenever you're ready."

I slowly sat and dangled my legs down the hole, feeling nervous at not having ground beneath my feet. My nerves were soon forgotten when I heard the sound of men yelling in the distance. I slid down the small hole, holding my breath.

The bottom wasn't as far down as I assumed it would be, and I slid easily into the vagrant's arms. Being so close to him, I could smell his stench. Like most vagrants, he needed a bath. It wasn't the worst scent I had smelled since I had been imprisoned, and I supposed I must have smelled just as bad.

He gently set me down and climbed part way back up the hole, reaching to pull the boulder back over it when I noticed another awful smell—human waste. I gagged and covered my nose with my hand.

"Apologies for the smell, my lady. This is the hole in which all of the waste from the household pots is emptied. There are tunnels down here that lead out to the village's market."

I nodded, still trying not to breathe the scent in.

He took my arm and guided us down the tunnel and into darkness. I still clutched my dress to keep from exposing myself to this vagrant.

We stumbled through the dark tunnels, twisting and turning. Once my eyes had become accustomed to the dark, I could make out a bit of the dirt and rocks that made up the tunnel walls. Still, I had no idea where we were going, and had to trust this strange man to get us out of there, lest I become lost and die of exhaustion—or thirst.

He had to ease his own pace to help me along. I knew not why he had shown me this kindness, but I didn't have the strength to even ask him at that moment. On and on we walked in silence until I started to shake with exhaustion.

He must have noticed, because he stopped and stated, "We can rest for a moment, but not for long. We're nearly out anyways."

I nodded and sank against one of the dirt walls, sucking in huge gulps of air.

"I'm sorry I don't have any water to give you, or I would."

""Tis alright—" I managed to choke out before he cut me off.

"Shh, hush. Save your breath. You will need it to finish the journey out of these tunnels."

I shut my mouth and nodded in reply before laying my head back against the dirt wall and closing my eyes.

I must have fallen asleep. When I felt a tap on my shoulder, I almost screamed out, thinking he was Algor coming to take me again.

"Shh. It's okay. We're in the tunnels, remember? We must get going. I'm sorry, I know you're tired."

The memory of my escape rushed back to me, and I felt a single tear run down my cheek as he helped me to my feet. I didn't know if he noticed, he kept his silence if he did.

We continued on through the tunnels for a while and just when I began to suspect we were lost, I noticed a faint light and paused.

"Look, that's moonlight just up ahead. Not much longer now," he urged.

I didn't need any urging. I felt a rush of energy at the sight of the moonlight and quickened my pace, though still dragging my feet against the ground.

At last, we'd come to an opening in the tunnel. It was a bit steep and rocky, but the vagrant held my arm firm, helping me along the way.

I stumbled on a sharp rock once and almost fell backward, but he held my arm tight and helped me gain my feet. My arm began to hurt where he clutched it, but I didn't complain, because without his hold, I wouldn't have made it.

When we made it up and out of the tunnel, I breathed in fresh air for the first time in…I didn't even know how long it had been. The fresh air felt like paradise. I had to blink back tears of joy.

Looking around, I saw we had come out at the end of a cobblestone road; the outline of houses and shops were etched in the dark. It seemed we were in the heart of the village. I started to ponder what my next move would be. I still had to find someone to take me to Terra. As much as I wanted to go home to my own kingdom, I didn't know if my mother still plotted against Adelaide. I decided I couldn't take the chance.

I had come this far. *I must go on to Terra and find a new life for myself there,* I resolved. Once I was settled, I would write to Adelaide and tell her of Algor so she could sentence him to death before he harmed any other women.

Feeling determined, I turned to my savior and put one hand on his arm. "Thank you, good sir. I shall be forever in debt to you for saving my life. I wish I had something to give you, but as you can see, I have nothing. You may leave me now and go on your own way." I heard my raspy voice shake with the effort it took to speak.

"Oh—no, my lady, you must come with me. You'll surely die out here on your own."

"But I must—"

"I cannot, in good conscience, let you go off on your own."

Panic rose within me when he grabbed my hand, not roughly but still too firm for me to escape.

He must have seen the fear in my eyes, for when I looked into his aqua-coloured ones, I saw only sympathy.

"Let me go! You cannot keep me! I must go!" I started to yell at him while he shushed me. This couldn't be happening again. I couldn't let myself be someone else's prisoner. "Help me, someone!" I called out to no one; not a soul was out this late at night.

He swiftly pulled me against himself and covered my mouth and whispered into my ear, "I'm sorry."

And then darkness overcame me once again.

CHAPTER 24

I BECAME AWARE of a softness I hadn't felt in ages beneath my body. *Could I be in a…no, I couldn't be, could I?* I opened my eyes. I was, *truly*, in a bed.

I took in a deep breath and stretched, taking in my surroundings. I was in a room with soft pink décor. The furniture was dark wood framed with bronze. The room had a warm ambience to it. Sunlight filtered in through the sheer pink curtains that covered the window, particles of dust dancing in the beams of light.

My vision landed on the corner across from where I lay, and my eyes connected with those of a strange man who sat staring silently at me. I didn't recognize him. He was clean shaven, with short-cropped hair that was black as onyx. His eyes, though…they seemed so familiar.

And then it all came rushing back to me; the memories of Algor and my imprisonment—of the vagrant who'd saved me.

I sat up, my breath rising and falling quickly in my chest.

The man stood and put his hands up, "It's alright," he cooed in a soothing tone.

"Wh—who are you? Where am I?" I heard the scratchiness of my own voice and swallowed. It felt as though my throat were filled with dirt and glass.

"I'm Percifal Lacrima, and you are at The Golden Lilly Inn—"

"But how?" I cut him off, not caring that I was being rude.

"I brought you here after you fainted in the streets." He looked at me pointedly. "You need to rest. You were nearly dead when I found you."

"You?" I shot. "*You're* the vagrant who helped me? How can that be?"

"Well, my lady," he looked down at himself, a small smile tugged the corners of his lips upwards. "You've been asleep for a couple of days. In that time, I decided I should clean myself up—"

"*A couple of days!* Dear Celestia, I really must be going." I started to get up, still not trusting this man who wasn't who he'd seemed. I doubted I would ever trust another man again, not after what had been done to me.

"Please…sorry, you didn't give me your name."

"Zephyra, Zephyra Caldura," I said as I started to peel the blankets off myself. I stopped just in time, remembering my gown had been torn. Pins were now keeping it in place, which made me blush. "Did you put these pins here?" I asked accusingly as he watched me.

"No, not I. That was Ginnie. Apologies. Did you say your name is Zephyra Caldura?"

"I did. Oh dear goddess. You know my name, don't you?" I asked, reprimanding myself for being so foolish.

He narrowed his eyes and paused for a moment before answering. "I do. You are a royal of Solis."

I narrowed my own eyes back at him. Why did he hesitate?

"You should be careful who you tell your name to. It could get you into more trouble."

I nodded, deciding he was right.

I swung my legs of the edge of the bed, but when I went to stand, my knees buckled with the weight of my own body. In an instant, Percifal was there to help me.

"Don't touch me." I shot him a look that made him back away while I steadied myself against the bed.

"Again, apologies. I can't fathom what you went through in that cell. I just didn't want you to fall and hurt yourself. I'll go fetch Ginnie."

Before I could ask who Ginnie was, he was gone.

Moments later, a petite woman who looked to be in her fifth decade entered the room. Her silver-streaked chestnut hair was pulled back in a bun, showing off her rosy cheeks. She had a sweet demeanor and reminded me of Gisela, only older.

"Oh dear," she exclaimed as she rushed over to help me back onto the bed. "You shouldn't try to stand on your own yet. I dare say you haven't got the strength."

"Thank you, madam," I said, letting her help me.

"Oh, please call me Ginnie."

"As you wish, Ginnie. I'm—Phyra."

"'Tis a pleasure to meet you, Phyra. I suppose you have many questions. I would ask you to wait until you've had more rest first."

"I suppose I can wait a bit longer. I would love a bath if I may, though." I wrinkled my nose, thinking about how filthy I was.

"Of course, dear! We would have cleaned you up sooner, but it seemed better to let you sleep in your state. I will get my maid, Amelia, to heat some warm water and prepare your bath. Just stay here until she comes to get you. I don't want you falling again."

"Thank you, Ginnie. I'm most grateful," I bowed my head to her.

She gave me a wink and was off, leaving me alone once again.

I sighed and sank back into the pillow, questions filling my head. How did I get so lucky? Was it even luck, or did Celestia have a hand in my escape? Surely I wouldn't have gotten away if not for the power I seemed to now hold. Did I even set Algor on fire, or had it been my imagination? I ground my teeth in frustration. I would never have these answers, so I tried to think of simpler ones instead; like, who was this man who seemed a vagrant but was now transformed into someone of good culture? And how had he found me, and why had he brought me here? I would ask Ginnie next time I saw her. It seemed she would answer my questions once I got some more rest.

Before long, the maid, entered my room wearing a plain black dress, holding two large buckets. "Good eve, Milady. I'm here to assist you with your bath."

"Yes, that would be lovely." The last time I'd washed was when I had first been captured. It had been even longer since I had a proper bath. I was looking forward to having all the stench and grime washed off.

Amelia came to my side and offered her hand to help me from my bed. I accepted it.

She led me to a small but cozy water closet and helped me peel off my old, torn dress, which was stiff with dirt.

"My, my, we're going to have to find you something else to wear, Milady."

"I have no money to pay for a new gown." I looked down, feeling embarrassed.

"I think Madam Ginnie and Master Irving's daughter left some of her old ones behind when she left to be married."

"Irving; is that Ginnie's husband?"

"Aye," she offered in her simple accent.

"And they own this place?"

"Aye, Milady."

Now fully stripped, I stepped into the tub. Amelia poured the buckets of warm water over me.

The water felt divine, surrounding me with its comforting warmth. Amelia grabbed a sea sponge and a block of soap, and began scrubbing the filth from my skin. I closed my eyes, letting her do her work in silence. It'd never felt so good to bathe.

Once she was finished scrubbing nearly every inch of my skin, she grabbed a vase and dowsed my hair with water, shielding my eyes with her hand. When my hair felt clean, she squeezed my shoulder in a comforting gesture. "I'll go and see about finding you something clean to wear. Stay here; I'll be back in a moment."

"I doubt I could even get out of the tub on my own…don't worry. I shan't move." I gave her a sad smile.

She nodded, leaving me alone with my thoughts once again.

It seemed Celestia had blessed me after all. I was getting a bath *and* clean clothing! I gave her a silent prayer of thanks and felt light-hearted for it. I lay back against the tub and closed my eyes, taking in deep, slow breaths.

The soap that Amelia had used on me made the whole small room smell of rose petals. It was quite lovely. I knew I was filthy, but I hadn't realized how much so until Amelia had scrubbed me clean. I'd probably smelt worse than that vagrant—er, Percifal. I didn't know what to think of him now in his cleaned-up state.

"Madam Ginnie has offered some of her daughters clothing for you to keep. She says her daughter can no longer fit into them, and would be happy to hear they'd gone to a good cause." Amelia interrupted my thoughts as she entered with a gown in her arms.

So I was a good cause now, was I? I was humbled by the gift anyways, and offered my thanks.

Amelia helped me out of the tub and into the light peach night-gown. It wasn't as fine as my own had been, but it was a comfortable enough, and much better than the grubby, torn dress I'd been wearing.

Back in my room, I noticed my bedding had been changed, and in the open wardrobe now hung three gowns. I lay back in the bed, feeling fresh and cleansed. I was overjoyed by the kindness I had received. I couldn't help but smile.

"You look happy, Milady. May I assume the bath and clothing are to your liking?"

"Oh, but of course. Thank you, Amelia. 'Tis more than I could have ever asked for."

"Well, be sure to thank Madam Ginnie too, for it was her idea. I simply follow her orders."

"Of course I shall. Anyways, I thank you for your kindness."

"You're welcome, Milady. Now, you must be hungry. You've been out for nearly two days. Supper should be almost ready for the night. I'll go and fetch you something light to eat."

"Oh, yes." I felt my stomach grumble at the very thought of food, "That would be wonderful."

With that, she left my room, closing the door behind her.

While I waited, I thought of what I would do once I regained my strength. I certainly couldn't stay here forever. Perhaps Ginnie and her husband would know of someone with a carriage I could commission to take me to Terra. I didn't have any gold or silver to pay with currently, but mayhap I could write to Adelaide and have her send some to whoever took me. Addy would surely assist me. I would explain that I was alive and well, and that we would meet again one day.

There was a gentle knock at my door before I saw Ginnie enter with a tray in her hands.

"Ginnie." I gave her a smile from my bed while I adjusted my position to allow for the tray to rest on my lap. "I expected to see Amelia."

"I know, dear, but I wished to see how you're faring myself. You're looking much better with that bath and in clean clothing." She raised her brows.

"I feel a lot better for it, too. Thank you for everything."

"No matter, Milady. Any good person would aid someone in your condition."

"Anyways, I'm grateful—and please, call me Phyra."

"As you wish."

With the tray now in my lap, I saw she had brought me chicken soup with biscuits and some water. I sipped the water first, glad that it wasn't poisoned with whatever potion Algor had been giving me. It was just plain, cool water.

The soup was warm and smelled delicious. I hadn't had warm, never mind fresh, food since I'd run away. As I put the wooden spoon to my lips, I closed my eyes with pleasure as the flavourful broth took over my senses.

Ginnie sat silently by my side while I ate. Once I was finished, she took the tray from me.

Not wanting to be alone with my question again just yet, I decided to ask, "Who is Percifal really, Ginnie? He seemed as though he was a vagrant when he found me, but now he seems to be a different man altogether—and why did he bring me here?"

Her lips drew upward. "He brought you here because we are friends of his. You see, he once helped us out too. As to whom he really is…that, you'll have to ask him yourself. Only he can give you that answer."

I sighed and sank back down, deciding to ask something else. "Do you know of anyone I can commission with a carriage to take me to Terra?"

She gave me a look of sympathy, her lips drawing into a thin line. "Apologies, but I don't. Is Terra your home?"

"It is to be soon, I hope."

"I will keep my ear out for one. One of our guests might know of someone. We do get a lot of travelers here."

"My thanks, again."

She nodded in reply and then left me.

Now clean and fed, I finally felt content and drifted off to sleep, the questions in my head leaving me at peace—for the moment.

I spent the next few days in bed, trying to regain enough strength to be able to stand without assistance. I was very grateful to Amelia, who brought me my meals and told me stories of others she'd met during her employment at the Golden Lilly. It seemed she had met a lot of interesting people; even a couple who claimed to be from a land outside

Sarantoa. I gaped at that, wondering how long they had travelled for—surely at least two full seasons. I had never even given thought to the lands that lay outside of Sarantoa, but when Amelia told me of these people's bronze coloured skin, bright clothing and stories of their magical gods, I thought perhaps I should try to find books on them so I could learn more.

Eventually, I grew restless from being confined to my room. One morning, as the sun shone in through the sheer pink curtains into my room, I decided to try my strength. Placing my feet on the wooden floor, I stood and found I was able to hold my own weight. I made my way to a chair that sat in front of a wooden table and small round mirror.

I felt a wave of shock roll through me as I stared at my reflection. I hadn't seen myself since I'd first been captured, and the woman who now stared back at me looked frail with sunken cheeks and a pallor even paler than the normal Solis skin tone. My freckles stood out like cinnamon on sugar. I couldn't fathom how I must have first looked when I'd been rescued in the dungeon.

I shook myself and picked the comb up off the table. Enough resting; it was time to regain my strength—and perhaps let the sun kiss my sickly skin.

For the first time since I had come to The Golden Lilly Inn, I stepped outside of my room to find myself in a long stone hallway and noticed the doors to other rooms. There were about a dozen doors with six on each side of the hallway. I heard my own heart beat in my ears as I made my way down the silent hallway until I came upon a narrow wooden staircase. I guessed the stairs that went up led to more rooms. The stairs leading down seemed to end at the main floor.

I stopped and leaned against the wall beside the staircase and listened. The sounds of men's laughter and the smell of warm food rose up to greet me. My mouth watered in reply to the smell. I took in a deep breath and steadied myself before taking slow, careful steps down the stairs.

When I reached the bottom, the floor creaked beneath my feet and I looked up to see if anyone had noticed me. No one did…there was simply too much other noise going on. Straight ahead, just to the right, stood a large bar and to the left there were large square oak tables with a little over half a dozen men sitting at them; stuffing their faces with warm oats and biscuits.

Growing closer to the men, I could smell scents of sweat and spice—

a scent I wasn't used to.

I spotted Ginnie just as she noticed me, bending down to clear empty dishes off of a table. She caught my eye and smiled, her round cheeks reminding me of little red apples.

I returned her smile as she came over to me, dishes in hand.

"G'day, Lady Phyra. I see you've made it out of your room on your own. How splendid. You're regaining your strength. I'm delighted."

"Good day, Ginnie. I am indeed regaining my strength, thank you. Soon I'll be able to continue my journey and be out of your way."

She waved her hand at that. "Never mind that. It's no trouble at all. We're happy to have you here."

"Well, anyways," I raised an eyebrow, wondering why she was so keen to have me when I hadn't even a piece of silver to give her. "I must be on my way soon. As grateful as I am for your kindness, I mustn't remain here for long."

She tilted her head. "I know it's not my place to ask, but are you running from something besides the awful man who captured you?"

"There's more cruelty in this world than that man," was the only response I could think to give her.

She pressed her thin lips together, but nodded in acceptance. "Well, please have a seat at one of the tables. Don't mind the men. Most of them know their manners when it comes to ladies." She gave me a wink. "I'll bring you some food to break your fast. My husband Irving will be back from the market soon. He's been eager to meet you."

"Thank you, Ginnie. I would very much like to meet Irving and thank him as well."

With that, she left to fetch my morning meal.

I observed the men, who seemed oblivious to my presence, before gathering enough courage to make my way to a small table in the corner next to the unoccupied bar. No one worked behind the bar yet. It was too early for ale.

Before long, Ginnie returned with a bowl of hot oats, biscuits and fresh water for me. She set it down without a word and began clearing empty dishes from the other tables.

Eating my meal, I began to relax. No one paid me any attention. Soon most of the men had finished their meal and cleared out of the dining hall, leaving behind a more peaceful atmosphere.

Deep in thought about what I would do if I couldn't find a carriage to take me to Terra, I didn't notice my mysterious saviour come up beside me. I jumped a little when he spoke.

"Good day, my lady. I see you're doing better."

I turned as he pulled up a chair beside me without invitation. It still astonished me to see how he had transformed from a poor looking vagrant into a...well, a good-looking man, if I was being honest, with his short-cropped hair and a couple days of stubble.

I folded my hands in my lap and sat back. "My thanks, good sir. I actually have a few questions for you, if you wouldn't mind."

"Ask away. I will do my best to give you the answers you seek."

I cleared my throat, not sure where to start. "Well—uh—first off, how did you find me there in that dungeon?"

He replied without hesitation, "I use the tunnels to get into the kitchens of rich manors, such as the one you were in, to take food for myself—not a lot, just enough to keep me from starving. Anyways, I was in the tunnel when I heard your screams and so I went to see what the matter was. That's when I saw what that horrible man was doing to you."

"...I see," I paused to think, smoothing my skirt. "And just why do you need to steal food? I mean, why did you look like a vagrant when you rescued me? I can see now that clearly you are no vagrant." I eyed his clean black trousers and white tunic.

"That—is a long story. One you're better off not knowing."

I narrowed my eyes. Either he had some deep dark secret, or he didn't trust me—or perhaps both. So be it. "Okay then, tell me why you chose to bring me here."

"I brought you here because you would have died if I left you on your own, and because Ginnie and Irving are my friends. I knew they would take care of you properly. Now it's my turn to ask you something." He leaned towards me and held my eyes with his warm aqua ones. I felt like I could get lost in those eyes forever. When he spoke next, it was so soft, I barely heard the words. "How did that man catch fire?"

My eyes went wide at his question. "I don't know, sir. He must have hit himself on one of the torches." I decided if he wasn't going to trust me with his truth, I wouldn't trust him with mine.

"The lanterns were on the outside of the cell though, my lady," he said pointedly, still holding my gaze.

"Are you accusing me of lying? I don't know! I was about to be *raped!*

Perhaps Celestia did it," I retorted.

"Ah, our beloved goddess. Apologies. Please don't be upset. I'm only trying to understand what happened."

"As am I, sir. Now, if you'll excuse me, I think I've had quite enough excitement for today."

He placed his hand on mine as I stood to leave. Panic rose within me and he quickly removed it. I was sure he meant it as a comforting gesture, but I couldn't keep the memory of Algor's hands on me away. I scolded myself inwardly for my weakness.

"Yes, of course," he replied after an awkward silence. "And please, call me Percifal." He looked up at me, sympathy etched in his features.

I didn't want his pity; all I wanted was to get out of this village. "Good day, sir," I muttered, ignoring his request. I left without looking back.

I sat on the edge of my bed and put my head in my hands. The memories that our conversation had brought back caused me to shudder. I didn't know if I would ever overcome my fear and mistrust of men again. Not after what had happened in that dungeon.

Slowly, my thoughts came back to my mysterious rescuer. His eyes held so much concern when he spoke to me. Not at all like Algor's. But then, why wouldn't he tell me the truth about himself? I let out a frustrated groan and decided mayhap I would never get all my answers.

Chapter 25

That evening, Amelia came to my room to inform me dinner was ready to be served. I decided to go back down to the dining hall for the meal. The kind maid had offered to bring my meal to me, but I was tired of being in my room and knew I now had enough strength to eat with the rest of the guests.

The hall had a very different feel to it at night. It was full of men, like it was during the morning, but now ale flowed in abundance. The men were louder too. Some of them laughed and goofed around with each other, while others argued over who could drink more ale or who had better fighting skills. Maids came around with trays of meat, sweet potatoes and even more ale. Behind the bar, a tall, slim man with a beak-like nose was busy filling jugs with the frothy ale. He pushed up the spectacles on that nose as he finished pouring the golden liquid.

Noticing me standing there, gaping like a fool, he beckoned me over to him. As all of the tables were already occupied, I decided a seat at the bar was the best place for me anyways. A few other loners ate their meals at the bar too.

"You must be the Lady Phyra. My wife's spoken pleasantly of you." His smile only held warmth.

I gave him a friendly smile in return, "Why yes, and you must be Irving."

"Ah ha! Right you are, Lady Phyra. I'm pleased to meet you." He put out his hand to take mine, and I offered it in return.

Oddly, I didn't feel any fear towards this man. He hadn't a threatening bone in his body. "The pleasure is mine. I wanted to thank you for your kindness and hospitality."

Just then, Amelia set a tray of food down on the bar before me and gave me a wink. I bowed my head in reply and went back to my conversation with Irving.

"Any friend of Percifal's is a friend of ours," he said, pouring more ale for another maid to take away.

"Oh, I wouldn't exactly call us friends. He rescued me, but I barely know the man." I waved a hand in dismissal.

"No matter. Who are we to turn away a damsel in distress, eh?"

At that, I laughed. My heart warmed. I could see why Percifal would call Ginnie and Irving friends. They were easy to like and seemed to have nothing but kindness to offer.

"Some ale to warm your spirit, my lady?"

"Sure, why not?" I shrugged.

He poured me some of the sparkling golden liquid and left me to my meal. This was the first time I'd ever tasted ale. I always drank wine at the palace when I had wanted something to 'warm my spirit.' Taking a sip, I found the taste wasn't a bad one, but I still preferred the fruity taste of wine over this fizzy, wheaty one.

During my meal, I listened to the conversation of the men behind me. One with a gruff voice spoke to one with a higher-pitched, younger-sounding voice.

"Do you think we'll really make it to Terra with these materials before it's been six sunrises and get the extra gold we were promised for being quicker than the other tradesmen?" the younger one asked.

"Aye, I bet you two gold pieces we will. We just have to travel faster and sleep less than the others," the gruff one replied.

"Alright, two gold pieces if we do make it in six sunrises or less."

"It's going to be a rough trip."

That was all I needed to hear to gather the courage to talk to them—well, the ale probably helped too. I got up off my stool and was about to make my way to their table when Percifal came out of nowhere and blocked my path.

"I know what you're trying to do, but don't. Those men are gamblers and not to be trusted. I'll take you back to Solis in a few days," he said in a low tone, his expression serious.

Taken aback by his rude interruption, I straightened my shoulders and lifted my chin. "What, were you watching me this whole time? I can take care of myself. And I'm *not* going back to Solis."

"Clearly, my lady, you can't take care of yourself. With your family is the only place you will be safe. I won't have your death on my conscience," he stated, ignoring my question.

I scoffed at his words. Perhaps he was right, but I simply couldn't go back to Solis. Not when Adelaide's life would be put in danger upon my return. "You don't understand. I can't go back; else something horrible shall happen."

"What will happen that's so horrible? Tell me."

"That is a long story. One you are better off not knowing," I repeated his own words back to him.

He raised his brows and then sighed in surrender. "Fine. These men are not your answer though. Promise me you'll not speak to them."

"Fine," I lied. I'd have said anything to get him to leave me be at that moment.

"Good. Now, I promised Ginnie I'd help her clean up the kitchen tonight. I trust you will keep to yourself and enjoy the rest of your night."

"Don't worry about me. I'm going to finish my ale, and then I shall retire for the night."

"Good night to you then, Lady Phyra," he bowed his head.

"Good night, Sir Percifal." I nodded in return, and he left.

Good, I thought. Now I could ask about passage to Terra without any interruptions, but when I turned back to the table, the men were already gone. Feeling utterly disappointed, I decided I may as well indeed retire for the night. I'd have to try again in the morning. If only that damned Percifal would stay out of my way.

I went to break my fast early the next day, in hopes of spotting those two men again. To my disappointment, it seemed they'd already left for the kingdom of earth, because they were nowhere in sight. So I ate in silence, listening for any other conversations about travel. I heard none.

I decided to spend the day with Irving to get my mind off my predicament for a while. He was going to the market to buy fresh vegetables for the night's meal. I thought it would do me good to get outside anyways.

"Do you go to the market every day, Irving?" I asked him. We walked along the busy cobblestone road that was lined with tented shops and their goods.

When we came upon some bins that held fresh fruits and vegetables, he stopped to feel and smell some carrots. "Aye, we only prepare the freshest meals for our guests. During the winter, it's a different case of course. We stock up before autumn's end, but in the summer, we take advantage of the market." He smiled at the short, round man who took his silver piece in exchange for the bag of carrots Irving now held.

"You treat your guests well, you and Ginnie."

"That's how we keep the business doing well." He winked at me as we strolled on. "Business wasn't always so good, you see. Actually, it was Percifal who helped us when we almost went under," he added with a note of gratitude.

"Did he?" I asked, unable to keep the surprise from my voice.

"Indeed. The hotel was in dire need of repairs; the stove that we heat water on was broken, and business wasn't doing well. Then he showed up and asked if we had room for him to stay in a while. He heard about our misfortune, and without us even asking, he fixed the stove and did the repairs and even gave us enough gold pieces to get us back on our feet. Then, out of nowhere, he told us he had to leave. We thanked him for everything and told him if he ever needed anything, we would be there for him. So when he brought you to us and asked for our help, we were glad to be of service."

"Huh." I was lost in wonder when a small boy almost ran right into me. I veered right to avoid crashing into him. "And he never said where he came from or why he was leaving?"

"No, he really didn't say much about himself, and we thought it rude to ask. He was the kindest man we'd ever met. That was enough. Poor Ginnie cried with joy when he gave us the gold. We tried to refuse, but he wouldn't take no for an answer."

"I'm glad your inn was saved. It is a nice place, and you and Ginnie are good people."

He chuckled humbly, but changed the subject as we headed back to the inn, "Any luck on your quest to find passage to Terra?"

"Sadly, no. I think I'll just start asking around."

"Well, I will keep listening for you and let you know should I hear anything. In the mean-time, I hope you're enjoying your stay with us," he offered, pushing his spectacles up with his wrist. They seemed to always be sliding off his nose.

"Very much so," I beamed.

As we walked on, he told me stories of how he and Ginnie met and of how they came to be owners of The Golden Lilly Inn. I listened, feeling lighter than I had since I'd left Solis, while the sun kissed my skin.

When we got back to the Inn, Irving left me to take the carrots to the kitchen for Ginnie to prepare. I sat in the dining hall, watching two men play a game of dice. They both looked a bit grubby and wore worn clothing; it was obvious they were travelers.

I lifted my chin and decided to put a brave face on and ask these men for passage while no one else was around to stop me. What harm could it do?

They were laughing as I approached their table, keeping my hands folded in front of me to stop them from shaking. Noticing my presence, they both stopped and turned towards me. One had scraggly, long blonde hair while the other was almost bald.

"Well, what do we have here?" The one with blonde hair said in a strong, deep voice.

"Good day, sirs. I—I'm looking for a way to Terra and wondered if you might be willing to take me there?" I looked the blonde one in the eyes, trying to appear confident.

The bald one threw his head back and howled with laughter. The blonde one just continued to stare at me before asking, "And what kind of payment might you have for us taking you all that way?"

"I—uh—I have nothing right now." I looked down before quickly adding, "But I know Queen Adelaide personally. I shall write to her. She'll pay you generously for your kindness to me."

"Hmm. Is this some kind of joke?" The blonde one looked suspicious. His friend stopped laughing.

"Oh, come now, Vanard! I know what we can take as *payment*," the bald suggested, winking at his friend.

Knowing what he meant, I began to shake my head and step back just as the bald one did the unthinkable. The-slime ball grabbed ahold of my arse and shouted, "Come on now, lass! Don't ye wanna have some fun?"

I was in such a panic, I didn't even feel the heat rising inside of me before the candle that sat on their table exploded and set the wood ablaze. I froze in silence as both men yelled and poured their ale onto the flames to drown them before they got out of control.

Before I had a chance to react, I felt an arm around my waist and heard a familiar voice say, "Sorry lads, this one's mine. Come now, Phyra, let's leave these men be."

"She owes us each an ale!" the blonde one shouted back.

Percifal tossed a gold piece at them, then directed me away from the table and out of the dining hall.

Once we were out of sight, he stopped and turned to face me, putting both of his hands on my shoulders. I couldn't explain the feeling within me at his touch, I knew I should pull away, but I felt safe with his strong hands on me at that moment. He had, after all, just saved me from another dangerous situation.

"What do you think you're doing?" He looked into my eyes. His features were stony.

"I can't stay here forever!" I shook out of his grasp and folded my arms, daring him to argue with me.

"No, you can't. I'm afraid you'll burn down poor Ginnie and Irving's whole business if you do."

I felt my heart stop at his words. "What do you mean?" I asked, feigning ignorance.

"You know what I mean," he shot back at me. "I know for sure now that you lied about how that man caught on fire back in the dungeon…mayhap you don't even know it yourself yet, but I know, Lady Phyra. I know you hold the power to the element of fire. I'm sure of it after that display with the candle I just witnessed."

I sighed, surrendering. "I don't know why I have this power. It just came to me when I was in that dungeon."

I knew I might have had it since I was a child, but I'd only recently been able to use it. I didn't feel like explaining all the details of my childhood to him.

"Well, I don't either, but I do know someone who can help you."

"And who might that be? Pray tell."

"My sister," he said, turning to leave. His next words came out so low I barely heard them. "Be ready for travel at dawn. We're going to Aquila."

Chapter 26

My head reeled with more questions than ever. Upon entering my room, I'd found Amelia making up my bed.

She turned, hearing me enter. "Oh—hello, Milady. I'm just making up your bed then I'll be out of here. How are you today?"

"I'm well enough, thanks, Amelia. Um, is there a messenger here I can give a letter to who'll deliver it to the palace in Solis?"

"Yes, actually, there's a boy who comes around every couple days to send and receive letters. Would you like me to fetch you some parchment and ink?"

"Yes please, and thank you, Amelia," I replied.

She nodded, now finished with my bedding. "I'll be back in a moment."

Now alone, I plopped down on my bed and ran my hands through my loose hair. So, I was going to Aquila. Sure, it wasn't Terra, where I'd originally wanted to go. It also wasn't anywhere near Solis, and that was good enough for me. In fact, it was even farther from Solis than Terra was. This was going to be a long journey. I hoped we would make it there before the cooler season approached. I didn't relish the thought of sleeping on the cold ground.

A knock on my door interrupted my thoughts. "Come in."

It was Amelia, back with the parchment, ink and a feather pen. "Here you are, Milady. If you give it to Ginnie once you are finished, she'll be sure the messenger gets it."

"Right; thanks again Amelia—not just for this, but for everything you have done for me."

"I was only doing my job, Milady. I'm pleased to be of service to you. It's been pleasant having a lady guest here. As you've probably noticed, most of our guests are men."

I raised my brows. "Indeed. Anyways, I'm glad we met and I shall always remember your kindness."

She started to smile, but then realization took over her features. "Does this mean you're leaving us, Milady?"

"Yes, I shall be gone at dawn. It is time for me to move on."

"Oh, you've found someone to take you to Terra?"

I paused and decided there was no reason I couldn't tell her the truth. "No, Percifal has offered to take me to Aquila."

"Oh! Aquila!" she exclaimed, clasping her hands together, eyes sparkling with wonder. "I've heard Aquila is a beautiful place. And you'll get to see the sea! I'm sure you'll be happy there."

I felt my lips curve up at her excitement. "I hadn't thought much about it, actually. I'm just grateful to be going somewhere new."

"I wish you the best of luck."

"Thank you."

With nothing left to say, she placed the writing supplies on the small table and left me.

I took a seat at the table and sighed. Where to begin? After some thought, I dipped the feather pen into the ink and began scratching words onto the parchment.

Dearest Addy,

I am writing to tell you I am alive and well. I hope I have not caused you too much worry since I left. I cannot tell you where I am now, but I must ask a favour of you. Please send some gold to Ginnie and Irving at The Golden Lilly Inn in Lottenheim for me. I would pay them myself, but I do not have anything to give them at this time. They are good people who have helped take care of me. Without them, I am afraid I may not be alive to write this to you. I hope you are well and happy and know that one day we shall see each other again. Until then, always remember that I love you and hold you in my heart.

Love, Zephy

P.S Please also send some guards to search for a man named Algor who lives in Lottenheim as well. He has been keeping women as his prisoners. He lives in a grand manor somewhere on the edge of the village. I am sorry I cannot tell you more.

I felt sorrow as I folded the letter and sat back. I missed Adelaide dearly, and I truly did hope I would see her again someday. I just knew if I went back then, there would still be risk of her being assassinated. I would rather miss her because of distance than miss her because of death.

Just as I was about to go and find Ginnie, I heard another soft knock on my door. Ginnie opened it and poked her head in. "Lady Phyra? Amelia has told me you'll be leaving us on the morrow."

"Yes, that's right." I bit my lip and looked down so she couldn't see the sadness in my eyes. I would miss her. She was like a mother to me…the kind of mother I'd always wanted.

She came over to me and put her arm around my shoulders. "We're so glad we got to have you stay with us. You'll be in good hands with Percifal. He may have his secrets, but he has a good heart."

"I'm glad I met you all too. I would never have made it if it wasn't for your and Irving's kindness."

"Well, just you remember that you're always welcome at The Golden Lilly Inn." She gave me a slight shake, her grin dimpling her cheeks.

"I shall, of course." Remembering the note, I held it out to her. "Will you please see this gets to the messenger for me? I need it delivered to the palace at Solis."

"Yes, I'll give it to him. He should be around here tomorrow. Would you like to come down for dinner? It's almost ready to be served."

I groaned, "I want to, but the men down there are so intimidating."

"No matter, my dear. I'll have one of the maids bring a tray up for you."

"That sounds perfect. Thank you."

"You're welcome. You have a safe journey. Take care of yourself, and trust no one save Percifal."

"*That* you don't have to worry about." I barely trusted Percifal, let alone any other person I might meet along the way.

"Good, and please take what you like from the closet. My daughter isn't missing those clothes anyways."

We embraced, and then she left me.

I decided to go through the closet. In the end, I picked a simple dark green dress that was a bit frayed on the edges to wear for travelling. I folded another royal blue one that looked more formal. I figured it would be good to have something nice to wear when requesting employment, when that time came.

Soon one of the maids brought my tray of food up with a cup of water. I ate all of my cooked carrots, game hen and fresh bread. I did so, not only because it was delicious, but I didn't know when my next full meal would be.

After my meal, I brushed out my hair and donned my night dress. I was to be up before the sun so I decided I should try to sleep early tonight.

Sleep didn't come easily. I couldn't stop thinking about what my future held and wondering about my travel partner and how his sister might be able to help me. One way or another, I would get answers from him.

Before I knew it, I was being awoken by the sound of pounding on my door. I opened my tired eyes and saw the faintest light at the edge of a dark sky through my window. It was almost dawn.

"Lady Phyra? Get dressed; we must leave now." I heard Percifal's voice through my door.

I threw my blankets off and swung my legs over the edge of the bed. "Just a moment, I must dress and then I shall be ready."

There was a pause before he answered, "I will wait outside. Come when you're ready, but please make haste."

I quickly dressed myself in the green dress with long sleeves and loose skirt. I decided to braid my hair to keep it neat and manageable. I peered at myself in the mirror and put my hand to my face. I looked much healthier than the first time I'd seen my reflection in this mirror. I gave myself an approving smile, picked up the extra dress, and put on the pair of leather shoes that I'd found on the room's floor. They must have also belonged to Ginnie and Irving's daughter. Thankfully, her feet were only a little bigger than mine. Now that I was as ready as I could be, I headed downstairs and out the front door.

I found Percifal holding two horses, one dappled grey and one bay. Seeing me, he took the extra dress from my arms and placed it in the bay's saddle-bag. "The bay is yours. Here, let me help you up."

I put my foot in his hand so he could hoist me up into the saddle. "So you have the means to buy horses…you're pretty wealthy for a vagrant." I commented.

He just snorted, so I dropped the matter and changed the subject. "Does my horse have a name?"

"I'm sure she does, but I didn't ask it. Name her whatever you please."

"Hmm." I thought of Nova for a moment. I missed her, but I was glad she didn't have to make this journey. She was old and it would have been hard on her. "I shall call…her?"

"Yes, her."

"I shall call her Moonlight."

Was that a smile I saw on his face as he finished tying his own saddle bags? I didn't know, for next he put his foot in the stirrup and swung himself on top of the grey. His horse looked majestic. I guessed he was a stallion even before he told me his name. "Then I will call mine Sunny."

The matter of naming now complete, we set out. I studied Percifal in his brown trousers and leather armor. The sword at his side that caught my attention; polished silver and iron, with a giant sapphire embedded on the pommel. This wasn't just any sword; this was the sword of someone important. That thought scared me more than anything I had come to learn yet about him. I decided to keep my thoughts to myself—for now.

We rode in silence for the first while. The sky was wondrous once the sun began to rise. Shades of pink, purple and orange streaked the deep blue. Birds were beginning their morning song and the grass was still dewy from the fading night. I took in a deep breath of the crisp, fresh air. I, at least, was enjoying being outside again, finally free from the world and my royal responsibilities. Free from the horrible Algor and his dungeons. Free from my own weakened health. Even though my future was uncertain, I was happy that it would take place far away from Solis.

Away from Lottenheim, we made our way into the forest. Before long, the sun was high in the blue sky and flickering through the large pine trees, warming my back as I sat atop of Moonlight. The steady sway of her movement was relaxing. I felt my body move with her, as if we were one being. Percifal rode off to my side, ahead just enough that I could see his back. He sat tall on his grey stallion. It was obvious that he also was no stranger to riding.

As our horses clopped on down the path, I wondered who he was before he'd come to Lottenheim. I now had confirmation that he was indeed from Aquila, but why had he left? He must have done something bad; that was the only reason I could come up with. Maybe he had all this gold because he'd stolen it. If he had stolen it, I was happy that at least he gave some of it up to help Ginnie and Irving. They were good people. I wondered if I would even see them again; probably not.

Finally, when the sun was over halfway past mid sky and my legs were aching, Percifal halted his horse. "We'll stop here to eat and then we ride 'til dusk."

My stomach grumbled in agreement. I dismounted my bay mare and found that my legs were weak and a bit shaky. Percifal took Moonlight's reins and tied them to the saddle, leaving enough length so she could eat grass, but not enough that she would step on them. I noticed he'd done the same to Sunny's.

"Here," he offered, holding out a chuck of bread and dried apples.

"Thank you." I took it and sat against a large stump, my movements slow and stiff.

He sat across from me, studying me. "We have a long way to go. Are you going to be able to manage it?"

I rolled my eyes at him. "Of course. I'm fine. I just haven't been on horseback for quite a while. I shall get used to it."

He inclined his head in reply, chewing on his bread.

"So, your sister…how is it she can help me?" I decided to ask.

He paused and took a deep breath before answering. "I suppose it doesn't hurt to tell you, seen as how you will be meeting her anyways. Chelela, my sister, holds the elemental power of water."

I almost choked on the dried piece of apple that was in my mouth as he continued.

"She, unlike you, has known about her power since she was a child. She also had training with it and knows how to control it—unlike you."

I glared at him. "I'm sure with training I'd be able to control mine as well."

"I'm sure you would too. That's why I'm taking you to her. She can help you learn."

"And just why are you doing this for me? It can't be out of the kindness of your heart."

He chuckled at that. "I do happen to be a kind man, you know. But you're right, that is not why I'm doing this. Chel was informed that all the elementals would be needed to fight a dark power. I didn't believe it—until I found you."

My eyes widened and I had to put my hands on the ground beneath me to steady myself. "Excuse me? Did you say *I'm* meant to help fight against a dark power?"

"I did."

"No, I don't think so. You—you're mad. That's why you were a vagrant when you found me. I understand now." I stood, with effort, and went to Moonlight.

He followed me. "Stop, wait. Would you *please* stop?" He grabbed my arm.

I looked down at his hand on me. His touch was firm, but not painful. I felt a shiver roll through me. I turned and faced him. His eyes held concern; they didn't look like the eyes of a madman. In fact, they looked very warm and inviting, like deep turquoise pools.

I shook his hand off and sighed, "What?"

"I'm not mad, nor am I a vagrant." He spread his palms out, as if proud of his next words. "What other choice do you have? Come with me to Aquila, and my sister will tell you herself."

Because he was right, I gave in. "Fine, but I still doubt the part about me helping fight a dark power."

I tried to get back on Moonlight but found myself, embarrassingly, too weak.

Seeing my struggle, Percifal helped me up back into my saddle. "We make camp at dusk." With that, he went and mounted his own horse, and we were off once again.

Chapter 27

On and on we rode, deeper and deeper into the forest. Eventually, the trees grew so thick, the sky was barely visible. With the sun blocked from our view, the air grew chillier. Night would be worse and I found myself wishing I still had the cloak I had taken from Solis. I don't remember when, but I had lost it sometime while I was in Algor's dungeon; probably when he had tried to force himself on me.

No, I scolded myself; I wouldn't allow my mind to go back to that dark place.

Eventually, my legs grew numb from being horseback for so long. As the sun started to set, creatures of the night began their night songs. An owl hooted from a tree nearby, and crickets chirped from somewhere in the tall grass. I prayed to Celestia that there were no predators around. I didn't think we would make it through the first night if there were.

When we finally stopped, the bit of sky that we could see had taken on a shade of indigo. Percifal had to help me off Moonlight as my legs no longer seemed to work. At that moment, I was grateful he was with me. As mysterious and secretive as he was, at least he didn't seem dangerous. Another man might have taken advantage of my weakened state, and on my own, I would have been useless.

He helped me to a patch of grass, and then went and unsaddled our horses and rubbed them down. I watched from the patch of grass I sat on, feeling useless.

Once the horses were dealt with, he took his sword and cut some branches down and piled them together in the dirt. He looked over at me once the task was complete. "I don't suppose you can gather your power enough to help with this, can you?" He gestured towards the pile of sticks.

"I—uh—I can try," I said, feeling useless.

He shook his head. "No matter, save your strength."

He picked up two stones and began knocking them together. To my amazement, the stones sparked and flames engulfed the branches. He tossed the stones down and gathered more branches, putting some to the side for later.

He beckoned me over once his task was complete. "Come, sit and warm yourself."

"Thank you," I muttered while he placed a wool blanket he had taken from his saddle bag down for me to sit on.

"Wait here. I'm going to see if I can find us some dinner," he stated.

Where would I even go? I thought.

I sat there silently, feeling the fires flickering warmth on my face as it cracked and popped. I held the power of fire and yet I couldn't even gather the strength to help build one. How was I to help fight a dark power if I couldn't even conjure up a small fire to keep us warm?

I was so deep in thought, I barely noticed Percifal approach with a grouse in his hand and a grin on his face.

"Not a grand feast, but I've found us something fresh for dinner." He held up the dead bird.

"Spectacular," was all I said.

He began plucking the bird. "You sound rather enthused. Is there a problem, my lady?"

"I'm just weary." I closed my eyes.

"Ah. Once you have some food in your belly and some sleep, I'm sure you'll feel better."

I inclined my head in reply, and he went back to working on the bird.

Before long, he had it on a stick and roasting over the fire. Once it was cooked, he pulled some of the meat off and offered it to me. It wasn't the best meal I'd had, but it wasn't the worst either. The meat was a bit dry and bland with no spices, but it was warm and filling. I couldn't complain.

After our meal, Percifal handed me the water skin. I drank its refreshing contents and handed it back to him. He put it away and pulled a small flask from his belt and offered it to me. "Here, this'll help you sleep."

I accepted it and took a swig. I sputtered and coughed as soon as I swallowed the spicy, warm liquid.

"Whoa, whoa," he laughed. "Take it easy. It's strong stuff."

"Yes, I see," I sputtered in between coughs. "A little warning would have been nice. What is this?"

"It's only whiskey. Have you never tried it?"

"I haven't."

"Well, it's my honour to be the one to give you your first taste."

I smiled and shook my head.

"What? You don't like it?" he asked with a look of dismay.

"No, I do. It's strong at first, but—" I paused to search for the right words to describe it, "it brings a welcoming feeling shortly thereafter."

He laughed softly at that. "That it does, my lady. That it does."

We sat in silence for a while, each deep in our own thoughts. Darkness had now completely fallen, and I could see a few stars peeking through the trees. Were we lovers, this would have been a most romantic setting, but we were not.

I felt myself blush at the thought. I inwardly scorned myself for even letting that thought rise to the surface. I barely even knew this man, and he wouldn't even tell me who he really was. According to my past luck with men, I shouldn't even be thinking thoughts like that in the first place. Men only wanted to fulfill their own desires. I couldn't let myself forget that, else I might find myself in trouble yet again.

Stretching, I broke the silence. "I must relieve myself, and then I'm going to try and sleep."

"A good idea that is, my lady," he replied, getting up.

When I returned from the bushes that gave me some privacy, I saw Percifal had set out four wool blankets; one for underneath and one for on top of each of us, I guessed. He had also taken off his leather armor and now only wore trousers and a loose, white linen shirt. My eyes wandered to the muscles visible through the thin material. He looked strong, like he'd been trained and polished for battle.

He looked up, noticing me. I quickly averted my gaze and stared straight at the blankets he'd laid on the ground. I shivered, feeling a cool breeze upon my back.

He must have noticed me shiver for he said, "If we sleep together, the heat from our bodies will keep us warmer."

Appalled by his suggestion, I stuttered, "I—I don't need body heat. A blanket shall do just fine. Thank you, sir." I strode to my blanket and removed my boots.

"As you wish, my lady." He gave me a formal bow, which only annoyed me. I didn't need a man to keep me warm. And now he was mocking me!

I climbed between two of the blankets, silently seething. He followed suit.

I must have been totally exhausted, for I fell asleep in an instant.

When I woke, it was early morning and the fire had died down to slow burning embers. I felt warm, regardless of the dying fire. I sat up and found Percifal's spot empty and his blanket on top of me.

I threw the blankets off my body and instantly felt the morning chill. I heard footsteps and twisted to see Percifal coming out from the bushes.

"Ah, good. You're awake," he stated, not looking at me. "We must be off soon."

I rose and felt my stiff muscles complain. Sleeping on the hard ground had done nothing good for my pain, but I gritted my teeth and kept my mouth shut about it. Percifal handed me some bread and dried berries from one of the saddlebags. I ate in silence and decided not to mention the extra blanket he'd given me.

Shortly after I'd finished breaking my fast, Percifal had our horses ready, and we were off down the path through the forest that had become my temporary home.

We rode through that forest for many days, following a creek so that we would always have fresh water for ourselves and our horses. My whole body ached from being on horseback day after day. Eventually, I grew accustomed to being astride the majestic creature I called Moonlight, and then it wasn't so bad.

It seemed, thankfully, that Ginnie had given Percifal enough food to last us through our journey—though I was growing tired of bread, dried fruit and nuts.

The forest grew thicker the deeper we went. My dress had a few tears in it from the sharp branches that grasped at me like clawed fingers. My arms and legs even had a few scratches on them from squeezing between trees.

As the days went on, the nights grew longer and summer began to turn to autumn. Some of the trees leaves began to get a gold tint on their edges, a sign that soon the forest would be splashed with colours of crimson and amber.

Every night, Percifal and I went to sleep with our own blankets. Every morning, I woke up with Percifal's blanket on me. One night, I woke before morning to find him with no top blanket and shivering. Feeling guilty, I grabbed my own blankets and shuffled towards him. I placed his blanket back on him and positioned myself with my back against his. Slowly, I felt his shaking stop and felt his warmth against my back.

The next morning, he was up before I awoke, as usual. Later that day, as we rode he decided to comment on my act of kindness. "You didn't have to do that."

Lost in my current thoughts, he'd caught me off guard. "Pardon me?" I asked, dumbfounded.

"The blanket and your—" he paused, "body heat. I was fine without them. I know how uncomfortable contact with me is for you."

"You were shaking. I'm not so cruel as to let you freeze. It's fine. It's only our backs that need touch, after all."

His lips pulled up a little in the corners, but he stayed silent. So every night from then on, that was how we slept; each with one blanket, our backs pressed together.

I could feel the heat from his back against me each night and I felt it oddly comforting, a feeling that confused me. I tried not to let my mind wander to the way his muscles felt against my own back; hard, yet soft—contrasting.

Percifal wasn't like other men, and I was beginning to learn that. My body was reacting differently to him. I felt myself stealing glances at him when he wasn't watching. He was a beautiful creature, now that he didn't look like a vagrant. His short, dark hair complimented his strong, angular jawline and high cheekbones. His body was muscular like a warrior's; not big and bulky, but defined and well-proportioned. He reminded me of a wild cat, quick and agile.

I didn't think he appreciated my appearance as much as I did his. He probably thought of me only as a fragile victim that needed protecting. And then there were his secrets. I could never let someone close who kept so much from me. I kept my emotions guarded, pretended I didn't care what his secret was or what he thought of me. I thought if I kept pretending, eventually it would become truth.

One evening, when we'd stopped to make camp for the night, I sat by the fire while Percifal washed himself in the creek. I was so used to being alone with only Percifal and our horses as company that I had begun to feel safe from the rest of the world. That was a big mistake, for I barely paid attention when I heard the sound of breaking branches nearby. I assumed it was just the horses.

I found out instantly how very wrong I was. Out of the trees, two men riding bareback came straight towards me. I thought they meant to trample me where I sat, so I scrambled to my feet to run away, but I was too late. One of the bandits reached down and hoisted me up onto his horse with him.

"*PERCIFAL!*" I screamed.

The bandit slapped his big palm over my mouth. "Yee partner is surely dead by now. Johnno went after him while we came to take yee. Don't worry, though. We know how to take care of a lady." He laughed to himself. It was a high-pitched and cruel sound that made me tremble to my core.

My heart dropped as his words began to sink in. *Dead?* Could Percifal really be dead? Suddenly, it felt like the whole world was slipping away. All hope was lost. I felt myself sag against my captor, defeated.

I don't know how long we rode for, but when we stopped it was at a small clearing in the forest with three small wooden shelters, big enough to fit two or three people in each. A fire was lit in the center.

The bandit let go of me long enough to dismount before pulling me off the horse too.

"Got ourselves a pretty one, Horas. Look at this flaming red hair. She must be descended from Solis."

The man, Horas, just grunted in reply as he dismounted his own horse.

The bandit's words gave me an idea. I knew with Percifal now dead, I had no hope of making it through the forest alive on my own, and at that moment, I was filled with so much dread that I just wanted to go home and never leave again.

I said the only thing I could think of that would get me there. "I am descended from Solis; you're right. Actually, the queen is my cousin. If you take me to her, she'll pay you *graciously* for my return. You shall have enough riches to last you a lifetime."

"Oh-ho-ho! Did you hear that, Horas? The *queen's* cousin! Ha! Yee be *lying*, girl." He turned on me and put a short, thick blade to my throat. I swallowed hard, feeling its sharp edge against my delicate skin.

"Go ahead, then, kill me." I looked him in the eyes, daring him. "You've killed my friend, so what does it matter now anyways?" My heart beat faster at my act of bravery.

He grinned at that, showing off his crooked yellow teeth, and his eyes crinkled at the corners. "Not yet. Not before we've had some fun."

He took the knife from my throat and slid it into his belt. One hand around my skinny wrists, he hauled me over to the post of one of the shelters and tied me to it with a thick rope. Once his task was complete, he stepped back went back to his friend.

I tried to listen to what they conversed about, but I could only make out a few words; liar, chance, fun and on the morrow.

Eventually, the one who had tied up me came back over to me. "Yee sleep here t'night. Tomorrow, we head fer Solis. Horas decided we can't miss the chance if yee may be tellin' the truth. If we find out yee be lying…" he made a slitting throat motion on himself with two fingers, and then he left me again. I couldn't see where they went; my bonds were too tight, but I guessed it wasn't far.

I tried with all my effort to wriggle my wrists from their bonds. The rope only ate away at my skin as I did, making it raw and sore. I gave up and laid my head back against the post.

As the night went on, the air grew colder. I shivered, unable to sleep. I thought mayhap I would freeze to death on this night. I welcomed the thought. Now that Percifal was dead and I was on my way back to Solis, I didn't see the point in going on. Percifal had to be dead. I knew if he were alive, he would've been there to save me. I hadn't seen or heard any sign of him since he went to wash in the creek. If only I had paid more attention to my surroundings, I could've hid until it was safe and then…and then what? Travelled to Aquila on my own? I didn't know where to go. I surely would have died anyways, lost and alone. At least I would have had my freedom.

CHAPTER 28

I AWOKE TO the morning song of birds chirping. The rising sun beamed down on me with warm radiance. Surprised I had fallen asleep, and even more so that I hadn't frozen to death, my head snapped up. *What a beautiful day to be in such a horrible position,* I thought miserably.

I heard Horas and his partner speaking from somewhere behind me. "Johnno should've been back last night," said Horas.

"We wait one more day. If he isn't back then, we take the girl to Solis without 'im."

There was a moment of silence before I heard footsteps coming closer, and then a piece of salmon was thrown at me. "Eat."

I peered up and saw large, hairy Horas hovering over me. "I can't eat without hands," I shot back at him.

He bent down, untied my hands and stepped back. "Try anything, and we'll kill yee."

Slowly, I bent forward and picked the piece of fish up off the ground. My body hurt from sitting in one position all night. Thankfully, the fish was warm; it must have been cooked recently. It actually tasted good.

When I was finished eating, I cleared my throat. "May I have some water?"

He grunted and threw a water-skin at me. I picked it up and drank. When I was finished, I asked to relieve myself.

"Fine, but that's it! I don't have time to watch yee all day!"

He took me to a bush and stood by, not taking his eyes off me.

"May a girl have a little privacy?" I asked, staring back at him.

"Nay, I don't think so. I'm not taking my eyes off yee. I'm not stupid, yee know."

I glared at him as I squatted behind a bush and did my business, feeling I'd lost all decency. Once I was done, Horas took me back to the post and retied my bonds.

All day I sat there, tied to that post, and all day I tried to call upon my power to burn the ropes that held my wrists away. At one point, I thought I started to feel the rope grow hot against my skin, but nothing else happened. I decided it must have only been my imagination.

Feeling frustrated and defeated, I gave up. It seemed I couldn't conjure my power up at will. I had hoped Percifal's sister would be able to help with that, but that wasn't going to happen now that I was going back to Solis.

Oh, Solis, I thought. I wondered what awaited me back at my home kingdom. Mayhap Adelaide would be with child and my return wouldn't matter. If she wasn't, perhaps I would tell my queen just why I'd run away and beg her to banish my mother instead of ending her life. Or I could just ask her for a carriage to take me to Aquila, but then I would have to explain why I wanted to go there, and I didn't know if she would believe me.

I groaned and tilted my head back against the wooden post. I was driving myself crazy with these thoughts. If I was being honest, I really didn't want to go back to Solis at all.

I squeezed my eyes shut and felt a big wet drop hit my leg where my dress had come up. I opened my eyes to see the once sunny sky taken over with dark, looming clouds. More water drops began falling. *Great,* I thought. At least this weather suited my mood more, and it would wash some of the filth from me; it had been a couple days since I'd washed in the creek.

Once I was soaked through, my dress now heavy with water, the rain let up. I heard my captors speaking about the grouse they had caught for tonight's meal. I guessed they didn't think I would be able to escape because they'd both left me to hunt. I supposed they were right, because I hadn't.

I heard a fire crackle. Shortly after, Horas's partner, whose name I learned was Oren, came to me with some cooked grouse. Instead of untying me, he held the bird to my mouth. I bit the meat from the bones, giving him a seething look.

"Don't give me that look. At least we be feeding yee." He glared back at me with his dark, beady eyes.

"Oh, how kind of you. You are such gentlemen," I mocked, rolling my eyes.

"Shut up, or we'll gag yee, and then yee can just starve."

I winced at his poor accent and butchering of our language. "If I starve, the queen shan't pay you."

I guessed he had nothing to say to that, because he just spat on the ground beside me and watched me finish my meal in silence. Once I was done, he held the water-skin to my lips for me to drink and then left, saying over his shoulder, "We'll let yee relieve yee self before we sleep for the night. We ride for Solis in the mornin.'"

I guessed their third partner hadn't returned. *Good,* I thought. Perhaps Percifal had taken the man down with him as his own life was taken from him. The thought didn't make me feel much better.

I sat in silence while the two men spoke of the route we would take to Solis and how we would have to make haste to avoid the colder weather. It sounded like it was going to be an even tougher ride than the one Percifal and I had been on as we would be riding through the night and only stopping once they could stay awake no longer. There would be a high chance I wouldn't make it alive out of this journey. Surely I'd die from exhaustion or starvation…or mayhap I would freeze to death as the days grew colder.

I choked on a sob as I realized that I may never see my Addy again—or my father, or even a comfortable bed and a good meal at that. Perhaps my death was inevitable, and I should just force them to kill me when they untied me in the morning. At least then I wouldn't suffer a slow death.

I hadn't had thoughts this dark since my time in Algor's dungeon, and I didn't welcome them now. I didn't want to give up. I just didn't want to suffer any longer. I was stupid to have left the palace and believed I could make it on my own. Surely Celestia was trying to teach me a lesson. *Okay, I understand,* I thought, looking to the sky. *I made a mistake but now I'm ready to join you, my goddess.*

Just as I finished that thought, as if she'd had heard me, I heard a man's strangled cry of anguish and the sound of metal clashing. My breath caught, and I twisted my head to see two men fighting with swords and one lying on the ground. I couldn't make out the men's faces from my post, but I could tell the big one was Horas, and I was guessing the one lying on the ground was Oren. As for the other man…I had no clue who he was; only that he moved swiftly, spinning and ducking, his sword like an extension of his arm.

Horas moved slower. His strikes were choppier, but he was big and strong, and his sword was blocking every attempt the other man made to pierce him. I held my breath as they battled on, their swords singing each time they met. It was like watching a flawless performance.

To my dismay, Horas struck the other man's sword with such force that it was almost knocked right out of his hand. The other man seemed stunned but quickly recovered and cut Horas' sword arm.

Horas fell back and quickly scrambled over to me. To my shock, he took a dagger out from his belt out and held the point to my throat. "Come any closer, and I end the girl's life," he hissed. I felt the cold point meet my skin.

The other man halted. Our eyes met, and I felt my heart stop. There stood my saviour, the one man I had grown to trust…the one I believed I had lost forever.

I breathed in, my eyes filling with tears.

A resolved expression overtook his features. His eyes narrowed, growing cold. In the next instant, his leg shot out, hitting Horas' knees and taking him down. As Horas went down, Percifal stood over him, and in one swift motion, plunged his sword into the big man's chest. Hot, scarlet blood sprayed up and splashed across my face as I screamed in horror at the sight before my eyes.

Now that the two bandits were slain, Percifal let his sword fall to the ground and dropped to his knees before me. Placing his hands on the sides of my face, he looked at me with anguish, no trace of the coldness left in his eyes. "I thought I had lost you forever," he said with a tremble in his voice.

"As did I," was all I could get out before his lips met mine. They were soft and warm, and I felt my whole body melt as I let him kiss me. This wasn't my first kiss, but it was the first one I'd enjoyed. I was so lost in the sensation that I forgot reality for a moment.

Then he let me go, and the memory of what he'd just done came rushing back to me.

Hot tears ran down my face as feelings of both anger and fear began to surface from within me. "You—you killed so easily. This isn't your first time taking another's life. I—I don't know you at all."

He seemed taken aback with my words as he cut my bonds away. "I had no choice, Zephyra. They would have come after us and taken you—perhaps even *killed* you."

"So you don't deny that you have killed before? Is that why you won't tell me about your past? Because you're a *murderer?*" I rubbed my sore but free wrists.

He grew cold at my words. A calm sense that scared me more than any rage would have, over took him. "I'm *not* a murderer." And then he rounded on me, the coldness melting as fast as it had come on. "I don't tell you about my past for your own good. If we were to be captured by certain people and they thought you were aiding me you would be condemned. I won't have that!"

"So you admit you've committed some crime, then," I stated, rather than asking.

"It was a crime, yes, but I did it for the good of others. That's all I can tell you."

"Oh, great." I glowered at him.

"Come, now. Are you okay to ride? I have our horses over there." He dismissed my anger, wiping the blood from his sword.

"Yes, *sir*. I'm fine. Let us continue on to Aquila."

I followed him and saw our horses were saddled and ready to ride. I smiled at the sight of Moonlight. I didn't think I'd ever see the beautiful mare again. She seemed happy to see me as well, for she nickered softly as I rubbed her velvety nose with my palm.

Once we were mounted, we wasted no time, off into the dark we rode at a gallop. When at last we stopped to let our mounts rest, I'd worked up the courage to ask, "So the third bandit, you killed him too?"

"You should not ask questions to which you don't want to know the answer," he answered, letting Sunny drink from the creek.

I rode up beside him and let Moonlight join in. I felt her sigh beneath me as if in thanks. "I just wish to know what exactly happened and how you escaped to find me, is all. I'm tired of being kept in the dark about everything when it comes to you."

He looked up at the night sky and I thought for a moment he might not answer. He broke the silence with a sigh of his own. "I heard someone coming when I was washing in the creek. My sword was nearby. I snatched it up just in time. A bandit upon his horse almost cut me down, but I was quicker than he. When he leaned down to make a fatal blow to my heart I blocked his move and pulled him from his mount—and then I sliced his throat. After that, it took me a while to find you. I would've been there sooner otherwise. I'm sorry you had to endure being tied to that pole."

I tried not to picture the image that came to mind when he mentioned slicing the bandit's throat. It came anyways. I forced my face to remain expressionless. I didn't want to seem ungrateful. If it hadn't been for him, I would be on my way back to Solis come sunrise. "Thank you for, once again, coming to my rescue. It seems I'm just an incompetent damsel in distress."

"Don't be so hard on yourself, my lady. The world beyond the walls of a kingdom is a dangerous place. It shows strength that you've made it thus far."

I didn't agree, but decided to take his compliment. I didn't wish to insult him any further this night. He had, after all, saved me for the second time; even if he'd killed three men to do it.

He'd already turned his mount and didn't see me shudder at the thought.

"Enough rest. We must go on. We've lost at least a day because of those bandits."

I groaned and edged Moonlight onwards.

We rode on through the night, the moonlight flickering through the trees like a bright candle in the sky and lighting our path. I tried not to think about the kiss I'd shared with Percifal as I listened to the hypnotizing sound of our horses' hoof-beats. As exhausted as I was, the memory haunted me. Did he really like me that way? Or had it just been a result of him thinking I was gone forever? I didn't know how I even felt about it myself. Best to just pretend it had never happened.

My legs grew numb the longer we rode, and I had to focus on holding onto Moonlight's lustrous mane to keep myself from sliding off. Finally, when the first edge of bright orange marked the eastern sky, we halted. I was relieved; I didn't think I could have gone much further.

"We'll rest here, but only for a short while. We still have far to go, and the nights are getting longer. We don't have warm enough blankets and garments to keep us from freezing once the weather grows colder,"

Percifal stated.

"You must be trying to kill me," I said as I slid off Moonlight onto wobbly legs.

He snickered as he helped me along, "Truly, I'm not. In fact, I'm trying to do the exact opposite."

I was grateful for his strong arms. I didn't think I could have walked on my own. He helped me to a grassy patch and laid me down. His face close to mine, I could see his expression was soft. His scruff was starting to grow back, hiding some of his sharp features, but his eyes were warm as ever in the dark shades of dawn covering us like a blanket of indigo. He brushed a piece of hair from my face and whispered, "Sleep now, Zephyra. I will take care of the horses."

I must have passed out instantly, for the next thing I knew, he was waking me with a gentle shake. The sky was now bright blue, and a blanket had been placed on top of me.

I shivered, now aware of the chill in the air. Percifal handed me dried berries and some stale bread. My stomach ached to be filled, regardless of the state of our food. I had never missed the scrumptious meals I'd once enjoyed at the palace more than I did in that moment.

I sat and broke my fast. My whole body ached from the hard ride through the night. I felt as though I hadn't slept in a decade. I knew that soon we would be off again. It took all my strength to keep from breaking into tears.

Percifal must have seen the defeat etched in my face. "I know this journey is a tough one. We'll be out of the forest soon though, and then it won't be long until we reach the village of Ambedar. We can have a good meal and rest in a proper bed there. Can you gather enough strength to make it until then?"

I nodded, afraid my voice would betray my feelings of weakness.

He gave me a sympathetic smile, and I felt my heart skip a beat. That got my mind off the current situation. What was this warm feeling beginning to grow inside of me when he looked at me so? Could I be growing to care for this man who wouldn't even tell me who he really was?

I inwardly scolded myself. It was only because he'd shown me compassion. That was all. Once we made it to Aquila, he could let his sister take care of me. He felt responsible for me. That was why he was being so kind…but deep down, I knew a part of me hoped it was more than that. *Stupid girl,* I thought. *Don't be getting your heart mixed up in this mess. You'll only get hurt again.*

He interrupted my thoughts by holding out a hand to help me up and back onto Moonlight. I felt sorry for our horses. They were doing even more work than us, carrying us through this never-ending nightmare of trees and bushes. I hoped there would be a nice green meadow waiting for them when we reached Aquila.

For the rest of the day, we rode through the forest, making camp at nightfall. But the next day, to my fascination, the trees began to grow thinner; our path became grassy. Soon we were riding through a meadow of tall grass that came to the horses' knees. A few times, I had to edge Moonlight on with my heels to keep her from stopping to enjoy a snack.

The air felt thicker and damper, with a fog that hadn't been in the forest. I knew then we must have been growing nearer to water. I shivered, feeling the dampness seep through to my bones. Regardless of the chill, I couldn't stop myself from grinning.

"Happy to be out of the forest, my lady?" Percifal asked, noticing my delight.

"I am. I thought we'd never make it out of that damned forest."

"We'll reach Ambedar by nightfall. We'll purchase lodging for the night and be off again on the morrow. It will take us three more days to get to Aquila from there." He halted his horse and gave me a pointed look. "You must be sure not to use my name from here on. We're close to Aquila now, and I don't want anyone to recognize it."

I raised one eyebrow at him. "Pray tell, then, what shall I call you, sir?"

He answered without pause, "Vernovus, and you are travelling with me because I'm your guide, who's taking you to your new place of employment."

"My guide, you say? Well, that's true enough. I suppose I shan't say you were a vagrant who rescued me and now is taking me to see his magical sister then?" I teased.

His eyes grew wide at my comment, not noting my sarcasm. "Please don't! It could cause a lot of trouble for Chel."

"You really can't tell when I'm jesting, can you?" It wasn't really a question. I rolled my eyes and pushed Moonlight onward, leaving him to catch up with me—which he did before passing me.

The meadow eventually turned into a valley of hills and craters. I imagined this land was beautiful and green in the summer. Being that we were now on the brink of autumn, the grass had turned brown. The sky was full of dark puffy clouds and it rained on and off throughout the day. If it weren't for the chill, I wouldn't have minded. The earthy smell from the rain was refreshing, and I took in deep breaths. We didn't have the lushness this place did in Solis. It was always so dry and dusty there up on the sandstone cliffs.

I let my thoughts wander as we rode on. It would feel nice to finally be able to change into the other dress I'd brought. The green one I wore now had grown filthy. I hoped I would be able to take a bath. I wasn't as dirty as I had been after being rescued from the dungeon, and the rain did its job at washing away any bad odor that may have clung to me, but I still didn't wish to go to the palace of Aquila looking like a peasant.

Shortly after the sun had set and the sky was a deep shade of sapphire, a few stars beginning to sparkle on its surface, we came upon a carved wooden sign that read, "Welcome to Ambedar."

It seemed like a quiet, peaceful fishing village. The smell of salt in the air told me we were close to the sea.

The buildings there were made from stone, and the streets were dirt that had been packed down from the many hooves and feet pounding them down over time.

"Welcome to Ambedar," my 'guide' said, pulling his hood up to cover more of his bearded face.

"What shall you do when we reach Aquila? Surely people will recognize you there regardless of your disguise, Sir Vernovus," I mocked his fake name.

"I'm not going to the kingdom of Aquila, my lady Phyra. I'll take you to the gate, and then you will ask the guards to take you to Lady Chelela, my sister. If they ask why, you will tell them she's employed you to be her seamstress."

My heart sank. He was going to just leave me once we reached Aquila? I scorned myself. Well, of course he was—*coward.* I stopped Moonlight and shook my head.

"Come now. I can't risk being seen. My sister will take care of you," he offered while I tried to find my tongue.

At last, words came to me as he wrapped a piece of material from his saddlebag around the sapphire hilt of his sword. "So what, you—you're just going to go back to being a vagrant? Hiding and pretending to be someone you aren't?"

"I will spend the winter here, and then yes, I must go to some place far away and remain hidden."

"But *why?*" I screamed in frustration, which only gained me a panicked look and a gesture to be quiet.

"You know I can't tell you why. Chel will fill you in once you explain everything to her. So rest your mind. Now, let us go find food and sleep. My stomach aches," he said as he turned Sunny back towards the street, dismissing me.

"So be it," I replied, following him in silence until we reached our destination for the night; a busy fishermen's lodge with a tavern inside called Oceania's Den.

Chapter 29

PERCIFAL HAD ME wait while he paid the owner of the lodge. I took in my surroundings while they bargained over a price. We were currently in the tavern full of fishermen, on their way to or from sea, I guessed. A few wenches preened over the fishermen; others simply seemed to be enjoying food and drink.

The room was small, with dark wood walls and dim lanterns. The floor was also wooden and looked like it had seen many feet over the seasons. There were small round windows on the one outside wall and paintings of a seascapes upon the others. It was cozy for a tavern, though I stilled preferred The Golden Lilly Inn.

"I have acquired us a room and a meal for the night," Percifal stated, coming to stand beside me.

"One room?"

"It's all we need. You can have the bed. I'll sleep on the palette."

"Oh," I shrugged. "If you say so. Did you happen to inquire about bathing?"

"There's a washing basin upstairs to the right."

That would have to do for now. "Thank you, Sir Vernovus." I bowed my head, spun on my heel, and marched towards the stairs with purpose.

"Our room is the last one on the left. I'll wait for you in there," he called after me.

The washing basin wasn't quite as nice as a full bath would've been, but it still felt good to sponge the dirt from my body, and there was even a piece of lavender soap that smelled wonderful.

I had stripped down to my under garments and washed as best as I could. Once the task was complete, I realized that I hadn't brought my clean dress with me. I rolled my eyes at my own foolishness in my excitement to be clean.

Luckily, there was no one in the hall. I quickly found our room and slipped inside saying, "Turn around. I need my clean dress."

He did as I asked, holding out the blue gown I'd brought from The Golden Lilly Inn. "I figured as much."

Feeling myself blush behind his back, I grabbed the dress and quickly donned it. "Would you be so kind as to help me with my stays?" I asked, holding the gown in place while he came around behind me to do so.

I felt his fingers gently brush the skin on my back a few times. He did my stays up firmly, but still loosely enough to allow me to breathe. "You seem as though you know what you're doing." I turned my chin so I could just make out his face, which looked focused on the task I had given him.

"I used to help my sister with hers sometimes." His lips pulled upwards slightly at the memory, though his eyes remained on my back.

I felt his breath on my neck, causing goose-bumps to rise up on my skin. I cleared my throat, feeling awkward.

He stepped back. "There, all done."

"My thanks again, sir."

"Of course. Now shall we go find something to eat? I'm quite famished."

"Indeed, as am I."

He let me lead the way.

Downstairs, we found a small table in a dark corner of the tavern, where we were served fish stew, fresh biscuits and ale. We sat quietly, all of our attention focused on our warm, delicious meal. It had been quite some time since either of us had had something fresh and warm, other than the meat Percifal had hunted and cooked for us over our fire, of course. The ale went down quickly and smoothly, a nice change from the water and whiskey that we'd been drinking since we had left Lottenheim.

I felt my muscles relax as I sipped on my second mug of the amber liquid. Percifal was telling me stories about himself and his sister from when they were children. I listened closely and actually started to enjoy myself…until he stopped speaking and his expression grew alarmed, eyes widened and a twitch in his jaw.

"What's wrong?" I asked, about to turn and look.

He reached across the table and caught my hand to stop me. "Dance with me." He pulled at me to get up.

Confused and a bit dizzy from the ale I'd consumed, I protested, "Whoa! I am not a good dancer, Sir Vernovus!"

"Shh! Just do it." He spun me around, not giving me a choice.

Halfway through my spin, noticed three well-dressed men getting a table. Percifal's eyes were locked on them.

The musicians played a light, bouncy tune that consisted of fiddles and a flute. I let him lead, as I didn't know this dance he'd dragged me into. I was used to the formal dances of high society. This was different, with its light, quick steps; Percifal held me steady. His grip was firm but gentle; it seemed most things about him were always contrasting.

I raised my chin so that my mouth was almost touching his ear and whispered my question. "…Those three men?"

"Peers of Aquila," he confirmed. My breath caught when he spun me again and then caught me. "Laugh like you're having a good time, Lady Phyra."

I smiled as he dipped me and let out a whimsical laugh. "My, you are a good dancer, Sir Vernovus."

"I've had practice," he winked.

Though a few others danced around us, I paid them no attention. I forgot we were even hiding from the three peers for a moment as I let Percifal guide me as though we were one, lost in the music. I suppose the ale had had a hand in my being so mesmerized. I didn't care. It was nice to let go and actually have fun for once. I couldn't remember the last time I had.

The song ended, and he gave me a bow before taking my hand and leading me off the small dancefloor at the edge of the tables. As we made our way past the table of peers, one in a black and gold velvet doublet stopped us. "Forgive me, sir, but you look quite familiar."

My heart sank before I let out a nervous laugh and answered for my partner, "Oh, you must be mistaken, my lord. I'm Lady Phyra, and this is my guide, Sir Vernovus. This is the first we've been to this area of Sarantoa."

"Ah—nice to meet you, Lady Phyra," he replied, eyeing us with interest. "I am Kelen, this is Haynis," he gestured towards the dark-haired man in a dark blue tunic. "And this is Gestiss," he finished, gesturing towards the other dark-haired man wearing a grey and black embroidered tunic. They were all clean cut and reminded me of the high status snobs I'd seen in my own kingdom.

"Nice to meet you—" I started, shaking his hand.

Percifal cut me off. "Apologies, gentlemen, the lady has had too much ale this evening. We were just about to retire for the night. Good evening." He bowed to them and pulled me away.

Kelen gave us a calculating look, one eyebrow raised.

Percifal all but dragged me up the stairs and into our room.

"Ouch! You're hurting me!" I pulled my wrist from his grasp as soon as we approached our door.

"I'm sorry." He opened our door and gestured for me to go in.

"And I haven't had too much ale." I put my hands on my hips stubbornly, even though I'd probably had enough for the night.

He closed our door behind him. "I know."

I waved a dismissive hand and plopped down on the small bed that occupied about half of the small room. "You know those men?"

"I have met two of them before, Kelen and Gestiss. I only met them once, briefly, so I don't think they've figured out who I really am. But nonetheless, we will leave before everyone wakes…just to be sure we don't run into them again."

I sighed and reached back to untie my stays.

Percifal came over and helped me. "Soon we'll be at the palace, and you can rest all you want," he offered, trying to alleviate my obvious distress.

"Yeah, right after you abandon me," I scowled in return.

"It's for your own good." Did I hear regret in his voice, or was that just my imagination?

I decided to let it go. He turned around to let me strip down to my undergarments and crawl under the covers of the small bed. I was exhausted, and the bed felt most welcoming. As hard as it was, I hadn't slept in an actual bed since The Golden Lilly. I closed my eyes and fell asleep without any trouble.

To my confusion, Percifal shook me awake shortly after. He was fully dressed, darkness still upon us. "Zephyra, wake up. We must go now," he whispered loudly, using my actual name for once. It felt strange hearing him speak it…almost intimate.

He tossed my blue dress on the bed beside me. "Get dressed. I will explain once we're gone from here."

I groaned, rubbing the sleep from my eyes and sitting up to let my legs dangle off the edge of the bed.

"I'm sorry to have to wake you earlier than expected, but we'll find somewhere else to rest."

"Okay, I'm up," I snapped in annoyance, which he didn't seem to notice. He busied himself with ensuring our saddlebags were all packed up.

Within the next few moments, I had my dress on; he had done my stays up for me once again, though this time with more haste, and I was following him down the dark stairs of the Inn. All was quiet, as everyone else was asleep in their nice warm beds. I envied them.

We crept out the front doors. Once outside, we headed for the stables. The stable boy who'd taken our horses upon arrival was nowhere to be seen, which led me to believe he was also asleep in his bed…like I should have been. I scowled at the thought while Percifal readied our horses.

It didn't take long before he brought Moonlight to me. "Ease your mind, Zephyra, there's an abandoned shack close by."

I scoffed. "Oh good, then you can tell me why we must leave this nice cozy Inn in the middle of the night."

"Of course. I just need some time to think."

"Well, think quickly," I shot, squeezing Moonlight with my calves.

The wind whipped at my face and disheveled hair as we rode at a gallop down the dirt road and out of Ambedar. We rode through the meadow by which we had come to the village, only this time we were going in a different direction. It dawned on me that we were going around the outskirts of Ambedar.

The sky was clear above us, a black blanket of full of stars and a pale glowing, round moon lit our way. The sight would have taken my breath away were I not so tired, cold and confused by our sudden departure.

No, more than that was causing my sour mood. I wanted to know just who Percifal really was and what he was hiding from. I would *make* him tell me. I laughed inwardly at that thought. *Sure, Zephyra, how are you going to make this dangerous man tell you anything?* Perhaps I would threaten him, I decided. *Threaten him with…*before I could finish my thought, an abandoned shack come into view.

It was small, made of rotten wood, and with broken windows and no door. It seemed quite abandoned, like an orphaned child.

We came to an abrupt halt just outside of the shack. I was wide awake now and wanted answers. Percifal worked in silence as we dismounted and started the task of unsaddling the horses. He seemed to be deep in thought, so I stood and waited idly. Once he was finished and the horses were tethered, I followed him into the shack.

There wasn't much to the inside of the small building; a small, worn table and a couple of tipped-over chairs that were now decaying. The floor was made of soft, packed earth and there was a pallet that must have once been the owner's bed. I imagined a shepherd had once occupied this place during the summer months, needing only the bare necessities while he watched his flock.

I looked over to the man who'd saved me twice and had been my guide on this trying journey to the kingdom of water. He had his dagger out and was shaving the beard that had begun to grow scraggly again.

I clenched my fists in frustration. He said he would explain once we got there, but there we were and he was as silent as a statue, and ridding himself of his disguise.

"Won't someone recognize you without your disguise, *sir?*" I asked in a vexed tone.

He winced, as if I'd caused him some pain with my words, or mayhap he'd nicked himself with his dagger. "Please, just call me Percifal from now on."

I shook my head and started pacing in front of him. "I shall call you by your name when you tell me who you *really* are, if Percifal is even your *real* name!" I knew I was being cold, but my patience had run out.

"It is my real name. Percifal, that's who I am."

"Then tell me what you are! Everything! And tell me why you ran away to pose as a vagrant. Tell me now, or I'll—I'll…"

"Or you'll what?" He strode towards me with a daring look in his eyes, looming over me. He was a great deal taller than me, but I didn't feel threatened by him. He had only ever saved me, he would never hurt me.

"I'll…" I hadn't gotten that far in my thoughts yet, so I rolled my eyes and said the first thing I could think of. I instantly regretted the words as they left my lips. "Or I'll go back to those men at the lodge and ask them to take me to Aquila instead of you." I lifted my chin and stared into his eyes, only to see how much pain my words had caused.

He began to back away, and I reached for him, feeling ashamed of myself. "No, wait, that's a lie. I wouldn't do that, but I'll find everything out from your sister anyways once I meet her, so you may as well just tell me now. Please."

A spark grew in his eyes at the mention of his sister. "My sister…yes, of course. Everything's happened so that you two can be brought together. Celestia works in mysterious ways."

I gave him a blank stare because I had no idea what he was going on about.

"Okay," he sighed and raked a hand through his onyx hair, sitting down on the palette. "I can't let you go to Aquila without me now. That's why I no longer need the disguise."

My heart grew surprisingly warm at his words and I took a seat beside him. "Okay, start from the beginning."

He paused to gather himself, and then he told me everything. "It all began about two springs ago, after Noctis De Celestia. You see, I was once not a very good man…I was blinded by my duty to King Zaeden De Thryst, the king of Aquila. Before I ran to Lottenheim and met Ginnie and Irving, I was one of King Zaeden's most trusted men. I was the constable of his army."

I felt my jaw drop. All of this time, I thought him to be just some thief, or maybe an assassin; not the constable of a whole damn kingdom! It surely explained his skill and finesse at fighting with a sword. Still, I could not believe my own ears.

I shook myself, as I noticed he was waiting for my reply. "So, you were the constable of Aquila. Why did you leave?"

He looked straight ahead with a distant gaze as he continued, "Well as I said, I was blinded by my duty to King Zaeden, although I was close to the royal family right from birth. My father had helped King Zaeden take the throne from our previous ruler, so my parents had been friends of he and Queen Thea before me and my sister even came into this world. I'm sure that fact helped once I proved my skills in fighting to King Zaeden, for he then appointed me constable of his armies. I was only sixteen when I was given the role, but I was well prepared for it.

Growing up to always honour my king, of course I never questioned him."

He paused, a frown creasing between his brows. "That was until my second decade on this earth, about three springs ago, when he learned of an island called Gwon. It was just off the coast of Aquila, and it was said that it flourished with women and gold. The women, he wasn't interested in, but the gold…he was a greedy king. He believed he was doing right by his people, because if he didn't get the gold from Gwon, he would increase his kingdom's taxes.

"At first, he sent me with his chancellor to the island to inquire with their ruler, Khadji, if he would trade some of his gold for goods such as wool and grain. Khadji laughed in the chancellor's face and told him he didn't need anything from Aquila. We left Gwon at once to inform our king. King Zaeden was outraged by the refusal and decided if Khadji wouldn't trade with him, he would take what he wanted instead."

I took a deep breath, shaking my head. "I'm beginning to dislike this king of yours."

He gave a short laugh. "You haven't even heard the worst of it yet. I begged King Zaeden to leave well enough alone. I told him we had no need for their gold anyways, but he wouldn't listen. He told me that I must sail with my men to Gwon and take some of the gold. He threatened to give someone else my position should I refuse. Feeling I had no other choice, I did as my king bade, and my men and I were successful in getting a large amount of gold back to Aquila. I'm not proud of it, trust me. But at the time, we rejoiced."

I shook my head and pressed my lips together, not liking what I was hearing.

"Our victory was short-lived though. Our kingdom was ambushed by Khadji and his own army shortly after our return. They came at night, whilst most of the kingdom slept, myself included. They took our guards down with their giant, foreign swords and gained access to the king's chambers. Woken by the sounds of fighting, I grabbed my own sword and headed towards the noise. It was then that I found Khadji with his sword to the queen's throat, spitting out the words, 'You take my gold, I take your queen!' And then he did it, he slit her throat. I can still remember the blood as it spilled out from her neck and onto the white silk sheets."

"Dear Celestia!" I gasped.

I noticed his hand shake a little before he folded those defined arms of his and continued, "King Zaeden was outraged. My parents came into the scene moments after Queen Thea's death. While I tried to get my mother out of the chamber, King Zaeden, fool he was, decided to try to go after Khadji barehanded. My father noticed and tried to stop him, only to be cut down by Khadji, who was trying to get at King Zaeden." Percifal stopped and put his head in his hands.

When he looked up a moment later, his eyes were rimmed with red. I put my hand on his shoulder to offer some comfort.

He continued, "I was trying to protect my mother, when instead, I should've protected my king so my father wouldn't have had to. He would still be alive if not for my mistake."

I couldn't believe what he was saying, that he was blaming himself for his own father's death. "No, what King Zaeden did *was* foolish. Don't blame yourself. If he would've stayed put, surely no one else would have died. It wasn't wrong of you to protect your mother."

"Nonetheless, I should've known King Zaeden would be blind with rage. Khadji left after that, taking his men with him. The whole kingdom was left in shock. Everyone mourned for my father, but even more so for their beloved queen.

"King Zaeden went into a silent rage after that night. After the funerals, he drafted up three letters; one to be taken to each of the kingdoms of Sarantoa, asking them to join him in a war against the island of Gwon to avenge his queen—and my father."

"I've never heard of this letter," I interrupted, and then bit my lip, realizing my rudeness.

"That's because it was quietly refused. I doubt your queen would've said anything about it to you. The other three kingdoms decided that King Zaeden had been careless by stealing the gold, and that this was his own battle to fight. They didn't want to risk their men for his mistake, which I understood, but King Zaeden did not. As I said, he is a greedy man who mostly thinks of himself.

"After the deaths of his queen and friend, he didn't seem quite right in his head. I think the refusal from the other sovereigns was the final blow. He decided that there was no point in being a king if he couldn't have his queen—or anything else he wanted. So instead he came up with a new plan, a plan to become the ruler of all of Sarantoa."

"But that's impossible." It was my turn to pace. All this time, there was so much going on that I didn't even know about. I wondered if Adelaide even knew, or if our grandmother had kept the letters details from her too.

"Not if you conquer all of the kingdoms."

I halted and faced him, but he wouldn't look at me. I felt my heart begin to race with the panic that coursed through my entire body. "Do you mean to tell me *war* is coming to the other three kingdoms?! To *my* kingdom, where my dear cousin, Queen Adelaide, now rules?"

"No—well—maybe. I don't know!" His hands shot up to grip the sides of his temples. He squeezed his eyes shut for a moment and then continued, "When King Zaeden told me of his plans to attack the other kingdoms and over throw them one by one, and that I was to lead his army, I refused. I knew it would be wrong to break the treaty."

"So you—you what? Told him *no?*" I let out a bitter laugh.

"I told him it was unwise and that the outcome would likely be a bad one for him, being that the odds were three against one. He refused to listen to me though. He told me if I wasn't with him, I was against him. I feared we were all doomed, but then one of my men came to me with a plan. He told me he thought he had enough support to take the throne from King Zaeden. I told him it was a good plan, but I couldn't stand against the king my father had helped put on the throne, the king who was once my family's friend. I told him I wouldn't stop him either. So I decided I had to leave Aquila.

"I told my mother and sister I was leaving for the good of everyone. I knew I would be deemed a traitor for abandoning my king. It's a fact I'm still ashamed of, but my heart was torn."

"So you just left…abandoned your kingdom in its time of need?" I asked incredulously. Though I had done the same, my kingdom hadn't depended on me as his did.

"Yes, I felt that was the only way to save our land. I ran far away, to a small village where no one would find me. That village was Lottenheim, where I met Ginny and Irving.

"Their Inn wasn't doing so well back then, so I offered to help them if they promised not to ask me any questions. When there wasn't anything left to fix, and The Golden Lilly Inn was doing well, I asked them if I could keep my stuff there until a time came when I needed it. They, of course, agreed. I didn't wish to use up all of my funds, and I certainly didn't wish to be discovered should a traveler from Aquila ever arrive at the Inn. So I went off and fended for myself, getting what scraps I could from the kitchens of large rich manors. That's how I came to find you."

"So you rescued me, and were going to take me back to Solis and then go back to being a vagrant—until you found out about my power," I stated, knowing this part of the story.

"Exactly." He got up and grabbed both of my shoulders, looking into my eyes with desperation. "Once I learned of your power, I knew I had to get you to my sister. You see, we know this sorceress. She told my sister that one day she would find others like her, that she had seen it in her vision pool. I didn't really believe it was true, and then I found you and I knew it was Celestia's plan for us to meet."

I looked up at the dilapidated wooden-beamed ceiling, feeling a weight suddenly upon my shoulders. "Okay, now tell me why we've left Oceania's Den in the middle of the night. And tell me what you have learned that caused you to change your mind about coming with me to the palace."

He shook his head and stepped away from me. "The worst, I fear. While you were asleep, I decided to sneak back downstairs to listen to the conversation of those three peers. As they spoke, I realized that I've made a tragic mistake. I should have stayed to fight alongside my friend, my duty to King Zaeden be damned! This is all my fault. I may have been a traitor if I fought against my king, but I wouldn't be a coward."

I stared at him, his words sinking in. No wonder he hadn't told me his story before. He was ashamed of himself. Regardless of what he thought, his regret at running away now could only mean one thing. "So King Zaeden is still on the throne," I stated.

He sighed and then said the words that made my blood run cold. "Yes, and they said that he's going to use a dark power to conquer all of Sarantoa."

CHAPTER 30

HIS WORDS RENDERED me speechless, and I had to blink a few times to clear my head. "So, what now? You want to use *me* to fix *your* mistake."

Did he actually look hurt by my words? His brow furrowed, and a muscle in his jaw twitched. "Believe me. I would rather you were *not* a part of this. Do you think I want to place you in harm's way?" He didn't wait for my answer. Instead, he grabbed my hand and pleaded, "War *is* coming, Zephyra, whether you want it to or not. Would you stand by idly when you know you may have the power to help stop it?"

"Ha!" I let out a strangled laugh. *Oh, the irony.* "I may have this power within me, but I don't know how to use it. I can't even light a small fire to keep us warm! What good am I for fighting some dark power?" I pulled my hand from his and threw my arms up in the air with exasperation.

"That—" He shook his head and pressed his lips together before continuing in a calmer tone, "That is why I'm taking you to my sister. Whom I also wish didn't have to be a part of this, by the way. She can help you, as I've said before."

He looked away from me and spoke in a voice so low I almost didn't hear him. "There's something else I haven't told you."

"Oh dear Celestia, what else could there possibly be?"

"I lied when I said I only knew your name due to your royal lineage."

I raised an eyebrow, "Oh? Then pray tell, how else *did* you know my name?"

"You have to understand, when I first saw you in that dungeon, I didn't recognize you. You were in bad shape, and it had been eight springs since I'd last seen you."

"Eight springs?" I echoed, confused.

"Yes, eight springs since I had the pleasure of sitting with you at Noctis De Celestia, when I was only a boy of a decade and a half."

"You?" I stopped short, taking his words in with disbelief. He had been the boy sitting at my table. This whole time, he'd known and not told me.

Suddenly, a horrific thought occurred to me. "I—I *cursed* you that night! You and those other two girls from Terra." I sat frozen, staring straight ahead. "That means this is actually all my fault. What has befallen you is because of me."

He tilted my chin so that I had no choice but to look into his eyes. "Listen to me. This is *not* your fault. I have never believed that. You said so yourself; you can't even light a small fire, never mind curse three people—"

"Is that supposed to make me feel better?" I cut him off.

"No. What I'm trying to say is that I didn't tell you how I knew of you because of some fake curse you tossed at me when we were children. I'm telling you because I don't believe it's purely coincidence that we've crossed paths before. Celestia has put us in each other's way again for a reason."

I lifted my head, hearing the memory of Celestia's voice in my head. "*You are a special girl, Zephyra.*"

I inhaled sharply at the memory, which snapped me out of my sullen state. Perhaps he was right. It seemed Celestia did have plans for me. If I really did have the power within me to stop this war, I must at least try. Otherwise, this demented king of Aquila would try to take over all of the kingdoms in Sarantoa, including my Adelaide's.

I straightened my back and held my head up high with resolve. "Alright, I'll help you try to stop this war. It seems that is, indeed, what our goddess wants. Who am I to deny her?"

The look of relief in Percifal's face was enough to make me glad, for the moment at least, that I had agreed to help him.

The next thing I knew he was kneeling before me, peering into my eyes with the most sincere look. "I'm sorry I did not tell you all of this before. I'd hoped King Zaeden to be dead, but it seems that he's the one who will conjure this dark power of which the sorceress spoke."

"I forgive you, Percifal." How could I not, after everything we'd been through together?

The look that came over him as I spoke those words…was it adoration? No one had ever looked at me that way before.

We looked at one another in silence, and I found myself noticing him as if for the first time, his long dark lashes and sharp features. He was the most beautiful man I'd ever known.

His gaze fell to my lips, and the next thing I knew, we were kissing. I almost cried out at the sudden release of pressure between us. It was like a cold layer of ice had broken. The whole world seemed to pause around us in that moment. My heart soared as a groan escaped from his throat. I never wanted it to end.

And then I saw a flicker of light through my closed lids and heard the roar of fire. I did not care, but Percifal pulled away, and my eyes shot open.

The walls around us were covered in bright, hot fire, the flames reaching out like hungry fingers grasping to reach us. I shrieked and scrambled to get off the pallet.

"Zephyra! Control your emotions!" Percifal yelled over the roar of the fire.

"I *can't!*" I screamed back at him, feeling my heart race in my chest.

"Call the fire to you, or we'll lose everything! You can do it! I've seen Chel do it with water! Just concentrate and calm yourself!"

I sucked in a gulp of smoky air, about to argue back, but it was no use. He was right, I had to at least *try,* or else we'd be travelling bareback the rest of the way. Not to mention we'd lose our saddlebags and everything in them

I turned to face the fire and willed myself to calm down. I closed my eyes and thought of Celestia and my love for her. I pictured myself calling to the flames and them bending to my will. I held out my hands to draw the fire back into myself. At first, nothing happened. Just as I was about to give up and run out of the shack, I felt a rush of burning power so bright, I saw white light behind my closed eyelids.

For a moment, I thought that my life had ended, that I was now in the heavens with my goddess. And then my breath came back to me with a *WHOOSH.* I opened my eyes to see the wooden walls of the shack no longer aflame. They were a little charred, but at least they were no longer aflame.

I felt suddenly weak with exhaustion and sank to my knees.

Percifal came to me and helped me back up onto the pallet. "Here, here. That was brilliant! I knew you had it in you. Now rest." He bent and pressed his palm against my cheek. "We have only a couple more days until we reach Aquila."

I was so confused by the fire. Had my passion really ignited those flames? I would surely have to be more careful in the future if that was the case. And Percifal…what were these feelings that were blooming between us? I was too exhausted for so many questions and sleep soon claimed me.

When I awoke, it was to the sunlight beaming in through spaces in the ceiling. A wool blanket was placed over me, and I felt warmth at my back. I turned my neck to see that the warmth was from Percifal's body resting against mine.

I sat up quickly, and Percifal stretched. "Good morning, Zephyra."

I blinked as the events from last night came rushing back to me; Percifal's revealing story about his past, my role in the events to come, our passionate kiss and the fire that I'd caused because of it.

I felt a rush of nausea and had to put my head down between my knees.

Percifal took note of my state and sat up beside me. "Zephyra? Are you alright?"

I took a deep breath and sat back up. Keeping my back as straight as a board, I answered without looking at him, "Yes I'm fine. It's just that…the fire…"

"Yes, there was the fire, but you put a stop to it. Don't you see how *good* that is?"

I shot off the bed to face him. "Sure, it is lucky that I was able to stop those flames from burning this whole shack down, along with all of our things, but the fact that I started it because of…" my voice trailed off as I searched for the right words. "Because of what? My emotions?"

"Yes, your powers are tied to your emotions right now, it would seem."

"I thought they were only tied to my anger, but I guess all of my stronger emotions affect my power. Until I can figure out how to control my power, I must keep my emotions in check—or I risk burning us both to ash."

"I understand." His expression turned to one of disappointment at my declaration, knowing exactly what I was saying. "I suppose you're right. We have a demented king and a war to worry about anyways. We should focus on that."

That said, he pulled his loose white shirt on and began strapping on his leather armor. I realized I must have hurt his pride so I placed a hand upon his shoulder and gave him a reassuring smile. When he looked up at me, his eyes seemed distant.

I faltered and pulled my hand away. Not able to meet his gaze any longer, I looked over his shoulder and told him, "I don't regret last night. I just don't want to put us in any more danger."

"Of course, my lady. You need not worry about my feelings." And then he dismissed the subject. "We should make haste; who knows how long we have before King Zaeden begins to act on his plans?"

I nodded and stepped back to smooth the wrinkles from my dress. I knew he was right, but I couldn't help but feel a pang of hurt at his suddenly formality.

As I braided my hair he said, "I'll have to tell the guards you're my slave when we reach Aquila."

I frowned at that. "You aren't going to sneak in to the palace? Do you think they'll just let you walk back in after leaving like that? You said yourself you betrayed your king. In most places, that would earn you a death sentence."

"Even if I were to successfully sneak us in unnoticed, someone would see us eventually and then I would definitely look guilty. No, too many of the people know me there too well to be fooled by some disguise. And we don't have the luxury of remaining hidden if we are to visit my mother and sister in their apartment. Besides, as insane as King Zaeden may be now, I don't believe he would ever sentence me to death. As far as I know, the rest of my family is still in his good graces. I have a plan that should get us in and hopefully we will get out with Chel before King Zaeden even knows I'm there." He bent down to pack our blankets into his saddlebag. "I will tell everyone that I went to ask Solis to join us in hopes of balancing the fight, and when they refused, I took one of their own to be my slave."

"Would you ever have done that?"

"Done what?"

"Taken someone to be your slave?" I asked.

"Perhaps once…when I all I wanted was please my king."

I shuddered at that, but let the subject go. We readied our horses and took off through the meadow into the hills that were now turning brown with the autumn season.

CHAPTER 31

WE RODE FOR two more days, stopping only to sleep beneath the stars. We slept with our bodies together as before, though there was no intimacy between us; it was only for warmth.

Our landscape grew rockier. The air was thicker and damper, making it evident that we were getting even closer to the sea. It wasn't long before I heard the crashing of waves. The sound was new to me, and I found it soothing. At one point, we came to a clearing, and the sea actually came into view. The sight took my breath away. I took in its blue depths and the steep golden cliffs towering over its edge and reaching toward the clouds, which were rolling through the grey-blue sky.

Percifal's face was set in a mask of determination as we pressed on. He broke the silence by saying, "Almost there."

I realized he was right when I saw the palace looming in the distance among the cliffs. The palace was made of white limestone and had peaking towers of different heights. There was something beautiful about the way it was nestled in those cliffs, the sea stretching out forever at its base.

Percifal drew in his reins to stop Sunny, I followed suit.

"Hand me your reins." He beckoned.

I paused and looked at him, dumbfounded.

"If I'm to make them believe you're my slave, it must look like you are coming here against your will," he explained. "Now, hand me your reins."

I leaned forward in my saddle and did as he bade. He took my reins and tied them to his own saddle before straightening his back. "Welcome to Aquila," he mumbled, edging Sunny onward with me now in tow.

Watching him, I thought about how majestic he looked against the backdrop, like he belonged here with his eyes that reminded me of the sea on a warm sunny day and a body that looked as unyielding as those cliffs.

Head held high, with his mighty sword strapped to his hip, he suddenly looked the part of the constable, even in his mere leather armor. I wouldn't wish to have him as an enemy, but was glad to have him as a protector.

I checked my expression as we rode up the side of a steep cliff and neared the large iron gates of Aquila. I needed to look miserable if anyone was going to believe I was being brought there against my will. I turned my thoughts to the person I hated the most, Algor, and scowled.

Standing at the irons gates was one of Aquila's guards. He was a tall man with long, dark hair that blew in the wind. He shielded his eyes to see us better without being blinded by the setting sun. He wore silver chainmail under a black surcoat that had Aquila's blue emblem, a seahorse in front of two crossed swords, embroidered upon the chest.

As we grew closer, a look of dismay crossed his face. "By heavens, it can't be…Percifal? Is that really you?"

"Good day, Sir Dante. Yes, it is I."

His expression quickly turned angry, his eyes growing hard. I did my best to remain small and insignificant beside Percifal.

"You left us over two springs ago. We have no use for you now. Why have you come back to the gates of Aquila, *Sir Lacrima,*" he added Percifal's title with a sneer.

"Ease your mind. I don't wish to regain my position as constable. I left only to try to gain support for our kingdom. I understand how it must have looked."

He seemed like he didn't believe what Percifal was saying, but then I saw a shadow of doubt cross his face. "Well, you sure left at a convenient time, but perhaps you are telling the truth. Who am I to decide? You may enter. King Zaeden will be made aware of your return. If you were indeed trying to aid our kingdom, I'm sure he will forgive your absence."

"No need to make King Zaeden aware of my return. I will be visiting him first. He was, afterall, the one who ordered me to go to Solis." Percifal stared him right in the eyes.

Sir Dante blinked a few times. “King Zaeden was outraged when you left, so how could that be true?”

“Do you really believe King Zaeden tells *you* all of his plans? It was a scheme, you idiot.”

Dante laughed nervously and shook his head. “Well there you have it. I guess there’s more going on than most of us know.”

He was actually buying Percifal’s story. I couldn’t believe it. He really was an idiot…Percifal was also a good liar.

I felt Sir Dante’s hungry eyes look me up and down. “Now tell me, who is this fiery red head you’ve brought with you?”

I willed myself to ignore his gaze.

Without even a glance in my direction, Percifal answered, “When Solis refused me, I decided I would take one of their own. A keepsake, you could say, for all my troubles.”

I turned my face, molding it into a look of shame.

Sir Dante judged me with his icy blue eyes. “Pretty little thing. I never took you as the type of man who’d take a slave; I guess your travels have hardened you.”

“It’s the people in this world who’ve hardened me.”

“Very well; you may pass. I’m sure the king will be happy to see you, regardless of the news you bring him.”

“Thank you, Sir Dante.”

The two men nodded to each other as we rode through the gates. I cowered in my saddle, feeling Sir Dante’s eyes still upon me. Something about the tall man made me shiver to my core.

Even once we were away from the eyes and ears of Sir Dante, Percifal kept his own gaze straight forward and said not one word to me. I felt as though he’d forgotten my existence all together.

Feeling awkward I offered, “You were quite convincing back there. I think Sir Dante believes you.” My voice sounded more nervous than I’d expected.

“Hush!” he scolded. “There are eyes and ears everywhere, and slaves don’t speak to their masters unless bidden to do so.”

I felt my cheeks burn at the way he’d just spoken to me. Who did he think he was to treat me, cousin to a *queen,* that way? I knew we both had to play our parts, but this was inexcusable.

Or was it? I scolded myself inwardly for my reaction. He knew this kingdom and its people better than I. If we needed to really make others believe I was his slave, perhaps we also needed to believe our own charade. Still, I didn't like being treated this way. I wished we could've thought of a better plan.

I soon forgot my worries, taking in the gleaming palace of Aquila in awe. It was beautiful, with enormous peaked towers and shining stained glass windows depicting scenes from the sea. The large oval window at the center was stained different shades of blues and greens, with a mermaid looking down upon the rest of the kingdom, as though she would protect them from any harm.

Percifal steered us away from that window and towards the royal stables.

A young, gangly stable boy came out to greet us while we dismounted. "Good day, sir and—and lady—"

"Pay the lady no attention," Percifal instructed. "Take good care of our mounts, aye? They've had a long and tiring journey." He tossed the stable boy a piece of silver and grabbed one of my wrists.

I pretended to seethe with rage, though it wasn't a hard feat.

"Y—yes, sir," the boy stammered nervously, bowing, and then he led our horses away.

"Come now," Percifal finally spoke to me, leading me towards one of the apartments connected to the main part of the palace.

I let him lead me and kept my silence. I hoped we would soon find his sister and end this act.

When we came upon the large wooden door to the apartment, Percifal knocked once softly before opening it. "Mother? Chel?"

Peering around Percifal, I caught sight of a woman who looked to be in her fourth decade. She sat upon a chair, but jumped to her feet when she saw us and cried out with glee.

Her long, wavy hair was the same onyx colour that Percifal's was. I could see where he got his sharp, angular features from too. As she drew closer, I noticed her eyes were a deep blue colour, not turquoise like his.

Her eyes welled up with tears as she grasped Percifal's face in her palms.

"My dear Celestia! Percifal!" She started sobbing as he pulled her into his arms. "I—I thought I w—would never see you again," she cried into his shoulder as he stroked her hair.

"I've missed you too, Mother. I'll tell you everything. It's alright now. Shh," he soothed.

I stood back, feeling as out of place as a chicken among ducks. I smiled at the way he softened towards his mother. Gone was the cold facade he'd worn just moments ago.

Seeming to finally remember me, he let his mother go and beckoned for me to come forward. "Mother, this is Lady Zephyra. She hails from Solis."

"Oh, my dear," his mother shook herself. "Forgive me my rudeness. You see, I have not seen or heard from my son in over two springs. Though he told me why he had to leave, I didn't know if he would ever return."

"No apologies necessary, madam. I understand," I reassured her. She patted a chair for me to sit down.

"Zephyra, this is Lady Dulcina Lacrima. As you've probably already guessed, she is my mother."

"It's a pleasure to meet you, Madam Lacrima."

"As it is to meet you, my dear." She turned to Percifal. "Now, you will tell me everything. But first, the two of you shall wash and eat. You both look as though you've had a long journey."

I winced, knowing what a sore sight I must have made in my dirty dress and hair that had half come undone in the wind.

"Yes, Mother. I can take care of washing myself. I trust I still have some garments here to wear?" Percifal asked with an eyebrow raised.

"Of course. Go take care of yourself. I'll see to finding Lady Zephyra something to wear."

With that said, Percifal disappeared, and his mother gestured for me to follow her up the wooden staircase.

The apartment had a warm cozy, atmosphere and was scattered with fine furnishings of cherry-wood and blue and silver décor that made one think of the sea during a bright summer day.

Madam Dulcina's chamber was decorated with many beautiful crystal vases and silver candlesticks. Her bed was a large canopied one with soft white covers and sheer silvery curtains.

One could see the Lacrima's were surely favoured by royalty. In spite of all that had come to pass, it seemed the king didn't blame Madam Lacrima. If he had, I doubted she would still have this apartment and all of her things.

As Madam Lacrima threw open the dark polished wooden doors to her wardrobe and began rummaging through her many gowns, I remembered just who I was pretending to be in this kingdom and thought it best to speak up, "Nothing too fancy, madam. I—er I'm posing as a slave whilst here in Aquila and don't wish to others to question my attire. Forgive me."

"Oh?" Madam Lacrima started. "Slave girls must be dressed well for their masters anyhow, but I shall find something suitable. Oh, and you will tell me exactly why you are posing as a slave, once your belly is full."

"Of course, madam. My thanks." I bowed my head as she pulled out a gown that was both light and royal blue.

"Ah, here we are. I think this'll do just fine. You're a bit smaller in the waist than I, so it may be a touch loose, but other than that, I believe it will be quite comfortable," she exclaimed, giving me a wink.

She handed me the dress and pointed me to another small room at the back of the chamber. "The washing room is there. Wash up in the basin and come down once you are ready. I shall see that supper is prepared and set out."

I thanked her again as she walked past me, her own silvery gown swishing as she exited her chambers, leaving me alone.

How wonderful it felt to be inside the walls of a palace again—*and clean,* I thought, scrubbing the grim from my body with the sea sponge that I'd found in the copper basin filled with cool water. Not a full bath, but it would do for now.

The dress Madam Lacrima had lent me was quite exquisite for what she must've thought was simple. The bodice was a sky-blue shade and laced up the front with silver ribbon. The sleeves, which only covered my shoulders, were of the same colour and made of lace. The skirts were made of a soft royal blue fabric that seemed to float away from my body with each movement I made.

Though Madam Lacrima was correct in that her waist was slightly bigger than mine, it wasn't noticeable and I was grateful, for it kept the gown from being too constricting—like many of my own had been.

Once I combed out my disheveled hair and braided it, I checked myself in the silver-backed hand mirror that was on the desk by Madam Lacrima's bed. Satisfied with my reflection, I made my way back downstairs to find Percifal and his mother.

Descending the stairs, I saw Percifal was now dressed in a deep blue doublet and black leather breeches. I didn't think he could ever be more beautiful than he already was…I was wrong.

I heard his breath catch when he spotted me. He looked over me with approval in his eyes. There was a light in them I hadn't seen since our night in the shack as he took my hand. "My Celestia, Lady Zephyra. You look exquisite. Like a true royal"

"Oh no," I put my hand to my chest, feeling my cheeks burn. "You don't think our cover will be blown if someone else sees me in this, do you?"

"Perhaps the dress is a little fancy for a slave…" he waved a dismissive hand, "but Mother can find you something simpler to wear tomorrow. I daresay no one else will see you tonight anyways."

"Alright. If no one else will see me, then I don't see the harm. It *is* nice to wear something so lovely once again."

"I thought you looked just as pretty in your rags."

I gave him a nervous laugh, not knowing how else to respond to such flattery.

"I mean it, Zephyra."

"I have grown quite fond of you as well—Constable Lacrima." I inclined my head, but he only shook his.

"Don't call me that, please. It's just Percifal now," he said with what sounded to me like shame.

"I was only teasing. Now come, show me to your dining room. I'm sure your mother is eagerly awaiting us."

He nodded in agreement. Taking my arm, he led me to the small private dining room, where his mother was indeed waiting with our plates. They were also made of silver. A hearty amount of food sat on the center of the rectangular table.

Once our bellies were full and we each had a couple goblets of Aquila's fine wine, Percifal enlightened his mother with our story. She listened intently with a solemn expression while he revealed his time as a vagrant and how he had found me, the girl with the power of fire.

When he finished telling her every necessary detail, he asked, "So, where is Chel anyway? I thought to find her with you."

Madam Lacrima sat back, folding her hands in her lap. "I'm afraid she's not in Aquila. I thought it too dangerous for her to remain here, with King Zaeden's thirst for power. I had her married to Valron Michester—the Duke of Cansbroke."

"You *what?*" Percifal slammed both his palms against the table, causing the plates to rattle. "You married her off like some—some *prize?* I thought you and father had agreed never to do that to her!"

"Percifal, listen to me," Madam Lacrima commanded, trying to soothe him in a gentle, yet stern voice.

Percifal wasn't listening though; he kept going on as if she hadn't spoken. "I can't believe you. This is outrageous, Mother. I leave and you sell off my sister because you think she is at risk? Everyone is at risk, no matter where they are, with King Zaeden alive and trying to use this dark power—"

Her patience wearing out, Madam Lacrima shot out of her seat and shouted at him, "I said, LISTEN!"

He clamped his mouth shut and glowered at her. I felt like they both had forgotten I was even in the room. I would've excused myself, but I didn't wish to draw their attentions while they were both this heated.

Madam Lacrima sat back down and put her hand to her forehead. "King Zaeden has locked Sreda in the tower and siphons her power to use for his own dark needs."

Percifal's face paled at his mother's words. I felt my own heart sink.

Sreda, I repeated the name over in my mind until, finally, I recalled why it sounded familiar to me. Percifal had told me that Sreda was the sorceress who helped his sister with her power when she was a child. If the king was using her magic for his own needs, the situation was even direr than I'd imagined.

Percifal's next words shook me from my thoughts. "We'll leave tomorrow for Cansbroke to find Chel."

"I'm actually relieved to hear that," Madam Lacrima sighed. "She used to write to me often, but I haven't received a letter from her in some time now, and I'm starting to worry."

Percifal frowned. "Do you think something has happened to her?"

"I'm sure she's fine. Nonetheless, it eases my mind to know you shall be going to her see her, sad as I am that you must be leaving so soon." She reached across the table and clasped his hand in her slender one. "You have grown into the most handsome and honourable man. I'm so glad to see you here and well."

He patted her hand and looked into her eyes. "It's good to see you too, Mother. Anyways, it's better I'm gone before King Zaeden decides to question me about my sudden reappearance."

She smiled sadly at him and let go of his hand. "Ah, of course. Though I'm sure he would never truly harm you, even now. Your father was like a brother to him."

Percifal only smiled back at her. I was sure he didn't want to give her another thing to worry about, even if he doubted it himself.

Madam Lacrima turned to me next, as if suddenly remembering my existence. "Forgive us our rudeness, Lady Zephyra, you must be exhausted. I can show you to your room so you may get some rest," she offered in a sweet voice.

"That would be lovely. This journey seems to never end."

"I'm sure you shall find comfort in Chel's home as well. 'Tis only a day's ride from here." She rose and led me away from the dining room, leaving Percifal alone with his goblet of wine.

I was indeed tired, but I also wanted to give Percifal and his mother some time alone. His mother missed him, and Celestia only knew when he would see her again.

"You may sleep in Chel's old room. I say it is more comfortable than the guest room. She's not here to use it anyways." I heard a bit of sadness in the last words she spoke.

I smiled at her and tried to offer her some comfort. "Thank you, madam. We shall send you word of your daughter's well-being when we reach her."

"You are very kind. The way my son looks at you…I have never seen him look at another with such adoration. I hope you realize he's a good man, even though he keeps his emotions hidden most of the time. He has been through a lot."

"I know he's good. He's saved my life twice. It is something I shall never forget," I reassured her.

"Wonderful. I'm glad he was there to save you," she said with a note of pride as she stopped and opened the door to Chel's bedchamber. "Ah, here we are. There's a night shift on the bed. I asked my maid to lay it out for you."

"Thank you."

"You're most welcome. Goodnight, Lady Zephyra; rest well."

"Goodnight, Madam Lacrima."

She left me.

The room was as comfortable as promised, I thought, lying back in the silk blankets that made me think of water. From what I could make out in the dim light, it looked like Chelela had taken most of her belongings with her. The pale moon shone through a long window that was covered by sheer, silvery curtains, casting a milky hue about the whole room.

It felt strange to be sleeping in a giant bed all alone after spending so many nights on the hard ground next to Percifal. I should have been able to sleep with ease. Instead, I found myself tossing and turning beneath the covers.

I tried to quiet my mind, but dark thoughts of my time spent in Algor's dungeon kept creeping in. I decided to focus on something else, something happy—Percifal.

Without him, I would likely be dead, my body rotting away in that dungeon along with Mel's. He was the true hero in all of this, whether he believed it or not. I'd never felt so close to a man before. Actually, the only person I'd felt that close to was Adelaide. When all this was over, if we could beat King Zaeden—what would become of us? Would I go home to Solis and leave him here in Aquila? I felt a sharp pain inside at the thought.

Letting out a groan, I decided this wasn't working. My mind was simply too awake to let me sleep. I swung my legs over the bed and felt the cool stone beneath my bare feet. Perhaps a walk around the apartment would do me good. Surely everyone else was asleep by now.

I turned the knob, and the door opened with a creak. I jumped back with a squeak as a dark human-shaped shadow caught me off guard.

"Zephyra?"

I blinked hard a few times, trying to adjust my eyes to the dark hallway. "Percifal?"

"Apologies; I didn't mean to frighten you. I only wanted to check on you. I couldn't—"

"Couldn't sleep? I finished.

"Right."

"Me neither." I backed away, allowing him to enter the room.

His eyes were dark and serious as they held mine. Forgetting myself, I rushed to him, and we were suddenly locked in an embrace, his strong arms encircling me as our lips met.

Our kiss was long and heated with passion. His mouth felt soft and succulent as our lips parted and our tongues danced. I had never felt more alive. My heart beat fast with excitement; my eyes welled up with emotion.

Suddenly, I remembered myself and what had happened the last time I allowed myself to feel such passion. I broke away. "No—I can't. I'm sorry." I looked down, unable to meet his eyes.

He breathed heavily, trying to compose himself. When he spoke his voice came out rough. "No, I'm sorry. I just…the way you make me feel…"

I looked at him then and smiled reassuringly. "'Tis alright. I know. I feel the same."

He cupped my face, running his thumb across my jaw.

"Would you do one thing for me?" I asked.

"Anything."

"Would you lie with me until I fall asleep? I'm not used to being alone anymore. My mind, it won't leave me be."

"Of course."

I felt the heat from his body begin to relax my own as I placed a hand upon his chest and closed my eyes. He was now wearing only a white shirt and black trousers, having changed from his fancy doublet and breeches. I was able to feel the rhythm of his heart beat through the thin fabric.

It lulled me to sleep just as I heard him whisper, "I fear I'm falling in love with you…"

Chapter 32

I AWOKE TO sunlight beaming through the window, taking place of the moonlight from the night before. I lifted my head. Percifal was no longer there. He must have snuck away after I'd fallen asleep.

Stretching, his last words came rushing back to me. *"I fear I'm falling in love with you."* I sucked in a deep breath, feeling as though I needed more air. I knew we cared for each other, but I didn't know he had grown to love me. I had never been in love before.

Did I love him? I wasn't sure, but I hoped he would forgive me for not returning his words. I was in shock and was unsure of my own heart. After all I'd been through; I had never expected to find love.

My grandmother seemed so sure I would. I remembered her dying wish to me that I would wait for love and not marry out of duty, as my father did. Mayhap she was right; mayhap love had already found me. The thought made my stomach flip, and I couldn't stop myself from grinning.

A knock sounded at my door, interrupting my thoughts.

"Yes? You may enter," I called as the door opened with a creak, revealing a petite older woman with silver hair.

"Pardon me, Milady, but Madam Lacrima has asked me to give you this dress to wear."

So this must be the maid. I was beginning to wonder if she'd even existed. "Thank you. Please leave it on the chair. I shall dress myself."

"As you wish, Milady," she replied, setting it down and taking her leave.

Once I had donned the simple grey dress that was more appropriate for a slave, though a bit small for me, I made my way to the dining room to find Percifal and his mother breaking their fast.

Madam Lacrima gave me a bright smile and beckoned for me to take a seat beside her. "Good morning, Lady Zephyra. I hope you slept well."

"I did," I replied, taking my seat. I glanced at Percifal, who only inclined his head at me. I felt a tinge of guilt that I'd said nothing to his proclamation of love and took to studying the food Madam Lacrima put on my plate awkwardly. Percifal and his mother continued their conversation, which seemed to be about the trip we would be making to Chel's as soon as we were finished eating.

"If we take the northern route through the hills, we should be there before nightfall," Percifal stated, taking a bite of honeyed bread.

"Those steep cliffs leading out of Aquila are quite dangerous and will slow you down. I wish you would take the eastern route around the cliffs," his mother pleaded.

"We'll be fine, Mother. There's no ice upon the cliffs yet. And we'll be careful. You need not worry."

"It is not you I'm worried about." Madam Lacrima tilted her head towards me.

Before I had the chance to plead my case, a loud pounding at the front doors sounded throughout the apartment.

Madam Lacrima's brow furrowed. "We've delayed your departure too long, I fear."

The little old maid who had brought me the dress, which I could only guess was one of her own, entered with two guards in tow. Sir Dante must have opened his mouth about Percifal's return.

"Apologies, madam, but these men insisted." She gave them a scowl, causing the paper like skin on her face to crinkle.

"Sorry to disturb you, my lady," the taller of the two guards spoke. "King Zaeden has requested an audience with Percifal and his slave."

Damn! We should have left before dawn, I thought.

"Can this not wait? We are enjoying our first meal with my mother, as you can see," Percifal rose, standing over the guard. He was taller and broader than both guards, but there were two of them and only one of him. And they had weapons. Still, he held his ground, and I silently prayed they wouldn't restrain him.

The guard crossed his arms while his partner stood by idly, ready to help if needed. "Alright, King Zaeden has *demanded* an audience with you and your slave girl—immediately. I think you know what happens to those who defy him." He paused before adding, "Even those who were once like family to him."

"It seems we have no choice. Take us to see the king." He stood, grabbed my arm and hauled me out of my chair. Our charade was back on.

I was in utter shock, as I let him pull me out of the apartment, the guards leading the way.

The way he held me was firm, but not painful. I risked a glance at him and saw his eyes were cold and hard. He wouldn't spare me even a glance, keeping his eyes locked onto the space in front of him as we neared the main entrance to the palace.

The large doors were thrown open, allowing us entrance.

My mind whirling, I didn't notice much about my surroundings as I was all but dragged into the throne room.

"Your Majesty, Percifal Lacrima and his slave are here, as you asked," the guard announced and he and his comrade both bowed deeply.

The king, who sat upon his throne on the dais before us, was clad in blue velvet robes and sparkling jewels. A golden crown with sapphires on its spikes rested on his head of dark curls.

The room was well lit due to the daylight that the large arched windows let seep in.

Behind King Zaeden hung the royal coat of arms, which was the same design that the guards wore on their chests. That was all I saw before Percifal pulled me too my knees with him. I lowered my gaze to the blue carpet that we now knelt on.

"So it is true," the king confirmed. "The constable who abandoned his kingdom has returned with a slave. I was beginning to think you dead."

"Yes, Your Majesty. I assure you I only left on your behalf. I was hoping to tip the scales in our favour." Percifal rose but kept his hand on my back to keep me from rising with him.

My blood boiled, but I knew must keep up this act. On my knees I stayed, my gaze never leaving the floor. I bit my lip to keep the discomfort from my face, courtesy of the stone floor that jabbed into my knees from under the carpet.

Silence drew on, and I risked a glance at the king, only lifting my eyes and not my face. He steepled his fingers against his lips, deep in thought.

I felt Percifal stiffen at the king's next words. "A poor choice, that was. You say you left on our behalf, and yet you were never asked to do so. Nor would you have been allowed. We do not need the aid of those other imbeciles. No, after being gone for so long, we find we cannot trust you. Because your parents were so dear to us though, we shall not condemn you to death, as is custom. Guards, take Sir Lacrima to the dungeon. Give him one of the empty cells. See, your king is not so cruel as to even throw you in with all the other filthy criminals." He smiled at himself as I tried to get up off my knees in a panic.

Percifal's hand pressed down harder on my back, and I was unable to gain my feet. I glared up at him, but he wouldn't even spare one glance in my direction. He remained as icy and silent as a cold winter night while the guards came and took him.

"No!" I shouted when they pulled him away from me, finally allowing me to stand. But as soon as I stood, I found myself falling back on my knees again before the king, hands clasped in front of me.

I felt my heart sink, watching Percifal disappear from the room without even a fight, and a horrible thought occurred to me. I might never see my friend again. Friend? No; who was I kidding? I realized in that moment that he was more than just my friend. He loved me, and I loved him too, I thought, regretting not having told him so. "I beseech you, Your Majesty."

He looked down on me with a malicious smile. His eyes held no warmth. "Well, my dear girl, whatever is the matter? You should be gladdened. You are now free."

I quickly checked myself. If he knew I was friends with Percifal, he was likely to throw me in the dungeon along with him—or worse. If I ever wanted to see him again, I would have to make King Zaeden believe I was only a mere slave. That was my only chance in coming up with a plan to rescue him.

I lowered my gaze once again, "Apologies, Your Majesty. It is only that I know not what I shall do now—or where I shall go."

His gaze grew hard and he dropped his all formality. "I have much more important matters to worry about than what's to become of a slave girl who belonged to the man who betrayed me! Although," his expression softened, "I dare say, Lady Dulcina is quite lonely with her husband gone from this world and her daughter married off to my queen's cousin. And now even her son is rotting away in the dungeons. I'm sure she could use your services and company."

"Your Majesty is generous to think of Madam Lacrima." I decided to use flattery. "I shall take your good advice. My thanks, Your Majesty."

He waved a hand in dismissal. "Good. Now, off with you. Guards! Take this slave back to Lady Dulcina's apartment."

A guard took me by the arm and pulled me up and away from the king and his throne room. I let him drag me back willingly, too miserable to care.

Chapter 33

MADAM LACRIMA SAT listening to me in her drawing room, her lips pressed together as I revealed what had befallen her son.

When I finished all there was to say, she folded her hands in her lap and regarded me. "This is terrible. We can thank Celestia that King Zaeden hasn't ordered him executed, at least. Don't worry though, we shall free my son."

"I beg your pardon, madam, but I don't see how that's possible."

She looked pointedly at me. "You hold the power of fire, do you not?"

"Yes, but I don't have control over it yet. I—" I began, but she silenced me with a raised hand.

"That may be true now, but a visit to Sreda can change that." She raised her brows in earnest.

"But Sreda—"

"Is locked in the tower. Yes, I know. But that doesn't mean you can't pay her a visit."

"Surely the guards shan't let me see her if the king is indeed using her as you said."

"There's only one guard posted at the tower's entrance." She gave me a coy smile. "But don't worry about him; I shall make sure he never even sees you."

A puff of air escaped through my lips, and I felt my shoulders stiffen. "I don't know…"

"Just come to my chambers when the moon is at its peak and I shall take you to where Sreda is held."

A moment passed before I raised my chin and squared my shoulders, coming to my resolve. "Alright, Madam Lacrima. Percifal has saved my life twice. I must do whatever necessary to save his now."

"Good. Now, I have some things to take care of. You are welcome to bathe. I shall have my maid assist you. Meet me in the dining room for supper at sunset. We can discuss more then."

I nodded in agreement and left the room to take advantage of the bath I had been offered.

I hadn't been able to fully submerge myself in anything but a creek since the Golden Lilly. It felt wondrous to soak my whole body in warm clean water. Madam Lacrima's bath wasn't as large as the walk-in pools that royals used, but the copper tub was large enough that the water came up to my neck.

I tilted my head back as the maid, whose name was Pearl, poured lavender-scented water over my hair. I felt guilty taking such comforts while Percifal was left to rot in the king's dungeon. How he must hate me for not even telling him my feelings before he was taken away! So much so that he couldn't even look at me. I felt tears threaten as I resolved that I would tell him of my feelings as soon as I saw him.

If he died without ever knowing how I felt, I would never forgive myself. *No,* I thought, he wasn't going to die, because I was going to save him just as he had saved me.

Time seemed to stretch on forever before the sun finally set and I went to meet Percifal's mother for our final meal of the day; *mayhap my final meal on this earth,* I thought with dark sorrow.

I wasted no time with small talk. "So, just how do you plan to get me past the guard unnoticed?"

Madam Lacrima inclined her forehead as she took a bite of sweet potatoes before answering, "These guards…they don't get much attention from women. It shall be easy to distract one who is stuck sitting out at the tower night after night."

"Oh," I blushed, averting my eyes from her stare. "You would do that?"

"For my son's life, I would do anything."

I understood, because I felt the same way.

Wearing the black cloak Madam Lacrima had sent to my room, I tucked the loose tendrils of my red hair under the hood and knocked on her door. When she opened, it my breath caught at the sight of her.

I dare say, it would have been difficult for any man to resist her.

She looked like a mermaid, in a blue iridescent gown with a tight bodice that pushed up her pale white bosom. Her dark hair tumbled loosely in waves down her shoulders. Instead of a cloak, she wore a lighter blue cape that accented the dress.

She gave me a wicked smile as she caught me eying her. I could see where Percifal got his looks from.

"Come now. Follow me—and keep your hood up. We don't want anyone to see that bright red hair of yours, lovely as it is." As she walked past me, I caught a whiff of her fragrance, which smelled like roses and sandalwood.

I kept my silence as I followed her outside and towards the tower that held Sreda.

Without warning, she halted and held her hand out to stop me. Bending close to my ear, she whispered, "Wait here until you see me draw that guard away from the door. Once inside, go to the top of the tower. There you'll find Sreda in a barred cell."

I swallowed nervously, but gave her a curt nod.

"Good. Oh, and do try to make haste. I shall do what I can to keep the guard's attention for as long as possible, but eventually, he'll want to retain his position at his post."

"Of course, madam," I replied.

She patted my shoulder, then spun and made her way towards the tower, leaving me alone.

It wasn't long before I heard the sounds of giggling and flirting floating through the air. I kept a close watch from the shadows until I saw Madam Lacrima and the guard edging away from the door.

I crept quickly toward the tower; the sound of my heart was pounding so loudly in my ears, I thought the whole kingdom could hear it. Madam Lacrima and the guard were now out of sight, but I still held my breath as I tried the door.

It opened easily, and I slipped through, closing it behind me. I wasted no time once inside the dark tower, which smelled of thick layers of dust.

I found my way to the stairs and hustled up them as fast as my legs would carry me. When I reached the top, I was breathless. I bent forward, trying to regain air into my lungs.

"Well, well. Who do we have here?" a voice called out of the shadows, startling me.

I looked up and squinted, trying to adjust my eyes to the dark cell that was in the corner of the room."La—Lady Sreda?" I asked between breaths.

"Just Sreda. I'm no lady," the sorceress said, creeping up to the front of her cell. "Come here, child. Let me look at you."

I slowly made my way to her cell and pulled back my hood, peering at her behind the bars. The sorceress looked to be the same age as Madam Lacrima, though her hair was white as snow, and her silvery eyes seemed to hold all the wisdom of the world in them. I believed she was a lot older than she appeared.

She smiled warmly at me. "Daughter of Celestia, Lady of Fire. At last you have come."

"You know me?" I frowned in confusion. How could this be?

"Aye, I've been waiting for you. I've known you would come for many seasons; I just didn't know when. Thank Celestia you're finally here to help save us. Time is of the essence now."

Her words brought me back to my current task, and I remembered I hadn't time to waste. The guard could be back at the door any moment, and then this would have all been for nothing. "Ah well, actually, I can't control my power yet. I was hoping you might be able to help me so I can save Percifal."

"Percifal! Is he alright?" Her look of concern was humble.

"Yes—er—well, he shall be if I can get him out of the dungeon."

"Oh dear. Yes, of course I can help you with that. Tell me first, what is your name, child?"

"I am Lady Zephyra Caldura."

"Caldura of Solis. Of course there would be power running through your veins. Now come here, Zephyra, and take my hands."

I did as she bade and grasped her calloused hands in my own. I was surprised by their strength, even more surprised when I felt the shock of power pass through them and into me.

"Close your eyes," she ordered. "The power that's coursing through you, do you feel it?"

"Y—yes," my voice shook. It felt like my whole body was on fire, though I felt no burning sensation upon my skin.

"This power you're feeling, take it in, and when you feel you can take no more, push it out. Do not think, do *not* hesitate, just feel."

I felt the power fill me up until I thought I would burst from the inside. Suddenly, white light flashed behind my eyes, and I pushed from somewhere deep within myself. I opened my eyes to see flames erupt from my palms.

Sreda pulled back.

She looked at me with approval. "Good girl. You see, you do have the ability to control your power. It just needed to be awakened. It seems you had suppressed it. It'll take practice to fully control it, but that should come easier now."

I was speechless at what I had just accomplished. Never had I been able to call upon the fire unless I felt the strongest of emotions. I could barely believe what had just happened.

Shaking my head, remembering what my some of my emotions could also do, I asked, "But how do I control the power when my emotions run strong and the fire burns against my will?"

"Quite the same way. Only instead of pushing it out, you must push it down back into your depths. Concentrate on controlling your emotions. Your power is connected to them right now. Once you have more control of your power, keeping the two apart will come naturally."

I let out a sigh and rested my forehead against the cell door. "I will do my best. Much gratitude, Sreda. I must go now before the guard returns and I get caught."

"It is you and the others who hold the power of the elements who are owed thanks. Only the elementals will be able to beat King Zaeden once he has Vesirus by his side," she said gravely.

I froze, her words turning my blood cold. "The dark lord? Of Mnyama?" I asked in horror.

"I'm sorry, child, but yes, King Zaeden has found a way to channel my power. I would end my own life to save this world, but he won't let that happen."

I could see the regret in her eyes, so I sought to reassure her before I turned back down the stairs. "I shall find Chelela, and we shall stop King Zaeden." I said the words with more conviction than I felt.

She gave me a solemn nod in return. It seemed she had more faith in me than I myself had. I hoped I wouldn't fail her and the rest of Sarantoa.

At least Sreda was being kept comfortable in the tower. It was far from the nightmarish dungeon I had spent my time in, and the one I imagined Percifal was being kept in now.

I peered out the door before exiting the tower. Madam Lacrima was pacing back in forth, waiting for me. To my relief, there was no guard in sight. I stepped out of the tower and met eyes with her. Wasting no time, she grabbed ahold of my wrist and pulled me away from the tower.

Once the tower was out of sight, I asked breathlessly, "The guard?"

"He fell asleep, but could wake at any moment. Was Sreda able to help you with your power?"

"She was. I believe I can control my power enough now to use it to save Percifal." I bit my lip and looked away, suddenly unsure of myself. "At least, I hope I can."

Startling me, Madam Lacrima took ahold of my shoulders. "You *must,* or we are all doomed. You understand? He needs to take you to Chel."

Swallowing hard, I managed only to nod. There was a lot resting on my shoulders. As selfish as it was, I would be glad to have someone else to share this burden with.

"Good. We haven't a moment to waste. I'll take you to the dungeon now. From there, I shall leave you to make preparations for your journey to Cansbroke."

"Alright."

"Come now, follow me," she beckoned with impatience.

Madam Lacrima led me through the dark courtyard, which was abandoned this late at night. The sky was cloudless, and I shivered as we crept around to the back of the palace. I knew not if it was due to the frigid air of the season or the circumstance that lay before me. Perhaps it was both that caused me to quiver like a leaf in the wind.

Madam Lacrima stopped when we came to a small iron door. "No guards are ever posted here, but the door is always locked. It is time to call on your power to open it."

"But how? These bars are made from iron."

"Try to melt the lock, my dear."

I inclined my head at her in sudden understanding. I hadn't thought to use my power in such a way. The thought of melting something had not occurred to me, though it did make sense. I only hoped my power wouldn't get away from me and engulf Madam Lacrima in flames.

I had to try. There was no other choice. Taking a deep breath, I turned my attention to the door. I shut out all thoughts and focused on the warmth that was glowing at my core. Feeling it beginning to grow, I pulled at it harder and harder, until the world slipped away and there was only myself and the hot white light that was a part of my very soul.

It grew brighter and hotter, until I could contain it no longer. It was then that my eyes shot open and I focused all of that white, hot energy at the lock on the door. Placing my hand over the iron lock, I pushed at the energy within me with everything I had. To my surprise, the iron beneath my hand grew red with heat before turning yellow then white, and liquid molten dripped down the door.

I stepped back, my eyes wide. The lock was now completely melted away. I couldn't believe I'd actually done it.

It seemed Madam Lacrima had no doubt that I could do it. She looked at me with a big smile. "Good work. Now, this is where I must leave you."

I turned toward her to protest. "You would send me down there alone?"

"This is a task for only you, Zephyra. Besides, as I said, I must make preparations for your journey. I'll be waiting out here for you when you get out."

"But what if I fail?"

"You shall not, but if you did, I would still be here awaiting you. If I'm not here when you return, go to the stables, get on a horse and get away from Aquila."

"Yes, madam." I bowed my head and she left me.

I sucked in a deep, shaky breath of the cool night air to steady my nerves. Then I placed both palms on the door and pushed it open.

CHAPTER 34

THE AIR INSIDE of the poorly lit dungeon felt thick. Only a few torches flickered on the walls as I descended the slimy stairs that took me deeper and deeper below ground. I shivered in anticipation and pulled my cloak tighter around myself.

Once I reached the bottom, I froze. I couldn't stop myself from remembering being locked in Algor's dungeon. *What am I doing?* I began to question myself. *How can I go back into such a place?*

Fear coursed through every fiber of my being as dark thoughts drifted through my mind. What if I got trapped there and could never escape? I would die, and no one else, save Madam Lacrima would ever know what happened to me. I wondered if she would come to rescue me and Percifal if that happened. *Percifal…I must save him.* I couldn't just leave him down here. Besides, I didn't think I could continue on this journey without him by my side.

I took a deep breath of the musty air and tried to block out all thoughts, except the ones that told me I must save Percifal. If I couldn't save him, I must tell him how I feel. The memory of our last moment together was gnawing away at me. The way he wouldn't even look at me after having confessed he was falling for me just the night before. I couldn't let him die down here, believing I didn't feel the same way.

Determination pushed my feet forward, one step at a time. As I began to make out the shape of cells along each side, I donned my hood and grabbed a torch off the wall.

Sounds of moaning and crying came from some of the cells. Some even noticed me and rattled their bars, calling out to me with desperation. I winced and I walked on, not sparing them a glance. The smell was even worse. I had to use my cloak to cover my nose from the scent of the awful body odours. There were so many prisoners down there. A lot of the cells held half a dozen men and women. I ignored those, remembering that the king had ordered Percifal to be locked in a cell by himself. Still, it seemed nearly impossible to locate him in this never-ending cave of death.

I decided the only way I would find him would be to call for him. This would surely draw more attention than I wanted, but it was necessary.

"Percifal?" I whispered, loudly at first, then paused to listen. No answer.

"Percifal!" I called louder this time.

At last, I heard movement from a cell in a back corner of the dungeon. I raced up to it and grabbed onto the bars and peered in, hope fluttering in my chest. "Percifal? Is that you?" I placed the torch I was holding in a bracket on the wall and turned back to the cell.

"Zephyra?" He asked in a tired voice.

I threw back my hood and laughed with joy, feeling my eyes well up. "Yes, it is I. Oh Percifal! Thank Celestia I've found you."

He came slowly up to the front of the cell and looked upon me. "Phyra, what are you doing here? Are you insane? You must leave at once. If anyone see's you here, you'll be thrown in here with me."

"No, I'm quite sane. I just couldn't let you die in here without telling you that I—that I—"

"That you what, have a death wish?"

I threw my head back in exasperation, annoyed at myself for stalling, and at him for thinking me unable to take care of myself. "No, that I *love* you." Tears I couldn't stop spilled over as I said the words.

He placed his hands on the bars. "Truly?" he asked, his voice now soft.

I nodded and was suddenly unable to stop my words from spilling out, words that I'd been holding back for longer than I had realized. "Yes! So much so that I was afraid—afraid of loving you because I have never loved anyone like this in my whole entire life.

"When you told me how you felt the night before you were taken I knew I should've told you, and then you were taken. I thought I'd lost my chance and you would die never knowing the truth." I choked on a sob and looked away.

"Shh, it's alright. Honestly, I didn't even know you had heard me when I told you I was falling in love with you. I thought you'd fallen asleep. I know it was cowardly of me to only speak those words when I thought you wouldn't hear them, but I'm glad you feel the same way. Still, this is no place for you. You should leave now, before it's too late."

Frustrated with myself for forgetting my mission, and for babbling on about my feelings, I tore my hands away and shook myself. "That's not the only reason I have come. I'm here to get you out."

"The only way you could do that is if you obtained a key from one of the guards."

"That's not the only way. I've seen Sreda, and she has shown me my power," I said with my chin held high. I felt more confident since I had melted the lock on the door outside than I ever had before.

"Sreda? But she is locked in the tower."

"Yes, but I had help from your mother. She's a sly one. But never mind all that. We don't have time right now. I must get you out of here."

"Alright, alright." He put his hands up. "But if this doesn't work, you must promise me you'll leave and go find my sister without me."

I thought for a moment before answering. I decided I wouldn't fail, so I agreed. "I promise. Now back up. I still don't have full control of my power yet and I don't want to harm you."

He backed against the back wall of the cell.

I closed my eyes, placing my hands over the bars as I had on the lock of the entrance door, and concentrated.

At first, nothing happened. I felt my heart begin to race, but I knew if I let myself panic I'd lose control. So I squeezed my eyes shut harder and took slow deep breaths, trying to focus everything I had on the power within me. Percifal remained silent.

I began to feel the heat, which was becoming familiar, growing from within myself. I focused on my white hot center, coxing it forth. Once that heat filled my whole being, I opened my eyes and focused everything I had on the bars beneath my hands. Slowly, the bars turned red with heat before turning lighter shades and then melted into liquid molten, just like the lock had, leaving a space large enough for Percifal to escape through.

I stood frozen, stunned that I had done it. I had actually used my power to set Percifal free!

Standing there like a fool, I was startled when Percifal rushed through the space and gripped me in a tight embrace. "You did it! Zephyra, you've figured out how to use your power!"

I blinked back tears, griping him tightly in my arms, something I feared I'd never do again. "I love you, Percifal Lacrima. Don't you ever leave me again."

"I love you too. And I won't. We should make haste though."

I nodded, remembering. "Indeed. Your mother is awaiting us."

He took my hand, and we ran past the cells and back up the dungeon stairs to the door, prisoners yelling at us to free them the whole way. As afraid as I was of them, I couldn't help but feel some sorrow for them. They would never again see the light of day. I knew what it felt like to feel that hopelessness. But there was no time to pause.

When we burst out the door, Madam Lacrima was waiting with Sunny, who was saddled and ready. She held Percifal's sword in one hand.

Seeing us, she cried out with glee and embraced the both of us before taking Percifal by the shoulders and kissing his cheek. "My son, you are safe. Thank you, Zephyra. I owe you a debt for this."

"'Tis not necessary," I replied with a shake of my head. "I would do anything for him." I decided to add with a smile, "We have grown to love each other."

She beamed down at me, letting Percifal free. "That brightens my heart. Nonetheless, should you ever need anything, you may call on me."

"Thank you, madam." I bowed my head.

"Now you must be off. I fear it shan't be long before the guards realize what has happened here. I'm sure the king will conclude that magic was involved in Percifal's escape." She flicked her hair over her shoulder then added, "I was only able to get one horse without raising suspicion so you'll have to ride together. There's food and water in the saddle bags."

Percifal pressed his lips tightly together and then gave a curt nod before giving his mother a quick peck on the cheek. "Thank you, Mother." He turned and helped me onto Sunny before he placed himself in the saddle behind me.

"Don't thank me. Just return safely to me, both of you."

"We shall do our best." My voice sounded more confident than I felt.

"Farwell for now." She let go of the reins and we were off.

I hoped if I ever came back to Aquila, it would be on better terms.

Chapter 35

I WAS GRATEFUL Percifal had grown up in Aquila and knew ways to slip from the kingdom unseen. As soon as Lacrima was out of site, I felt him relax, a little.

I didn't want to take that away from him, but I knew I had to tell him about the conversation I had with Sreda.

"There's something else you need to know." I said with a sigh.

He stiffened at my words. "What is it?"

I bit my lip and hesitated. I decided there was no easy way to say it so I just came straight out with it. "She told me King Zaeden is working with Vesirus."

He pulled Sunny to a halt so fast, I almost flew off his back. "She what? No, that's impossible. If he's working with Vesirus there's no way you or Chel is getting involved."

"We have to. Believe me, I'd rather not, but Sreda foresaw the elementals being the ones to stop him." I turned so I could look up at him. His expression was grim and he shook his head.

"When I thought we were going against a mere mortal, I thought we had a chance, but now…he will kill us all."

"That is why we must stop him. We are the only ones who *can.* Otherwise, yes, he will surely kill us all."

He let out a groan of frustration and urged Sunny back into a walk. "I'm beginning to dislike Celestia's choice in elementals, but who am I to defy our goddess. I'm with you until the bitter end then, if it comes to that."

"I hope not," was all I could think to say.

He decided to change the subject, which I was glad for. "The terrain is a bit rough the way we are going, but sleep if you can, and I will get us to Cansbroke," he spoke into my ear.

"I shall try." I leaned closer to him and tilted my head back against his shoulder, glad for his warmth. The air held the biting chill of autumn.

I only able to sleep for a few moments at a time, for the terrain was indeed rough and bumpy, causing me to startle into wakefulness each time the horse stumbled. Up and down the steep cliffs we trod. I felt sorry for Sunny, who willingly did as Percifal asked, taking us the quickest and most hidden way possible to his sister's new home.

We paused only once when we were through the cliffs, and only then to water ourselves and Sunny before we were off again through the countryside.

Not realizing I had fallen into a light sleep, I was startled when we came to an abrupt stop just outside of the iron gates that stood in the entrance to a smaller palace, which was dark with slumber. I noted that dawn would come soon as the sky was beginning to awaken with its first light to the east.

"Who hales at this time of morning?" a voice grumbled from the other side of gate.

"It is Percifal Lacrima, brother to Chelela of Cansbroke. I wish to see my sister."

Silence followed for a moment. I began to wonder if the guard had fallen asleep when he finally answered, "I will let you through, but your sister's not here." The heavy gates then opened as we dismounted Sunny.

Percifal grabbed the man by the front of his tunic and peered into his face. "What do you mean, she's not *here?* Where *is* she?"

The burly guard held his hands up in surrender, "Whoa—ho ho. It's not my place to say. You'll have to speak to the new Duke about that."

Percifal held on to the guard for another moment, until I placed a gentle hand on his arm. Releasing the large but unintimidating guard he said, "Alright. Hold our horse while I seek out your master. We'll not be long."

As we started towards the quiet palace, the guard called out behind us, "Weapons are not permitted to guests."

"Then it's a good thing I'm family," Percifal shot over his shoulder.

I remained silent, praying to Celestia that his sister was only away on some sort of errand or visiting friends, and something horrible hadn't happened. My gut told me the latter was more likely.

Coming up to the large bronze-etched doors, I stood back while Percifal gave a thunderous knock and yelled at the top of his lungs, "Hello! I wish to speak with the Duke!"

Shortly after, a skinny middle aged man with a receding hair line opened the door. Bleary eyed, he yawned, "Who calls at this—"

He didn't get out the rest of the words before Percifal brought his sword up to rest beside his throat. The man's eyes were now as round as the full moon.

"Take me to your master," Percifal said in a low voice that left no room for disobedience.

I shivered, feeling the icy rage coming off Percifal.

"Yes, my lord. If you will follow me right this way," the servant's voice shook as he beckoned slowly with one hand.

Percifal released his majestic sword from the man's throat and pointed it at his back when the man turned to lead us. "Alright, but try anything, and I'll run you through."

We followed the cowering servant through the palace, which was dark save the torch he held in one hand. Down a long purple carpeted hall and to the right was a large golden door. That's where we stopped.

The servant turned around to face us in a pose of surrender. "This is the Duke's chamber. What would you have me do now?"

"Step aside," Percifal answered before banging on the door with his fist. "Get up, Sir Cansbroke, or I shall end your servant's life outside your door and burn your palace to the ground." He said the last part with a glance at me.

I shuddered. It was an empty threat. Even if I could burn the whole palace down, I simply wouldn't. Who knew how many innocent lives would be taken if the palace were set aflame? Surely there were other servants and maids there who'd done nothing wrong.

It didn't matter anyway. The next instant, the duke opened the door in his night shift with his own sword in hand. Both men's swords came to each other's throats. The forgotten servant stood frozen behind me.

"Who dares enter my household at this time of night with a weapon and threaten me?" the duke, Asked with a sneer. He looked disheveled, his dark mass of curls all out of sorts.

I knew I did not like this man right away. He reminded me of a rat, who only cared for himself. It seemed Madam Lacrima had made a poor choice for her daughter when seeking her husband. I couldn't believe she would deem her daughter to a fate with this man.

"I have come in search of my sister, Chelela. I've been told she's not here. So do tell me, where is she?"

"Ah, that." He raised an eyebrow and gave a smile filled with malice, keeping his sword raised. "If you lay down your weapon, I'll tell you."

Percifal paused for a moment. "If I let mine down, you will do so as well?"

"That's fair."

Slowly, both men lowered their swords. Nonetheless, I still felt tension in the air and couldn't relax. The scent of sweet incense wafted out from the bedchamber. It made my stomach turn.

"I'm sorry to inform you that you're correct, your sister's not here.

Unfortunately, my brother, who was her husband, took to illness and left our world two full moons ago. He left everything to me. I had no use for your sister, so I—" he paused with a pensive look before continuing on. "—I sold her. You see, I had no use for her, and—"

Either this man was stupid or overly confident in his own skill.

"You—you *what?*" Percifal raised his sword instantly. I had never seen him so furious, his face twisted and red with rage.

It pains me to say that in that moment, even I was afraid of him, but I knew I had to intervene, or else he would kill this man before he even told us who he'd sold Chelela to.

Gathering up more courage than I felt was in me, I said in a stern voice, "Percifal, *stop!* Killing this poor excuse of a man won't help us find your sister."

At first, it seemed as though he hadn't heard me; then he lowered his sword, just a little and said, "Alright then. So tell me, who exactly did you sell her to?"

"T—to some important man from Gwon." His voice shook as he held up his hands; his sword now lay on the floor by his feet.

"I need a name. Give me a name," Percifal demanded through gritted teeth.

"I believe his name was—Jehvad? He sells girls for their—er—talents." He winced as he spoke the last words.

So just stupid, I thought. My first guess was right.

"You sold her as a *sex slave?*"

Before the man could answer, or I could even blink, Percifal stuck his sword right through the duke's throat. I stood there shocked as the duke's eyes widened in horror. Percifal pulled his sword out of the duke's throat in one swift motion. The duke gargled on his own blood before crumpling to the floor with a loud *THUD.*

Before I could gather my wits, Percifal took ahold of my hand and led me away from the bloody scene and out of the palace. I walked behind him, my mind in shock at what had just happened.

The sky outside was now a lighter shade, which I noticed right before I bent over and wretched on the dewy grass. I felt like I was in a nightmare. Perhaps the duke deserved to die, but I still didn't like being there to witness it. I felt I didn't know this side of Percifal and hoped I wouldn't see it again anytime soon. If Percifal and the guard exchanged words when he took Sunny back, I did not hear them.

About to help me mount, Percifal took notice of my distressed state. Taking my shoulders, he looked into my eyes with…compassion? There wasn't a trace left of the rage that'd over taken his features as he ended the duke's life. It seemed to be replaced now with worry and fatigue.

"Zephyra," he whispered gently. "I'm sorry that you had bear witness to such bloodshed again, but we must go."

"Go?" I looked up at him with confusion. Chelela was gone. What were we to do now? "Where?" I asked dumbfounded.

"To Gwon. I have to save Chel from whatever hell she's in before we can even try to stop King Zaeden."

I put my face in my hands, squeezing my eyes shut. The whole world was suddenly spinning. Of course we must find Chelela first, but how much more could we bear? How did I get messed up in all of this madness? I was just a girl from Solis—just a queen's shadow of a cousin. Since when did my destiny have so much purpose? Oh yes, when Celestia saw fit to bless me with the power of fire. In that moment it all just felt like too much. I felt more cursed than blessed and I'm ashamed to say that I wanted to give up right then and there.

Percifal seemed to read my thoughts, and offered, "Listen, if this is too much for you, I can go find Chel, and you can stay in Aquila with my mother until we return—"

"No!" I cut him off, finally coming to my senses. I took a deep breath and continued, "No, I'm coming with you. You may need my power, besides, 'tis no longer safe for me in Aquila. I'm just not used to so much death."

"For that, I wish I could say I'm sorry, but I had to end him for what he did to Chel. He sold her like she was some *cow* for him to make a good fortune from."

"I understand why you did it. That doesn't make it any easier though. Now help me up so we can leave this awful place behind."

He did as I bade, and then got up behind me.

We rode in silence, and I didn't question our direction until the welcome sign to Ambedar came into view.

Exhausted; my voice sounded gravelly to my own ears, "Ambedar? Is it safe for us here?"

"I have a friend here who owes me a favour. Don't worry. We'll not be visiting any inns or taverns where I might be recognized this time."

"Oh." I didn't have the strength to question further.

I felt Percifal's strong arms tighten around me. He kissed the delicate spot behind my ear and spoke in a soft voice. "I am truly sorry for all that you've had to bear. I hope you know I won't let harm come to you though."

I felt goosebumps rise on my skin at his gentle touch. "I know. I'm just tired."

He squeezed me tighter in reply before reining Sunny to a halt. "Ah, here we are."

We had stopped at a small wood cabin right by the sea. I could taste the salt in the air as the wind blew off the endless body of water and whipped at my face and hair.

As soon as Percifal and I dismounted, he began removing our saddle bags and tack from Sunny.

"Well, here is where your journey with us ends, my friend," Percifal said to our dark horse as he patted his neck and set him free.

"You're just going to let him go?" I stood disbelieving.

"The sea is no place for a horse, and the admiral has nowhere to keep him for us. We'll purchase a new horse when we need one."

I raised an eyebrow, watching Sunny trot off. "I sincerely hope he finds a good new master to take care of him."

"He'll be fine. Come now, let's get out of the cold."

I nodded and followed him up to the small cabin.

Percifal wasted no time with knocking. He swung open the door and called in, "Admiral Ruess! I know you're in there, you filthy bastard!"

Silence…and then, "Who hales there?" called a gruff voice from within.

"It's your good old friend from Aquila."

"I have no—wait, Lacrima? Is that you?" The admiral came forth. He was a stout man with salt and pepper hair and a beard to match. I guessed him to be near his sixth decade, though his icy blue eyes still looked sharp with wisdom.

Percifal chuckled as the admiral embraced him and thumped him on the back in a friendly manner.

"By heavens, Lacrima, I thought I'd never set eyes on you again."

"You cannot get rid of me that easily, Admiral."

The admiral stepped back and took notice of me. "And who is this pretty lassie?"

"Admiral Ruess, this is Lady Zephyra from Solis."

Admiral Ruess bent forward, taking my hand, and planted a big wet kiss upon it. "It's a pleasure to meet you, my beautiful lady."

I grinned at him, feeling my cheeks grow warm. "The pleasure is mine, Admiral. Percifal tells me you two are friends."

"Aye, that we are." He eyed Percifal and then gave me a wink. "Perhaps I'll tell you that story later. It looks like you both have been to the ends of the earth and back, hey? Please make use of my washing basin."

"Do we smell so bad that a man of the sea is telling us we need to bathe?" Percifal wrinkled his nose in distaste.

"Well, the lady doesn't, but you, on the other hand…"

Percifal held up his hands in defense and laughed. "Well, I did just come from a dungeon. Give me a break."

"Now *that* is a story you must tell me."

"Alright. I'll catch you up while Zephyra takes use of the washing basin first."

I took that as my cue and asked, "Where am I to find this washing basin, Admiral?"

"Ah, yes, it's right this way." He beckoned me to follow him towards the back of the cabin, to a small closet which held the basin.

Percifal followed and handed me one of our saddle bags. "I noticed my mother packed you some clean dresses. I figure you might want some fresh attire."

"Thank you." I gave him a coy smile. He returned it with a warm smile of his own.

"My room's just over there. I'm sure you need rest, so feel free to use it," the Admiral offered, breaking my warm thoughts of Percifal.

I bowed my head in thanks, and the two men left me to catch up on the previous events.

The water in the basin was cool, but it felt good to wash the filth from my skin nonetheless. When I was finished and donned the simple, light blue dress that Madam Lacrima had given me, I stole quietly into the Admiral's bedchamber and took up his offer for rest.

Just a quick rest, I told myself. I just needed to rest my body and close my eyes for a moment. As soon as I closed my eyes, sleep claimed my exhausted self though. The next thing I knew, movement stirred me awake. I cracked my eyes open and saw Percifal peering down at me.

He must have finished telling Admiral Ruess our story and cleaned up himself. His hair was damp, and his face now shaven. The sight of him quickened my heart and stole the breath from my lungs.

The corners of his lips curled up, seeing that I had awoken. He gently kissed my forehead. "You look like a goddess who has just awoken from her slumber."

I blushed. Not knowing how to answer such endearments, I changed the subject. "So is Admiral Ruess going to take us to Gwon?"

His brow creased and I made room for him to sit on the bed by me. "Yes, though it wasn't easy to convince him."

"I thought he owed you a favour?"

"He does, but he argued that taking us across the sea when winter is nay upon us is no favour but a death wish."

I swallowed my fear and ignored the part about a death wish. "So why did he owe you a favour anyways?"

"Let's just say the only reason he has a ship now is because of me."

"Oh," was all I said as he brushed my hair from my face. The touch sent quivers of pleasure throughout my entire body.

"He only agreed because I told him it was to rescue Chel."

"Well, at least he agreed in the end."

"Yes. We leave at dusk, and then we are going to be at the mercy of the sea. I'm sorry you must risk your life for my sister," he apologized. His expression told me he was serious.

"Don't be. I'm risking it for all of us. Besides, if I'm to die, at least it is for a good reason—and I'll have you by my side."

At that, he took my face in his gentle hands and kissed me deeply. Flames coursed through my veins and warmed my very soul as we slowly peeled off each other's clothes and explored one another's bodies. For a moment, I worried that I might set us all on fire, but the warmth at my core was soothed to a warm glow by Percifal's touch. And when I finally let him take me, I didn't regret it.

I smiled to myself afterwards, feeling happier than I ever had in my whole life. We both fell into slumber in each other's arms, lulled by the sound of the waves outside the cabin.

Chapter 36

WHEN I AWOKE, the sunlight outside of the small window had transformed into darkness. The only light came from a candle that burned low on the table across the room. I heard a rustling beside me and rolled over to see Percifal donning his dark blue tunic. He looked quite refined.

He caught me eyeing him up and chuckled, "Keep looking at me like that and we're never going to make it onto that ship."

"It's just that you're so beautiful. I simply cannot help myself," I said innocently, batting my lashes at him. That earned me another laugh.

"Be that as it may, the admiral has *The Blue Angel* ready and waiting."

I sat up and yawned. "I'm quite looking forward to sailing, actually. I once dreamt of adventures to faraway places. Only, I'm sorry for the circumstances for which we're travelling," I added as an afterthought. Surely he wasn't excited about having to travel to a foreign land to rescue his sister.

"Well, I hope the sailing is smooth and the weather is in our favour. Come here, and I'll help you with your dress."

I went to him, thankful that this dress only had buttons and not suffocating stays. He finished with the buttons that went up the back of the dress and smiled in awe. "It seems blue is your colour. It suits you well."

"You think so?" I beamed at him. I always hated the way my own kingdom's colours looked on me. Perhaps I was meant to wear Aquila's. I gave him a wink, and he took my arm and led me out to *The Blue Angel.*

It wasn't a large ship by any means, but it looked sturdy and had rippling pale blue sails that caught the chilly wind blowing off the sea. We didn't need much room anyways. There were only four of us, including myself, Percifal, Admiral Ruess and his first mate, who we called 'Hobbles.' I guessed he'd earned his name from the way he limped when he walked. He was a kind, scrawny man, whom I quickly grew to like.

Unfortunately, the sailing wasn't very smooth. The excitement I'd felt at the notion of sailing soon gave way to a bout of seasickness that took me days to shake. The sickly scent of fish wafting through the air didn't help either. While I spent most of my time below deck feeling nauseous, Percifal spent his above, helping Admiral Ruess and Hobbles man *The Blue Angel* through the treacherous winds that the admiral had warned us about. When he wasn't helping up above deck, he was comforting me and holding my hair as I got sick into a metal bucket. I felt guilt that he had to worry about me while also helping the other two get us to Gwon in one piece.

One night, we sailed through a storm so treacherous, I feared we wouldn't make it out alive. Heavy winds slammed *The Blue Angel* hard against the water, rain pelted down upon us in buckets, and lightening hit dangerously close. The others made me wait below while they tried to take back control of the ship; saying that I would be of most help if they didn't have to worry about me. Who was I to argue with them? It wasn't like I had the power of wind or water to aid them. Fire would do no good in a storm.

Chelela would have been able to help us, but she wasn't here. Feeling useless, I did the only thing that I could think to do; I prayed to Celestia for mercy. As we began to lose hope that we would make it out alive, the clouds finally broke and the wind died down. It seemed our goddess had answered my prayers. I came up above deck as I felt the ship steady. The moon suddenly appeared as a beacon to light our way, as if Celestia herself was guiding our way. I gave her a silent prayer of gratitude.

After that night, it was only two more sunrises until I heard Hobbles bellow, "Land! I see land!"

I rushed up to the stern to join the others; my stomach had finally gotten used to the movement of the sea beneath us. What looked to be an island was growing closer and closer.

"Is that Gwon?" I could barely dare to let myself hope.

"Aye, that's Gwon, Milady," the admiral answered, in awe himself.

I laughed with glee. We had actually done it! We had made it to Gwon in one piece.

Percifal embraced me as tears of joy streamed down my face. His strong arms encircling me made me feel we could do anything, as long as we were together. We'd escaped King Zaeden's dungeon and braved the winter sea to reach Gwon successfully. Now all we had to do was find Chel, and she would help us find a way to stop King Zaeden. As Percifal peered down at me with those warm aqua eyes of his, I knew this was my destiny.

EPILOGUE

I SAT ON a wooden stool in what must have been our twentieth dim and musty tavern, filled with noisy, stinking men.

Percifal sat across from me, looking defeated as he stared into his mug of ale. "It's hopeless, I swear we have been to every brothel, every tavern—every *corner* of this damn island and still, there's been no sign of my sister."

"I know, but what other choice do we have but to keep looking? I'm sure she must have escaped and is hiding someplace we don't know of. 'Tis the only feasible explanation," I offered, touching his forearm to comfort him. It pained me to see him this way.

He looked at me with such regret that I almost winced. "No. It's not the only *feasible explanation.* She could also be dead." He slammed his mug down and squeezed his eyes shut in pain.

His words were so blunt, I had to look away to hide the hurt in my own eyes.

He noticed it anyways. "Forgive me. I don't mean to take it out on you. I only wish we could find Chel, but time's running out, and the more time we spend here the more time King Zaeden has to—"

"Did you say Chel?" a sultry feminine voice interrupted from somewhere behind me.

We both turned to see a tall woman with sleek, sable coloured hair standing with her hands on her hips. From the look of her, she was well off, and I guessed, not afraid of much in this world. Her tight leather corset showed off her bountiful bosom, and the golden jewelry around her wrists and neck glittered in the low tavern lamp light. She had full, dark pink lips and cat like eyes, and I'm sure, if her black skirts weren't hiding them, I would find her legs to be lean and muscular like the rest of her body.

I found my voice before Percifal. "And if we are, would you be able to tell us anything?"

"I might—for a price."

"Name your price," Percifal spoke before I could answer myself.

She gave a sly smile and turned her dark gaze towards Percifal. For a moment, I was worried she would name him as her price, but then she tilted her head and said, "Your sword. That's my price."

His eyes widened at the same time I gave her a stern, "No!"

"Zephyra—" Percifal began.

"You cannot," I cut him off. "That sword is important to you and we might yet need it."

"My sister is *more* important to me. And we can find another weapon. Besides, we have you." He eyed me, and I knew he referred my powers.

I rolled my eyes and gave in. "What does a whore need with a sword anyways?"

My words only seemed to amuse the woman more. She smiled wider and bent down to whisper in my ear, "This *whore* needs to protect herself. She also knows where your man's sister is. So bite your tongue, *my lady*."

She was mocking me, but before I could retort Percifal cut in, "The sword is yours; forgive my lady for her rudeness. Now tell me where Chelela is. Please."

"Alright." She straightened. "But not here. Follow me."

We did as she bade. A few eyes peered at us as we made our way towards the back of the tavern, but when our guide winked at them they looked away, blushing. To others, it looked like we were her customers. *Let them think that.* I thought to myself. It was a good cover.

We followed her to a wine cellar that was hidden from the regular customers. Once inside, she checked to make sure we were alone and then turned and held out her hand for the sword.

"First tell us what you know of Chelela," Percifal said, keeping his sword by his side.

"Alright then, but try to leave without giving me the sword, and I will scream and others will come to my aid. And then you will be taken to

Khadji for harming one of his precious *courtesans*." She raised her chin and stared into Percifal's eyes. I had no doubt she was telling the truth.

I bit my lip and decided to keep my mouth shut.

"You have my word that the sword is yours, once you have given us all the information you know about Chelela."

She held out her hand again, but this time, for Percifal's own. He took it and they shook on their agreement.

She sighed before starting and began to pace as she spoke. "I worked with Chel for a time. She was new and foreign to this land. I felt bad for her, so I helped her learn the trade. I told her it was her only hope of remaining alive, because in Gwon if you are bought as a whore and can't do your job properly, you are discarded. You're a mouth that's not worth feeding."

I saw Percifal grow cold at the woman's words so. Afraid he would end her like he had the duke, I asked, "We've checked all the brothels and taverns in Gwon. She's nowhere to be found. So where is she?"

"If you would let me finish," she replied, obviously annoyed, and then continued on in her singsong voice. "Once she figured out that strength came with knowledge of the trade, because that's when men are at their weakest, she escaped. How? I'm not sure. I've heard stories that she killed a man and disappeared to the sea. If it is true, I know not. I only know that Chel is no longer working as a whore. Some say they have spotted her at Alden's Cove, where there are myths of Sirens being sighted. Seems fitting for a runaway whore, if you ask me." Her laugh was like liquid honey.

"Don't call her that." Percifal spat.

"Percifal," I warned. "We have what we want. Just give her your sword and let's go."

The two stared each other down for another moment before Percifal tossed his sword to her. She caught it with a grin, examining its glory with her dark golden eyes. "T'was a pleasure doing business with you, Sir Percifal. Good luck with Chel," she offered, turning and walking away with her hips swaying, sword in one hand.

"Oh, and tell her Malyi misses her and wishes her luck," she called back over her shoulder. She disappeared out of the cellar and left us alone.

So there we stood, weaponless except for my unreliable power. At least now we had an idea where to look for Chel.

I knew now that I absolutely had to save Percifal's dear sister, the woman who could help us save our home. I also knew that I would do anything for this man. Steadying myself, I took his hand in mine and we left the tavern.

ACKNOWLEDGEMENTS

I would like to thank my alpha readers, Sarah Psiurski and Corey Lamoureux, for making sure everything made sense, finding plot holes and checking my spelling and punctuation. You were the first important part of helping this book come to life.

To my beta readers, thank you for taking the time to read this book and give your input.

Thanks to my cover artist, Yvonne Less at Art4Artists. The cover and promo material you designed for this book is gorgeous. You really captured Zephyra and the scenery of Solis the way I imagined. You were a pleasure to work with.

Thank you, John Renehan, for your work on my map. You brought to life what I had in mind. You're truly talented.

Another important person in helping me with this book was my editor, Michelle Browne at Magpie Editing. Thank you for helping me cut down on all my over used words and pointing out all the little things I missed.

Thank you to my husband for listening to me talk about my book and for everything else you do. This book wouldn't be possible without you.

Thank you to my mother, Sheila Watson, for always being my biggest supporter. You've always told me to do what makes me happy. I also believe I got my creative side from you.

I'm grateful to my formatter, Tami at Integrity Formatting, for making my book look so good on the inside.

I also want to give a shout out to my high school English teachers.

You were the first ones to tell me I should write a book, and that's where this dream began.

Thank you to all the Facebook writing groups I'm part of. I have been given a lot of good advice over the years from some of the members of those groups.

A special thank you goes to authors Kate Sparkes and Angie Grigaliunas for answering all of my questions about writing and self-publishing. You are both huge inspirations.

To all of my family and friends, I appreciate you always being there for me.

Finally, I want to give a huge thank you to my readers. I write for all of you! I hope you like my stories and the characters I've created. I hope my books help you escape reality, if just for a short time.

If you do like my books I encourage you to leave me a review wherever you purchased this book from and/or tell others about it so I can write even more.

About the Author

Andrea lives in Alberta, Canada with her husband and two cats. As an only child she had to be creative growing up to keep herself occupied. Reading and writing have always been two of her favourite activities. She got her artistic side from her mother and her persistence from her father. She's always been a fan of fantasy themes and even dresses up in corsets sometimes.

Apart from reading and writing, she enjoys dancing to her favourite music and horseback riding. She always tries to keep herself busy because she's a free spirit who gets restless easily.

If you'd like to be updated on her writing and when her next books are coming out you can find her online at:

www.AndreaBLamoureux.wordpress.com

She would also love to connect with you on Facebook at:

www.facebook.com/AndreaBLamoureux

and on Twitter @ALFantasyWriter